DARK DREAM'S UNRAVELING

THE CHILDREN OF THE GODS BOOK 27

I. T. LUCAS

ELLA

*E*lla woke up to complete darkness. Disoriented, she tried to move, but the strong male arms banded around her were holding her imprisoned.

No, no, no! It can't be. She was no longer the captive of the Russian.

Had her rescue been only a dream?

"Let me go!" She pushed on the hard chest she was plastered against. "Let me go, damn it!"

Her efforts were futile, but she couldn't just give up.

Ella shoved harder.

Unexpectedly, the arms fell away, releasing her, the force of the push sending her tumbling down the other side of the bed and all the way down to the carpet.

She landed on her butt with a thud. "Oof!" That hurt.

"Ella! Oh, dear Fates, I'm so sorry." He was on the floor beside her before finishing the sentence. "Did you have a bad dream?"

Getting all banged up had at least one positive outcome—Ella's brain fog was gone.

Those arms that had held her so tight hadn't belonged to

Gorchenco, they were Julian's, as were the glowing blue eyes regarding her with so much concern. Last night, she'd fallen asleep cradled in the comfort of his embrace, and he must have held her all night long.

And how had she repaid his kindness? By waking him up with a blood-curdling scream.

Twice.

Poor guy.

"I'm so sorry. It was completely dark, and I couldn't see anything. I thought I was still with the Russian and that the rescue was just a dream."

"Oh, sweetheart."

He hugged her gently, giving her every opportunity to pull away, but when she wrapped her arms around his neck and kissed him, he tightened his hold, lifted her off the floor, and sat on the bed with her cradled in his arms.

"You should've left a light on. There are too many scary ghosts in my closet for me to be okay with total darkness."

He hugged her closer. "Next time, I'll remember that." Reaching out with his long arm, he turned the bedside lamp on.

Now she could see the room, but since the shutters were closed, it was impossible to tell whether it was still night outside or if day had begun.

"What time is it? I'm supposed to be at the clinic at ten, and I still need to go home to get dressed."

Sleeping over at Julian's had been a last-minute decision, so naturally she didn't have a change of clothes at hand, and going to the clinic in the little black dress and high heels that she'd worn to Dalhu's exhibition was a no go.

"Why?" He chuckled. "Can't you go in my shirt? I can also lend you my briefs and socks again."

She'd done it once, right after her rescue, but that was because she hadn't wanted to take anything the Russian had gotten for her to her new home. Concern about appearances had been the last thing on her mind.

Things had changed since then. She'd embraced life in the village and the clan of immortals who'd become her new extended family. People here knew her, and parading around in the T-shirt she'd borrowed from Julian to sleep in was not an option. Even though it was long enough to serve as a mini-dress, she wasn't leaving his house like that.

"Very cute, Julian. Talk about a walk of shame to shame all others."

"But you have nothing to be ashamed of."

That would have been true even if they'd had sex, but doubly so since they hadn't done a thing. The headache that had assailed Ella every time she'd tried to talk about Logan had exhausted her, and after taking three Motrins and changing into Julian's well-worn T-shirt, she'd fallen asleep in his arms.

Which had been very nice.

Sleeping in the same bed with a man she actually cared about and wasn't afraid of was a new and pleasant experience. Julian made her feel safe, or at least he did when she was fully awake and knew it was him and not a dream walker, aka Logan, or a dream specter, aka Gorchenco.

"Do you have a new toothbrush I can borrow? My mouth probably smells like a garbage can."

Julian shook his head. "No, it doesn't. But yes. I have a toothbrush."

"Why are you shaking your head like that?"

"Because I've never met a girl who would mention a stinky garbage can in the same sentence as her mouth. Most try to appear delicate and refined."

Great.

Way to go, Ella.

Talking to Julian wasn't the same as talking to her younger

brother. Now that she was an adult, she should try to act more ladylike.

He hooked a finger under her chin and looked into her eyes. "Did I say something to offend you?"

Crap.

She also kept forgetting his super senses. Not that she could've done anything about it. Her body broadcast her emotions by emitting scents that only immortals could smell, probably dogs as well. She had no control over that, which meant that there was no hiding her feelings from Julian or any of the other immortals.

Her only consolation was that the others probably couldn't sniff her from afar, and she had no intention of sitting on any other immortal's lap.

Ella shrugged. "It's not important."

Holding on to her chin, he smiled. "Come on. Sharing socks and underwear means that we are close enough to tell each other everything."

That was a weird leap of logic. One had nothing to do with the other. But whatever. He probably thought it was something worse than what it actually was.

"I'm not refined and delicate enough for you?"

Julian's eyes widened, and then he laughed. "I love that you are such a tomboy. Beautiful girls are usually full of themselves and act entitled. You're nothing like that."

The tension left Ella's shoulders. It was a relief to know that she didn't have to put on a special act for Julian to like her. He accepted her the way she was.

His nice compliment deserved one in return, though. "Neither are you." She cupped his cheek. "You are every girl's dream guy, and yet you are not a jerk. I wonder why?"

He frowned. "Why would that make me a jerk? It's not a bad thing to be wanted."

She was proof that his statement was not true. "It can be

bad, but I digress. It's just that most successful, good-looking guys are exactly like the girls you were talking about. Too full of themselves and self-entitled. When guys get a lot of female attention, they think that they don't need to be nice."

Julian looked away. "I'm not successful. In fact, I feel like quite a failure."

This time it was Ella's turn to stare at him with wide eyes. "Are you nuts? What are you talking about?"

Raking his fingers through his hair, Julian sighed. "I spent seven years studying to become a doctor, and now I'm not sure that this is what I want to do. I can't work with humans because I can't handle the barrage of their intense emotions, and with Merlin here, the village immortals don't need my medical services."

Ella could understand that. Grief was a frequent visitor in hospitals, and feeling it day in and day out must have been draining for someone like Julian who absorbed it all as if it was his own.

Not a fun way to spend his days.

"You could become a plastic surgeon and have a private practice. Not much angst there."

"Are you kidding me? What about all those who are unhappy with their results, which I'm sure would be the case with my patients. I don't have any artistic talent, which I think is a necessary tool for a plastic surgeon. I would be doing people a disservice."

That was true. What else was there? "How about optometry?"

"That's a possibility. It's a bit boring, though."

"Psychiatry? That's not boring for sure, and it could be potentially beneficial to the clan. I bet that some people with special abilities think that they are crazy. It could be another way to identify Dormants."

He arched a brow. "Did you ever feel like that?"

"That I'm crazy? No." Ella pushed out of his arms. "I was born with my ability, and I thought that everyone could talk with their moms in their heads. Later, when I was older and realized that my mother and I were unique, I already had years of proof that our telepathic connection was real."

"It must have been difficult nonetheless. Being different, I mean. And hiding what you can do."

"Yeah, it was. The hardest part was hiding the truth from Parker. But he was too young to be entrusted with our secret. Besides, my mom thought that he would feel left out because he couldn't do what we could."

"I wonder what his special ability will be."

Ella shrugged. "He might have none, and then he's going to be very disappointed. I understand that not all Dormants exhibit special abilities, and that transitioning into immortality only enhances what is already there."

"Every Dormant is unique." Julian stood up and took her hand. "I have a feeling Parker is going to surprise us all. You and Vivian have such a powerful telepathic connection that it doesn't make sense for him to have no paranormal talent at all."

"Our telepathic connection may be strong, but it's quite useless because we can only communicate with each other. I hope Parker gets something better." She smiled up at him. "We can talk about all this later. I really need to get going."

"Let me give you a new toothbrush and a clean towel."

JULIAN

*a*s Ella emerged from the bathroom wearing the tight black dress and high heels she had worn last night, Julian rubbed his hand over his mouth and commanded his elongating fangs to behave.

Having a basically platonic relationship with her was pure torture, but it was a pain he was willing to endure for as long as it took. Hopefully, that wouldn't be too long.

"Ready to go?" he asked in the most nonchalant tone he could muster.

She wasn't fooled though. A light blush coloring her cheeks, she smoothed her hand over the side of the dress. "Yeah."

"Come on." He took her hand.

As they entered the living room, Ray looked Ella up and down. "Good morning." He didn't even try to hide his leering. "You look stunning in that dress. That look is so much better on you than the jeans with holes and Frankenstein boots from the other day."

The guy needed a serious attitude adjustment. Leering at a woman was rude and leering at a man's girlfriend was an invitation to trouble, but leering at an immortal male's mate was suicidal.

Taking a moment to indulge in imagining the various methods of showing Ray the error of his ways, Julian decided that a punch to the guy's smug face would be the most satisfying.

"Good morning, Ray." Ella smiled at his obnoxious roommate, but her smile was much less friendly than it had been the first time she'd met him. Evidently, she didn't like his attitude either.

She waved at him on her way out. "And goodbye."

As Julian followed Ella out, Ray nodded at him and lifted both hands with his thumbs up. "Congratulations, man."

Julian pinned him with a hard glare. "If you value your precious thumbs, which I know you do, I suggest that you keep them either in your pockets or on the piano keys. And I don't want to hear any comments about Ella from you either."

The smile evaporated off Ray's face. "Peace, roomie. I meant no disrespect."

His anger over Ray's behavior was disproportionate, Julian was aware of that, and if Ray's rudeness had been directed at him, he would have ignored it or made a joke out of it. But his roommate's behavior had been offensive to Ella, which was unforgivable.

Casting the guy another glare, Julian closed the door and schooled his expression for Ella's sake. "I'm sorry about that." He wrapped his arm around her waist. "I don't know what has gotten into him. Usually, he's a decent fellow."

Ella shrugged. "I told you. The walk of shame." She threaded her arm through his and pushed her hand inside his back pocket. "But I don't care. Let them think whatever they want."

It was such an intimate thing to do. Her hand on his ass made his jeans feel way too tight, and not because she was

8

pulling on them from behind. Nevertheless, he wanted it exactly where it was.

"It's not what you think it is. He wasn't trying to shame you," he said. "Immortals' attitude toward sexuality is different. The inappropriate smiles and leering was Ray's way of congratulating us. Not that it makes it right, and he was being rude, but in no way was it meant to shame you."

She shrugged. "I don't care about what Ray thinks. What I do care about, though, is the circus we are about to encounter in my house."

"Circus?"

"Yeah. My mom is going to be ecstatic, thinking that we've finally sealed the deal. And I don't even want to think what Parker is going to say. Hopefully, Magnus has left for work already, so at least I'll be spared his response. Although I can't even begin to guess what it would've been. I don't know him that well."

"Probably none." Julian chuckled. "It's funny how everyone is going to assume that we had sex last night when the truth is that we didn't even kiss."

"Sorry about that." She cast him an apologetic sidelong glance. "And thank you for being so patient and understanding. You're a true gentleman."

Julian wasn't sure what she was thanking him for.

For not kissing her?

Or for not having sex with her?

He'd known it hadn't been on the table when she'd asked him to take her to his house. The only reason Ella had gone home with him and had spent the night was that she'd been so shaken up over Dalhu's depiction of Navuh's son and her inability to say anything about it.

It must have felt awful to be controlled from afar by a puppet master, unable to use her own mouth and say what she wanted to say.

If Julian ever got his hands on that Doomer, he was going to exact payment from his hide for every little bit of discomfort he'd caused Ella.

She'd recognized Lokan as someone she'd met during her captivity, but she couldn't tell anyone how and where because he'd compelled her silence. Dalhu had filled in some of the information, like the bastard's name, and that he had the extremely rare ability to compel humans. Kian had added another piece of the puzzle. Apparently, Ella had told him about a lunch meeting she'd attended with a shady character the Russian was selling weapons to.

Come to think of it, there must've been more to it than the one business meeting Ella had told Kian about. Otherwise, her panicked response to Lokan's portrait didn't make sense.

He frowned. "Did Lokan ever touch you?"

Ella opened her mouth to answer, but then grimaced and shook her head.

"Damn. I'm such an idiot. I shouldn't have asked you about him. I'm sorry. Did I give you a new headache?"

"Yeah, but it was only for a moment."

He should have been more careful and avoided mentioning Lokan at all. Every time Ella tried to say something about the Doomer, she suffered severe headaches.

Julian gave her hand a light squeeze. "I'm sorry for causing you unnecessary pain."

She squeezed his hand back. "We are apologizing too much to each other. I don't like it."

"Right. It's not a good way to start a relationship."

Ella didn't respond to that, but the expression on her face bothered him.

What was going through her head?

Hopefully, she wasn't reconsidering being in a relationship with him. Was she?

"Well, we're here," Ella said as they climbed the steps to her front porch. "Brace yourself." She opened the door.

Maybe that was what her troubled expression had been about. She'd been bracing for facing her mother.

"Oh, good," Ella whispered. "There is no one in the living room." She took off her high-heeled shoes, motioned for him to follow her, and tiptoed to her room.

"Ella? Is that you?" Vivian called out.

"Damn. Busted," Ella whispered. "Yes, Mom. I'm just going to change before going to the clinic."

Vivian's footsteps got faster, her house slippers flapping a rapid tempo on the living room floor. "The clinic? Why? What's wrong?"

Ella turned a pair of pleading eyes at him. "Julian?"

"Go, I'll take care of this."

"Thanks." She gave him a quick peck on the cheek before ducking into her room.

"What's going on?" Vivian asked.

"Let's go back to the living room."

Vivian shivered. "You're scaring me, Julian."

He took her elbow and turned her around. "Ella asked me to tell you what happened yesterday at Dalhu's exhibition."

"Should I call Magnus in?"

"Is he home?"

"He's out in the backyard with Scarlet."

"I thought he went back to work."

"He did, but he has the morning off. This evening he's going out on a mission." She grimaced. "I hate it, but I knew what I was signing up for when I allowed myself to fall for him."

"Magnus is a good man."

"The best."

"I'm sure he will want to hear this too. But if possible, I don't think Parker should be here. Not that any of this is age-inappropriate, it's just that you should decide what he needs or doesn't need to know. Not me."

Vivian nodded. "Parker is in his room, studying. I'll get Magnus." She walked over to the sliding door and opened it. "Can you come in for a moment? Julian needs to tell us something."

The Guardian stepped in with Scarlet trotting behind him. Sensing the tension, the dog tucked her tail between her legs and plopped down on her doggie bed.

When the couple sat on the couch, Julian took the armchair across from it and debated where to start. Ella hadn't told him whether Vivian and Magnus knew about her meeting with Lokan, but he shouldn't assume that she had.

"While still with Gorchenco, Ella attended a meeting he had with a business associate. She heard them talking about the Russian supplying the other one with weapons and about an island, which later on she figured out must've been the Doomers' island. She told Kian all of that, but without mentioning the guy's name. Yesterday, at the exhibition, she recognized him from one of Dalhu's charcoal portraits. According to Dalhu, his name is Lokan, and he is one of Navuh's sons. Lokan has the unique ability to compel humans."

Vivian frowned. "Is there a difference between a thrall and a compulsion?"

"A compulsion is much stronger than a thrall and lasts longer. Sometimes it can last indefinitely. It depends on the strength of the compeller and the susceptibility of the compelled."

"What does it have to do with Ella?"

"Apparently, and for unclear reasons, Lokan compelled Ella not to mention him. When she recognized him and wanted to say his name, nothing came out. When she tried harder, she got a bad headache. Bottom line, Ella can't tell us anything about him."

Magnus smoothed his hand over his goatee. "I don't understand. You said that she told Kian about meeting him. So, mentioning him was okay but saying his name wasn't? That doesn't make sense."

"I agree. That's why I think there is more to it than that one meeting. Unfortunately, Ella can't tell us what it is. That's why she's going to the clinic. Merlin is preparing what he calls a tongue relaxer for her. Hopefully, it will help her tell us a little more."

3

ELLA

"*F*ates, Merlin. Do all your potions have to be this stinky?" Julian held out the small decanter to Ella. "I know that we've decided we shouldn't apologize to each other so much, but I have to apologize in advance for this."

She took the bottle and held it away from her. "If this helps with my problem, I don't care how vile it smells or tastes."

"Hold on. I'll get you a Godiva chocolate." Merlin rushed out of his office.

Her favorite, but one was not going to cut it. She was like an addict with those. Once Ella got a taste of one, she craved more.

"Do you know where he hides them?" she whispered.

"The chocolates?"

She nodded enthusiastically.

"No clue."

"Then follow him." She waved her hand, shooing him on. "We can raid his stash later."

Merlin was such a scatterbrain that he wouldn't notice some of it missing. Or most of it. Besides, he was a chill guy,

14

and she knew he liked her. He wouldn't mind if she pilfered some of his chocolates.

Julian crossed his arms over his chest and affected a stern expression. "I'm not raiding anyone's stash. I'll buy you as many chocolates as you can possibly eat." He leaned to whisper in her ear. "But then you'll run the risk of gaining those extra hundred pounds you've mentioned."

For a moment, she wasn't sure what he was talking about. Was it something she'd said? It sounded like it.

The headache had done a number on her last night, and everything was kind of fuzzy. But then she remembered Julian picking her up and carrying her to his home. He'd said something about her weighing nothing, and then they'd joked about it.

Gasping dramatically, Ella put a hand over her heart. "God forbid. Don't say such things when I'm about to risk my life, drinking this stuff." She lifted the decanter. "Nasty things are floating near the bottom. Do you think Merlin used spider webs to make it? Or was this just a very dirty container?"

"No spider anything." Merlin returned with a small box of chocolates. "I brought you four, so you'll have enough to share with lover boy."

Crap. Was everyone assuming she and Julian got it on last night?

And how did Merlin even know where she'd spent the night?

Apparently, Julian had been right about gossip in the village. These immortals needed to get a life, which apparently they didn't have because they couldn't find anyone, immortal or Dormant, to have a relationship with. That would also explain their excessive fascination with any new couple and their sex life.

"Okay, young lady. I suggest that you pinch your nose, drink up, and follow with a chocolate."

"Do I have to finish the whole thing?"

Merlin nodded. "As much as you can stomach. The more, the better."

Ella eyed the floating unidentifiable objects, hoping they were just residue from the herbs or whatever else Merlin used to cook his potions from.

Once she removed the stopper, the smell almost knocked her over, but she was determined to do whatever it took to remove the freaking compulsion. Pinching her nose with one hand, she lifted the decanter with the other, gulped down its contents, and then snatched the chocolate from Julian's palm.

Popping it into her mouth, she chewed it up and then reached out her hand. "Quickly. Give me another one."

She ended up eating all four and not leaving any for Julian. "I'm sorry. It's just that it tasted really awful, and I can't control myself with these small pieces of divine goodness."

He shook his head. "No apologies. I'm not a great lover of chocolates."

It was on the tip of her tongue to ask him what he was a great lover of, but that would have been cruel considering that she wasn't ready to let him demonstrate.

Instead, she asked, "What now? How long before we know if it worked or not?"

"Twenty minutes or so." Merlin pulled a fob watch out of his pocket. "You can sit in the waiting room if you want. Or you can take a walk and come back by eleven o'clock."

"I'd rather take a walk."

"Let's go." Julian tossed the empty chocolate box into the wastebasket.

A few minutes into the walk, Ella started feeling the potion's effects. It reminded her of the time she drank too much wine at Gorchenco's prompting.

"I don't feel so hot." She leaned on Julian.

Without heels, she was so much shorter than him that her

16

head barely reached his armpit. If he wanted to, he could have tucked her head under his arm.

"Do you want to sit down?" He eyed her worriedly.

"Yeah. I'm getting dizzy."

As they found a bench, Ella motioned for Julian to sit down first and then sat in his lap. "I hope you don't mind. But I want you to hold me."

"Mind?" He wrapped his arms around her, propping up her back so she could get comfortable. "I love it."

"Good. Because I'm planning on doing it a lot." She cupped his cheek and smirked. "I'm so evil."

Julian frowned. "Why would you say that?"

"Because I know what it does to you. I can feel you getting hard under me, and I know it must be torturous."

What had possessed her to say that?

Tongue relaxer.

Well, now she knew what it meant.

"I'm sorry. Crap. I keep saying it. It's the freaking potion's fault. I mean, about what I've said before. And about apologizing. Damn. This is hard. I didn't realize how compelling it is to say sorry."

Julian rubbed her back. "It's okay. No need to feel bad about pointing out the obvious." He kissed the top of her head. "I have a beautiful girl sitting in my lap. It's a natural response."

"Right? That's so true. I should feel good. If you didn't get hard, I would've felt way worse."

He laughed. "I think the potion has done what it was supposed to. We can head back to the clinic."

"We should." She tried to lift her head, but then let it plop back on his chest. "I can't. You'll have to carry me."

"No problem. I love doing that too."

Merlin opened the door for them. "Back so soon?"

"I can't lift my head," Ella complained.

"You must be very sensitive." He followed them inside into his office, then pulled out a chair for Julian and one for himself.

"Let's give it a try, shall we?"

Ella nodded.

"What can you tell us about Lokan?"

She opened her mouth, tried to speak, but nothing came out. Shaking her head, she tried again. "I can't."

"Headache?"

"No. I just can't talk."

Merlin smoothed his hand over his long beard. "At least there is that. But that's a temporary effect. Once the potion is out of your system, I'm afraid the headaches will come back every time you try to talk about him."

"What I don't understand," Julian said, "is how come Ella could tell Kian about the meeting and what was discussed, but not anything else. Did Lokan just compel her not to say his name?"

Ella shook her head, but that was all she could do.

She'd wondered the same thing. It occurred to her that the trouble had begun after Logan had made her promise not to tell anyone about his dream visits. The first and second dream encounter had happened while she'd still been with the Russian, and she'd told him about them. The compulsion hadn't been there yet.

Damn, how she hated this.

Even here, in the hidden village, he was controlling her from God knew where. He could be on the other side of the planet for all she knew.

The big question was what Lokan aka Logan wanted.

Why was he doing this?

Was it his way of amusing himself?

Or did he really plan on coming after her?

And if he did, how?

She had to find a way to keep him out of her dreams.

Sleeping in Julian's arms might have helped, but on the other hand, Logan's visits hadn't been nightly. He might have just happened to skip last night.

There was no guarantee that Julian's presence was helpful. She'd dreamt about Logan while sleeping with Gorchenco. If his presence hadn't deterred Logan, Julian's probably wouldn't either. Ella doubted that her feelings toward her bed partner made a difference.

The thing was, she couldn't even ask anyone's advice on keeping her dreams private because she couldn't talk about it.

Or maybe she could if she didn't mention anything specific?

It was worth a try.

She turned to Merlin, who seemed to know a lot about many things. "Is there a way to guard dreams against intruders?"

Once the question had left her mouth, Ella clapped her hands in glee. It worked. She'd voiced it, and her head didn't feel as if it was going to explode.

Merlin shook his head. "There isn't. If you have disturbing memories or thoughts, they might manifest in your dreams. Even thralling you to forget them won't help. The subconscious is very difficult to control."

Ella's smile melted away. Merlin hadn't understood the meaning behind her general question, and neither had Julian.

Damn. There must be a way around the stupid compulsion, and she was going to keep trying until she found it.

JULIAN

"I think I can walk by myself," Ella said as Julian pushed to his feet, still holding her in his arms.

He could understand her embarrassment about being carried around the village in broad daylight, but she was still a little woozy. Merlin had brought coffee for the three of them, and it had seemed to help with Ella's dizziness, but she was still slurring her words, and her eyes were unfocused.

"Let's give it a try. Lean against me, and I'll prop you up."

Merlin shook his head. "We should have a golf cart here for cases like this."

"There is one for deliveries. I'll go get it." Julian was about to put Ella down on the chair when she clutched his sleeve.

"Don't go. Please, just help me up. I'll walk home."

When she looked up at him with those big blue eyes of hers, pleading for him not to leave her, he was helpless to refuse even though getting the golf cart was the smart thing to do.

"Okay."

Lifting Ella off the chair, he tucked her against his side and wrapped his arm around her middle. "On one."

For several steps, he had to hold her up, but the movement

combined with the fresh air seemed to be helping, and Ella tried to walk on her own. That lasted for about ten steps, and then she leaned against him again.

"Are you sure Merlin's potions are safe? The only other time I felt like this was when I got drunk on too much wine. My bodyguard had to carry me up to the bedroom."

"The one who tried to save you from the fake explosion?"

She nodded. "Misha. I hope he's okay, and that Gorchenco hasn't killed him for letting me die in that explosion. I liked him."

As the jealous bug gripped him with its poisonous pinchers, Julian forgot all about being a gentleman and took unfair advantage of Ella's drunk-like state. "How much exactly did you like this Misha guy?"

"A lot. He was huge." She lifted her hand as high as it would go. "Tall, almost like Yamanu, but twice as wide, and he had a crooked nose that looked like it had been broken once or twice, and scars. And the back of his head was flat." She chuckled and patted the back of her own head. "Like Frankenstein's monster. But he was nice to me. I know he was only following Gorchenco's orders, but he could've been grumpy about it, or mean. He wasn't. Misha always had a smile for me."

As a tear slid down her cheek, she wiped it away with the sleeve of her hoodie. "I hate not knowing what happened to him and having no way of finding out."

It dawned on Julian then that Ella was holding in a lot, and not all of it was about enduring Gorchenco. What he wondered, though, was whether she was putting on a brave face just for others or for herself as well.

At some point, the dam was going to break, and all those suppressed emotions were going to burst out to the surface. It wasn't a question of if, but of when.

Poor girl.

And her ordeal wasn't over yet.

What did that fucking Doomer want with her?

Had he suspected that she was a Dormant and was planning on getting his hands on her?

Did he want to use her to find the village?

What if there was more to this compulsion, and he'd planted a command in her head to contact him with information about her location?

But that didn't make sense.

When Lokan had met Ella, she had known nothing about the clan or who the people organizing her rescue were. So even if that Doomer had thralled her and scanned her memories, he would've found nothing of interest there.

Nothing other than her telepathic ability. But that could only make him suspect that Ella was a Dormant, not her connection to the clan.

Unless Vivian hadn't followed their instructions and had revealed something to Ella that had given Lokan a clue.

When Ella's step faltered once more, Julian lifted her into his arms. "We are almost at your house, and there is no one around."

"Thank you. I was about to ask you to carry me." She chuckled. "No matter what, I'm never drinking one of Merlin's potions again."

Unexpectedly, his heart sank a little when she said that. What if they wanted a child sometime in the future? Without help, that future might be very distant.

But that was a silly thought and way too premature. They hadn't even had sex yet, and Merlin's fertility potions might not work. In fact, Julian was pretty sure they wouldn't. He had more faith in the human fertility treatments that had been proven to work. Those, if adapted to immortals, might actually be successful.

As Julian took the steps up to the front porch, the door opened and Vivian came out.

"What happened?"

"It's the potion. Apparently, Ella is very sensitive to it."

"Hi, Mom." Ella waved a hand. "Don't worry. I just feel like I'm drunk. It will pass."

Vivian kissed her cheek. "Will coffee help?"

"I already had some. I think that it's best for me to sleep it off."

"As you wish, sweetie." Vivian led the way to Ella's bedroom and opened the door. "Let me know if you need anything."

"I will, Mom. I love you."

"Love you too." Vivian closed the door, leaving them alone.

Since Ella was dressed in street clothes, he put her down on top of the comforter. "Do you want to get undressed before I tuck you in?"

"No. I'll just take a short nap. My clothes are clean."

"As you wish. Let me take your shoes off."

She toed her sneakers off before he had a chance to get to them. "All done."

Leaning, he kissed her forehead. "Are you going to be okay here by yourself?"

"Yes." Closing her eyes, she tucked her hands under the pillow, and a moment later her breathing became deep and even.

Adorable.

When he left Ella's room, Julian closed the door quietly behind him and then strode to the living room where her family was waiting for him.

"Did it work?" Magnus asked.

Julian shook his head. "She still couldn't tell us anything."

Magnus's eyes began glowing. "I hope that son of a bitch is not planning anything."

In the corner, Scarlet whimpered.

Julian lowered his voice so as not to scare the dog. "I was thinking about it on the way here. Lokan had no way of knowing that Ella would end up with the clan. When she met him, she didn't know about us, so he couldn't have thralled the information out of her. The only thing I can think of is that he guessed she was a Dormant and wanted her for himself. The question is how he's planning to do it. Did he plant a secret command in her head to contact him?"

"If he did, she would've done it already," Vivian said. "Why wait so long?"

It wasn't long at all, but still.

"We have to assume that he pulled the rescue plan out of her head. So he knew there was a chance she'd get free. Planting a command like that would've made sense. There is one more possibility, though." Julian pinned Vivian with a hard stare. "If he knew who the people rescuing her were, he might have planted a different command in her head. To disclose the village's location to him."

Vivian's eyes widened. "But how? Ella didn't know anything about the clan until you told her the story after the rescue when she was already on the plane."

"Are you sure? Maybe you let something slip during your telepathic conversations?"

"I did not. I was very careful not to reveal anything about the clan. Turner warned me not to."

"Yes, I know he did. But sometimes people blurt things out accidentally."

Even without the immortal glow, Vivian's eyes blazed with anger. "You can ask me the same question in a hundred different ways, Julian, but my answer will still be the same. I didn't tell Ella anything about the clan or about immortals, and I didn't let anything slip either."

5

ELLA

*A*fter Julian had left, Ella tried to nap, breathing slow and steady and counting sheep floating on fluffy clouds, but it was no use. She felt too nauseous to fall asleep.

It was like having a hangover combined with an upset stomach.

Merlin's potion was vile, and it went beyond the taste. Maybe she was having a reaction to it?

It wasn't like over the counter medications that she could get in the supermarket. Those had been tested and approved, while the things Merlin was cooking in his kitchen hadn't been checked by anyone other than the loony doctor, and he'd probably tested them only on other immortals.

Hopefully, the effects would dissipate soon because she had things to do. Like figuring out how to circumvent Logan's compulsion so she could tell Kian and the others about his dream intrusions.

Just thinking about it made her head hurt, but it was probably the concoction's fault and not the compulsion's. Propping herself up on a pile of pillows, Ella closed her eyes and once again tried to deep-breathe the headache away. Sometimes it worked, though that was when the headache was stress related, which could have been the case now, but she had a feeling that this one had been caused by the potion.

When deep breathing didn't help, she got up, padded to the bathroom, and pulled out a container of Motrin. Popping three capsules into her mouth, she washed them down with tap water.

The next weapon in her arsenal of natural remedies was a shower. There was something rejuvenating and relaxing about the heat and the moisture, and it was very effective for headaches.

On second thought, though, a bath would be better. It was more conducive to thinking.

It took a good five minutes for the tub to get full, and when it did, Ella got in and sighed with pleasure. This was such a nice, big tub. She could actually lie flat in it and submerge her body completely. The bathroom she used to share with Parker in the old house had only a basic tub that doubled as a shower, and even though Ella was small, she couldn't get comfortable in it. Even worse, it hadn't had a working lock, and her mother had refused to fix it, claiming it wasn't safe.

Not safe from a little brother, that was for sure. Ella had had to prop a chair against the door to prevent him from *accidentally* barging in.

Her mom was such a worrywart. Vivian would go into a full panic mode if she entered the room and didn't find Ella right away, and only then think of checking the bathroom.

Opening the channel, Ella sent her mother a quick message. *In case you're looking for me, I'm soaking in the tub.*

Are you okay? How are you feeling?

I'm fine. A headache started, so I took three pills.

Can you keep the channel open? I worry about you being in the tub when you don't feel well. I've heard of people drowning in shallow bath water because they fainted.

26

Ella rolled her eyes. *I can't keep it open because it's draining my energy. But I can talk to you every five minutes. Okay?*

Don't forget, or I'll have to come in.

The door is locked.

As if I can't open those locks. I don't know why you even bother. Parker knows how to do it too.

Which means that I need a better lock.

Ella closed the channel before a new argument started. She loved her mother, and she even tried to be understanding about the super-charged protective streak Vivian had developed, but it was annoying.

Thank God for her mental barriers. If her mother could enter her mind whenever she wanted, it would be awful.

Hey, maybe telling her mother about Logan via their private channel would work? What if only speaking about him out loud was a problem?

Mom. And that was it. She couldn't send anything about Logan or her dreams.

What is it, sweetheart? It hasn't even been five minutes yet.

Oh, then never mind. I love you.

Love you too, sweetie.

Well, that was a bust.

Perhaps she could try to write it down and then let Kian read it.

No, she shouldn't think about showing it, just about writing it down. Logan had said not to tell anyone about him, and the command was literal. As long as she tried to communicate information about him to others, she was going to get blocked. But what if she wrote it in her personal journal?

Not that she had one. But it was never too late to start.

Excited about her new idea, Ella got out of the tub, pulled her bathrobe on, and padded back to her room.

I'm out of the tub, so you can stop worrying, she sent to her mom.

Do you want me to bring you something to eat or drink?

Just thinking about food makes me want to barf, but I'd appreciate some black coffee.

Coming up.

You're the best, Mom.

Pulling out a notepad and a pencil, Ella started writing. To get herself going and forget about the purpose of it, she decided to start by making a list of things worth putting in a journal.

What was her first memory of telepathic communication with her mom?

There had been so many of them.

She would think of it later. For now, she was just jotting down major turning points in her life, like Parker's birth and her father's death. Again, she didn't want to start writing about it because once she did, she would never stop. Almost twelve years later, she still missed her dad and thought about him nearly every day.

Wiping away a tear, she continued to her graduation from high school, the prom that had been such an underwhelming event, her job at the diner...

Meeting freaking Romeo. Stupidly falling for his fake charm and false declarations of love. She'd been such a painfully naive idiot.

Damn, it was hard to keep writing with a hand that shook, and once again she decided to only put down bullet points. Falling for Romeo, lying to her mother and going with him to New York for what she'd thought would be a fun weekend, meeting the scumbag's uncle and realizing that she'd been lured into a trap. The auction house, getting bought by the Russian and what that had entailed, and then she got to meeting Logan.

Now it was time for putting down details.

Ella wrote about going to lunch with the Russian, his handsome lunch guest, hearing them talk about weapons and then about some island Gorchenco used to vacation at.

So far so good.

Dreaming about…

And that was it.

She couldn't continue, and the headache that assaulted her was so bad that Ella felt like vomiting.

Crap, crap, and triple crap…

Throwing the pencil across the room, she got up and rushed into the bathroom. Leaning over the sink, she cranked the faucet open and splashed cold water on her face.

It helped with the nausea, but not the headache.

Except, the headache was what had caused the nausea, so she needed to eradicate it too.

Simple, everyday thoughts, that was what she needed. Like planning to go shopping for shoes online. She needed a pair of pumps that weren't as high-heeled as the ones she'd borrowed from her mother.

The longer Ella distracted herself with mundane, unfocused thoughts, the more the headache subsided, until she felt safe to return to her room and not barf all over the carpet.

Her mother entered with a coffee mug. "Are you okay? You look pale."

"I'll be fine. Thanks for the coffee." Ella took the mug.

Thankfully, her mother had gotten the hint. "I'll be in the kitchen if you need me. I know you're nauseous, but if you feel better, I'm making soup and salad for lunch."

Ella shook her head. "Maybe later."

When Vivian left, Ella started pacing. What else could she try?

Her laptop caught her eye.

It was probably a stupid idea, but it wouldn't hurt to try. Snatching it off her desk, she sat on her bed and opened a new note.

This time she skipped the preamble and went straight to the point, but decided not to mention the name. She typed: *Dreaming about Mr. D.*

D for Doomer and for dream-walker.

Without letting herself get carried away by the small success, she wrote: *Mr. D can enter my dreams. He calls his ability dream walking.*

Ella's relief was so monumental that she felt dizzy, but for a good reason this time. Her first instinct was to run out and show Vivian her laptop, but her mother could miss the reference and start asking questions that would bring the headache back.

Having Julian around, filling in the missing pieces, would work better.

Instead of texting like she would normally do, she called him. "Are you very busy?"

"Not at all. What's up?"

"I need you to come over. There is something I want to show you."

"What is it?"

"I can't tell you. You need to see it."

"I'll be there in five minutes."

"Thanks."

To make it in such a short time, Julian would have to jog, not walk…

Crap. She was still in her bathrobe.

Rushing into her closet, she pulled on a pair of panties, skipped the bra and grabbed a sweatshirt off the shelf. A pair of leggings and her house slippers went on next.

She looked like a hobo, with mismatched clothes and wet pink hair that was sticking out in all directions because she hadn't brushed it after getting out of the bathtub.

Finger combing would have to do.

6

JULIAN

*E*lla hadn't sounded scared. She'd sounded excited. Still, Julian dropped the stack of estimates he'd gotten for the remodeling of the halfway house and then ran all the way to her place as if his tail was on fire.

"Hi, Vivian," he said as she opened the door. "Ella called me. She wants to show me something."

"Come on in." Vivian threw the door open. "She's in her room."

"Thanks." He headed down the corridor.

"Can you stay for lunch?" Vivian called after him. "It's nothing fancy. I made soup and salad, but we would love for you to join us."

"Thank you. I would be happy to."

"I'll tell Ella to open the door."

He stopped with his knuckles an inch away from it. With Ella's human hearing, she might not hear him knocking on the soundproof door.

As she opened it, looking like she'd gotten dressed in the dark and with her pink hair in disarray, he wanted to pick her up and kiss her.

Adorable.

But it was apparent that Ella was pumped about something that she couldn't wait to share with him.

"That was fast. Come in. You have to see this." She pointed at the laptop propped on a cushion on her bed.

Sitting down, Julian lifted it and put it on his knees. There were only two lines of text on the screen.

Dreaming about Mr. D.

Mr. D can enter my dreams. He calls his ability dream walking.

"Who is Mr. D?"

Rolling her eyes, Ella affected a stern and haughty expression, lifted her chin, and turned her face slightly to the side as if posing for a portrait.

Did she mean Lokan? But why Mr. D and not Mr. L?

"Is the D for Doomer?"

She nodded enthusiastically and pointed to the word dream.

"And for dream walker?"

Jumping up and down, Ella squealed and clapped her hands.

"You found a way around the compulsion?"

She nodded again, then snatched the laptop from his hands, put it on her desk, and started typing.

It seemed like Ella was afraid to say anything out loud. Even a yes.

When she was done, she handed him the laptop. The third line said: *I need to know how to block Mr. D from visiting my dreams.*

"This is big. We should tell Kian. I've never heard of an ability like that."

He reached for her hand and pulled her into his lap. "I'm so glad you found a way to let us know what's going on. I knew it had to be more than just one lunch meeting. Now it all makes sense. He didn't want you to talk about his dream visits. What does he want from you?"

Ella took the laptop and typed: *I'm special because I can communicate telepathically. Mr. D wants to find me and take me.*

Julian felt his fangs elongate and his venom glands swell. "Over my dead body. But that's an empty threat because he can't find you. You're safe here. Just don't give him any clues."

She rolled her eyes again and pointed to the previous line she'd typed.

"I get it. That's why you want to block him."

She nodded.

"Let me text Kian. Maybe he knows of a clan member who can help with that."

His text was short and to the point. *Ella found a way around the silencing compulsion. She can type what she can't say. Lokan is invading her dreams, and she wants to know how to stop him.*

Kian's answer came back a moment later. *Bring Ella to my office at five in the afternoon. I'll get Turner and Bridget.*

"Five o'clock at Kian's office. Turner and Bridget are going to be there too."

"Good. Can you explain this to my family?"

"Sure. Your mom invited me to stay for lunch."

As he and Ella entered the living room, Parker and Magnus were setting up the table.

"Right on time," Magnus said. "Take a seat."

Julian glanced at Ella. "Should I wait with this for after lunch?"

"What is it?" Vivian put a large salad bowl on the table.

"Ella found a way around the compulsion. She can type what she wants to say, but without mentioning his real name. She calls him Mr. D."

Vivian grinned. "My clever girl. I knew you'd find a way."

"I wasn't sure at all," Ella said. "It was a last-ditch effort after I tried communicating it to you telepathically and then writing it by hand."

Parker came in with a plate piled up with toast. "What is everyone talking about?"

"Remember what I told you about the clan's enemies?" Magnus said.

"The Doomers."

"Ella has met one, but she didn't know that he was a Doomer."

"There is more to it," Julian said. "Apparently, this guy has the ability to intrude on people's dreams."

Magnus lifted his hand. "Let's serve the soup before it gets cold. You can tell us the rest while we eat."

"Need any help?" Julian got up.

"Vivian and I got it." Magnus clapped him on the back.

When everyone was seated, Julian waited for Magnus's signal to continue. Perhaps the Guardian didn't want Parker to hear the rest?

Feeling Julian's gaze on him, Magnus lifted his spoon. "Eat your soup first, Julian. The story isn't going to get cold. The soup is."

For the next several minutes, no one talked. When Julian was done, he wiped his mouth with the napkin and glanced at the Guardian again.

"Go ahead," Magnus said.

Thank the merciful Fates. Sitting on exciting news like this wasn't good for digestion.

"What Ella typed on her laptop was that Mr. D has been invading her dreams. What I think happened was that he discovered her telepathic ability during that one face-to-face meeting they had, and he decided that he wanted her for himself. I'm guessing that he didn't act on it because he needed Gorchenco for the weapons, so he couldn't antagonize him by taking Ella by force, and he couldn't thrall the Russian to give Ella up either. Somehow, though, he must have established a connection with her that has allowed him access to her dreams."

Julian turned to Ella. "Is this a correct assessment so far?"

She nodded.

Vivian groaned. "Is this nightmare ever going to end?"

"I'm so sick of guys coming after Ella," Parker said. "Maybe if she gets married, has ten kids, and gets really fat, it will stop."

Ella threw a crumb of toast at him. "Oh, gee. Thanks, Parker. That's exactly what I want from my life."

"What?" The kid threw his hands in the air. "Isn't having ten kids better than being chased by every evil guy who sees your face?"

Chuckling, Vivian looked pointedly at Julian. "Why jump all the way to ten? One child might do."

Uncomfortable, more for Ella than for himself, Julian raked his fingers through his hair. "Ella is only eighteen, so this conversation is pointless. Besides, I don't think it would stop someone like Lokan. He'd probably want to get his hands on Ella's child as well."

7

KIAN

"I've never heard of a dream walking talent," Kian said. "Have you, Bridget?"

She shook her head. "Nope. I can ask Merlin. The guy is a fount of knowledge. We could also ask Dalhu and Robert."

Kian waved a dismissive hand. "I doubt they know anything. But go ahead."

"What about the goddess?" Turner asked. "Maybe there were dream walkers among the gods or the early immortals?"

"I'll do it right now." Kian pulled out his phone, at the last minute deciding to call instead of texting.

He hadn't called her in a while, and Annani would be on his case for being a neglectful son, contacting her only when he needed something. Which regrettably was true, and there was no excuse for it.

After all, he wasn't only her son but also her regent, and it was his duty to call her with regular updates, which he failed to do. She had every right to be upset with him.

"Kian, my beloved son. How good it is to hear from you."

"Hello, Mother. How have you been?"

36

"Excellent, my dear. But I know you are not calling to inquire after my well-being. How can I assist you?"

There was no point in denying the truth, especially not with the audience listening in.

"Have you ever heard of a dream walker? A god or an immortal who could enter another person's dream from afar?"

She took a long moment before answering. "It should be possible for someone like Yamanu to thrall people from afar while they are asleep. But I do not think he can pinpoint a specific person."

"I'm not talking about thralling. I'm talking about interacting with a person in his or her dream, conducting an actual face-to-face conversation."

"I do not see how it is possible. Again, an elaborate thrall can mimic a dream. But it would be like planting an entire scene in the person's head. They would not be really interacting. Do you understand what I am trying to say?"

"I do. Except, it seems that one of Navuh's sons has the ability."

"Are you sure? It could be trickery. I would not put it past Navuh and his subordinates to pretend to have powers they do not."

The thought had crossed Kian's mind. But to determine that, he needed to ask Ella some more questions. "Thank you. I need to investigate this more in depth. I'll let you know what I find out."

"Please do. It is very troubling. We could be vulnerable to dream attacks."

"Indeed. I'll talk to you later. Goodbye, Mother."

"Goodbye, my son."

Ella, who was the only one who hadn't heard the other side of the phone conversation, was looking at him expectantly. "What did the goddess say?"

"Annani has never heard of a god or immortal who could

interact with another person in his or her dream." Kian tapped his fingers on the conference table. "I need to ask you more questions. Are you going to type your answers?"

She opened her laptop. "I'll do my best."

"In those dreams, did Lokan try to get information out of you?"

Julian cleared his throat. "We should call him Mr. D from now on. It makes things easier for Ella."

"No problem."

In the meantime, Ella finished typing and handed the laptop to Julian. "You can read it out loud for everyone."

He nodded. "Ella says that he didn't ask her anything. Sometimes she felt as if he was leading her into revealing things, but she was always careful not to."

"How much in control of the dream are you, though?" Bridget asked. "Can he glimpse your thoughts while sharing your dream?"

When Julian handed the laptop back to Ella, she typed up a quick response and handed it back.

"Ella says that she's in full control. It's the same as if she were awake. Because of the telepathic connection with her mother, she has practiced blocking from a young age, and her shields are always up. She has to lower them to communicate with her mother. Mr. D can't see what she doesn't want him to."

Frowning, Ella took the laptop and typed some more before handing it back to Julian.

"The only exception was the sanctuary. In one of the dreams she was walking the grounds when Mr. D joined her, and as he commented on the landscape, she said that it was typical of the region. That could've given him a clue as to where the sanctuary was located. In another dream, he joined her at the diner where she used to work, so that's not a problem, and then he met her at her favorite San Diego beach. Ella is afraid that he might enter a dream while she's dreaming about the village and see it through her eyes."

"The village is not a problem," Turner said. "Seeing it through Ella's eyes will not tell him anything about its location. The sanctuary is another story, though. The Brotherhood might have records of the place from when it served as their base. He can recognize the landscape from pictures if they kept them, and if he suspects what and where it is, he can find old newspaper articles about the sanctuary from its monastery days."

Kian leaned back in his chair. "I don't think we should be overly concerned, but just as a precaution, it's a good idea to beef up the sanctuary's security."

"I agree." Turner flipped his notepad open. "I'm on it."

"The question is how to protect Ella from his visits," Bridget said. "This must be really hard on you." She cast Ella an empathic look. "Going to sleep is probably stressful instead of relaxing."

Ella grimaced. "It is."

"Killing Mr. D or putting him in stasis would solve the problem," Julian hissed through slightly elongated fangs.

Kian snorted. "For that, we would need to find him first."

Ella took the laptop from Julian and spent a couple of minutes typing away.

"Ella says she can do some snooping around and ask him questions. Maybe he'll tell her where he is. We know what he looks like. So, if we know where he is, we can catch him."

"That would require Ella to pretend she enjoys his company," Bridget said. "Can you do that?"

Ella snorted. "I fooled a paranoid mafia boss into believing that I liked him."

"That's true." Bridget looked at Kian. "Gorchenco had a reason to be suspicious of Ella's motives. Mr. D has none. He'd be much easier to fool."

I. T. LUCAS

Perhaps. An old and experienced Doomer would not be so easy for Ella to wrap around her little finger. Was Lokan old? Kian had forgotten what Dalhu had written in the dossier he'd prepared on the guy.

Besides, Lokan was likely spending most of his time on the island where they couldn't get to him anyway.

On the other hand, Lokan wanted Ella and was probably planning to lure her somewhere he could snatch her. He knew she was in California, so that meant that he knew he'd have to be in the States to get her.

Which would make catching him much easier.

It could be an incredible step forward for the clan. As Navuh's son, Lokan would know the location of the island. Not only that, they could hold him as a negotiating chip. Navuh didn't care much for his rank and file, but he must care for his sons, if not emotionally, then for their usefulness.

The question was whether they would manage to get Lokan to talk.

The Doomers the clan had captured in the past hadn't been privy to the information, and on top of that, they'd been under compulsion not to reveal any of the Brotherhood's secrets. Even Dalhu suspected that he'd been compelled before leaving for his mission in the States.

Kian wasn't sure he was right, though.

Dalhu had claimed that the compulsion had eased the longer he'd stayed away from the island. But that sounded more like a thrall than a compulsion. Then again, immortals could only get thralled by gods, and Navuh was no god.

Kian had the passing thought that maybe Annani's half-sister Areana had something to do with it, but he then dismissed it out of hand.

First of all, they had no proof that Areana was alive. Neither Dalhu nor Robert had ever heard of her. And secondly, Areana

40

was a weak goddess. According to Annani, her sister had been weaker than some of the more powerful immortals.

"I want you to keep me updated," he told Ella. "Every time you dream about him, text me the details. Or you can type it in your laptop and text me the page. Whatever works for you."

She nodded. "I'll do that."

8

ELLA

"*I*'m hungry," Ella said as she and Julian climbed the steps to her front porch. "I hope my mother saved dinner for us."

With all the excitement, she hadn't eaten much at lunch, and the meeting had taken longer than expected.

He rubbed his stomach. "We should've gotten something from the vending machines. I'm hungry too, and I don't want to impose."

"Don't be silly." She cast him an incredulous glance. "Even if there are no leftovers, I can whip us up a couple of sandwiches, or we can heat up a frozen pizza." Other than salads, which she had several good recipes for, that was the extent of her culinary expertise.

As she opened the door, Ella scanned the living room for her mother, but no one was there. It still felt strange to her that the front door remained unlocked at all times, even when no one was home, and stranger still that she had no need for a key.

Heck, she didn't even have one. Maybe there was no key?

She wasn't sure. On the one hand, it was nice to know that the village was so safe that no one locked their doors, but on the other hand, having no key to open the door with made her feel as if this wasn't her house.

It was just a passing feeling, a niggling in the back of her head, or maybe just an uncomfortable sensation in her stomach, not a conscious thought. Logically she knew that this was home, even more so than their old house.

Her family didn't belong in the human world. They belonged right here, in this village, and in this brand new, gorgeous house that was theirs to keep.

"Mom? Where are you?"

"I'm right here." Vivian entered through the glass doors with Scarlet trotting behind her. "I was reading outside. How did it go?"

"Good. Is there anything left over to eat? I'm starving."

Vivian waved them over to the table. "I would have waited for you, but Magnus had to leave. I have your plates in the warming drawer. You can tell me everything after your bellies are full."

Once they were done with the main course, Julian summed up the meeting for her mother.

"I don't like it," Vivian said. "Encouraging those dream visits is asking for trouble."

Ella couldn't argue with that assessment. Her mother was right, but she was going to do it anyway.

Finally, Kian was taking her seriously and seeing her as a valuable asset, and not the pesky human girl with grandiose ideas.

Ella hadn't missed the sparkle in his eyes when he'd realized that she had access to one of Navuh's sons and could get information for the clan that they couldn't obtain in any other way.

Julian put down the bread roll he was munching on. "Kian doesn't think it's dangerous. Even if Mr. D can see the village through Ella's eyes, it's going to be meaningless to him. Ella doesn't know the location, and there are no landmarks visible from here."

"The ocean is a big one," Vivian said.

He waved a dismissive hand. "It's only visible from the very edge of the village."

"And I never saw it," Ella added. "I'll just avoid that spot."

Vivian sighed. "Well, I guess that everyone other than me is in favor of this." She pushed away from the table and snagged an envelope from the counter. "While you were gone, Magnus brought your fake papers." She handed it to Ella.

"Oh, good. Now I can go to a club." Ella opened the envelope and pulled everything out. "A driver's license with an awesome picture, a passport, a social security card, and a birth certificate." She glanced at Julian. "You guys are thorough."

Popping the lid off a Snake Venom bottle, he smiled. "I'm only the doctor. I know as much about the production of fake papers as you do."

"This is freedom." Ella lifted the driver's license and waved it in the air. "Now I only need a car."

Her mother flinched. "It's not safe for you to go out by yourself yet. The danger from the Russian is not over."

"I can take you out," Julian offered. "We've just eaten, so a restaurant is not an option, but I can take you to a nightclub."

Across the table, Vivian sucked in a breath.

It's okay, Mom, Ella sent. *I'm not ready for a club.*

Relieved, her mother slumped in her chair.

"How about a movie?" Ella turned to Julian. "I haven't been to a movie theater in ages."

He put his beer down. "You know that we have one in the underground complex, right?"

"I do. But you probably don't have any of the new movies that are now playing in theaters."

He snorted. "Are you kidding me? Have you forgotten about

Brandon? We get new movies before they are released to the public. He gets us the early screening copies."

"Do you have *Vampires in Paris*? It's supposed to come out next month."

"I've never heard of it, but I can check." He pulled out his phone. "We have a list of available movies on the clan's virtual board."

"Let me see." She leaned closer and peered over his arm at the phone. "Anything else interesting on that board?"

He handed it to her. "Take a look."

"Class schedules, a list of movies, and some items for sale. That's uninspiring."

He took his phone back. "What do you think should be there?"

"A horoscope." She lifted a finger. "An advice column." She lifted another one. "Recipes. Short stories." She lifted two more. "Cleaning hacks. There is so much that can go there."

Julian lifted a brow. "Cleaning hacks?"

"Yeah, like shortcuts, or ways to remove stains. Things like that."

"All of the things you've mentioned can be found on the internet. They are not clan specific."

"True." Her excitement dimmed.

For a moment, Ella imagined having her own column on the board. "I'll talk with Carol and Eva. See if there is anything they would like to have there. Carol suggested that you should put up pictures of all clan members so the newcomers could familiarize themselves with their faces. I for one wouldn't want to run into a Doomer and mistake him for a clan member."

"There is a very slim chance of that."

She arched a brow. "Really?"

Not that she would've known what Logan was when she met him, but still. Out of the billions of people on the planet she'd gotten to have lunch with a Doomer.

"Yeah, you're right." Julian glanced back at his phone. "We have *Vampires in Paris*, but it looks like a horror movie. Are you sure you want to see it?"

"Pfft. It's a parody on the vampire lore. You're going to have fun watching it."

9

JULIAN

"*L*et's hope no one is watching a movie already." Julian held the elevator door open for Ella.

"Is it a popular hangout spot?"

"I don't know. If I watch movies at all, it's usually in my room on my tablet."

"Netflix?"

"Yeah."

"I used them extensively during my hibernation period." She chuckled. "Mostly Christmas movies. They are sweet and romantic, and I know nothing bad is going to happen. A guaranteed happy ending."

"It seems that we have the place all to ourselves." Julian pushed the theater's doors open. "Do you want popcorn?"

"Sure." She followed him to the enclave with the antique-looking popcorn machine. "It's just a replica, right? It's not a real antique."

"It's as modern as it gets. Makes awesome popcorn." Julian turned the thing on. "Three minutes."

"That's so cool. Where do you keep the movies?"

"Stored on a server." He picked up the controller and wrapped his arm around her waist. "Front row or back?"

"Back, of course."

As they sat down, he leaned and whispered in her ear, "This is the making-out row."

She laughed and waved her hand at the empty seats in front of them. "Obviously. So, all the people watching the movie won't see us kissing."

"We can pretend that the place is packed."

She cast him an amused glance. "Let's not. I like having the entire theater to ourselves." Sniffing, she turned in the direction of the popcorn machine. "I think it's ready."

"I'll get it."

Ella was so hard to read.

It was driving Julian nuts. His sense of smell and even his empathy were useless with her. She seemed to like him, was acting as if they were best friends, had worn his clothes, and had even slept in his bed, but that was it.

Here and there her arousal would flare for a brief moment, and then it would get snuffed out as if there wasn't enough kindling to keep it going.

Was it the result of what she'd been through, or was it him?

He'd never had a problem like that before. Throughout the ten years that he'd been sexually active, Julian hadn't encountered even one woman who hadn't responded to him right from the very first kiss.

Returning to his seat with an overflowing bucket of popcorn, he handed it to Ella. "Taste it. I bet it's better than any you had before."

And so am I, he wanted to add.

She popped a piece into her mouth. "It is. What makes it so good?"

"You'll have to ask Okidu. He's the one who buys the supplies for the machine and keeps it clean."

"I will. Now let's watch some bloodsuckers terrorize Paris."

Wrapping his arm around her shoulders, he pressed play and braced for an hour and a half of boredom. Parodies were usually too stupid to watch.

He ended up laughing his ass off.

When the credits rolled in, he clicked the movie off and the lights on. "I have to admit that it was fun." Despite the fact that no making out had been going on.

But he'd had his arm around her for the entire time, and when she hadn't been doubled over with laughter, Ella had been resting her head against his bicep.

"It's a sequel to *Vampires in London*. That's how I knew it was going to be hilarious. Maddie and I watched it together, and Maddie laughed so hard she almost choked on a piece of popcorn. I had to use the Heimlich maneuver on her." Ella sighed. "I miss her. That's my only regret about being here."

He offered her a hand up. "When you are an immortal, you can visit her and then thrall the memory away."

Her eyes peeled wide. "I'll be able to thrall?"

"You'll have to practice doing it, but yeah."

"Awesome. I can't wait. There are so many perks to being an immortal."

It was on the tip of his tongue to remind her what she had to do in order to become one, but he didn't want to push her. Ella already knew that.

When they passed the village square, Julian stopped. "Where do you want to sleep tonight? The way to my house is straight ahead, and yours is to the left."

Despite how hard it was to have her so near and not touch her like he wanted to, Julian hoped Ella would sleep in his bed again. Holding her throughout the night had forever changed how he wanted to spend his nights. It was going to be so lonely without her. So empty. So cold.

"I need to sleep at home." She put a hand on his chest. "You know why."

He nodded. She was anticipating a dream visit. But that didn't mean she had to be alone while it was happening.

"I can keep you safe."

"It's sweet of you to offer, but I can't. Having you in my mind is not a good idea. I need to put other people in there. People from my old life."

"I get it."

It was smart of her to plan ahead and fill her head with old memories, but that didn't help with his sense of disappointment.

As they reached her front porch, he turned her to him. "Can I at least get a kiss goodnight?"

Ella smiled and took his hand. "Let's do it like in the old movies from the fifties, sitting on the steps in front of my house and being very quiet so my mom won't hear us moaning into each other's mouths." She pulled him down as she sat down. "Except, in my case, instead of coming out with a shotgun, my mother would clap her hands in glee."

"We wouldn't want that." He lifted her and put her in his lap. "That's better."

As she wrapped her arms around his neck, the slight scent of her arousal reached his nose. "I agree. Kiss me, Julian."

He did, pouring all his feelings into that kiss, but at the same time making sure not to overwhelm her.

If she needed more, she would let him know.

Ella's comment from before had given him an inkling as to what she wanted. In those old movies, the girl was a virgin, and her parents wanted to make sure she remained intact until her wedding night.

He needed to treat Ella as if she were a virgin.

Because basically, she was. She'd never had sex with a male

of her choosing and had missed out on the wonder of joining for the first time with someone she cared about.

It had been stolen from her. She'd been taken against her will by someone she could barely stand.

The rage that bubbled up to the surface every time he thought of that was difficult to stifle, but Julian didn't want to add insult to injury by allowing himself to vent it in Ella's presence. Perhaps after they said goodnight, he should hit the gym and obliterate a punching bag.

"Julian? Your eyes are glowing. Is it because you're turned on?" She sounded like she knew it wasn't the case.

"I'm sorry. Every time I think about what was taken from you I get angry."

She cupped his cheek. "Forget about it. Let's focus on the future, not the past."

He rested his forehead on hers. "I want to make you happy, Ella. I want to erase every bad experience you ever had and replace it with a good one. But I know that you are not ready, and I'm not going to pressure you into anything. All the power is yours. I will never try to take it away from you."

10

ELLA

*I*n her room, Ella plopped down on the bed and draped an arm over her eyes.

This was hard.

To fool Mr. D, she had to distance herself emotionally from Julian, but by doing so, she was bound to hurt him. For her plan to work, she shouldn't have even kissed him goodnight, but he'd looked so disappointed, and a kiss was the least she could do to cheer him up.

He was such a sweetheart, so considerate, and hopefully patient.

Until the situation with Mr. D got resolved, she couldn't open up to Julian. Keeping her emotions suppressed was what had allowed her to put on such a convincing act for the Russian. She needed to use the same tactic on the Doomer.

It was like creating a blank canvas to paint a fake staging backdrop for her act.

Heck, maybe she should pursue an acting career. Except, more than a makeover would be needed to change her appearance enough for Gorchenco not to recognize her. Besides, once she turned immortal, she would have to avoid notice, like the rest of them.

For Mr. D, however, she needed to look like she had before. Which meant thinking and imagining her old self and not looking into the mirror, or at least as little as possible.

Perhaps she should tape a picture of her old self over the bathroom mirror? Eva had taken some before the makeover and had shared them with Ella. All she needed to do was to print one out.

She ended up printing her face on twelve pages and taping them on the mirror like a collage.

Changing into her pajamas, Ella got in bed and closed her eyes. If Logan showed up, should she treat him exactly like she had the Russian?

The situation wasn't the same, so she needed a different approach. Logan hadn't bought her, and except for that first dream, he hadn't tried to force her into anything.

Well, he was popping uninvited into her dreams, but that wasn't even close to what the Russian had done. And Mr. D was handsome.

Heck, he was gorgeous. A true Lucifer if she'd ever seen one. Perhaps it painted her shallow, but it was much easier to pretend attraction to a guy who looked like that. And if she cared to be frank with herself, not much pretending was needed.

But what if Mr. D remembered her saying Julian's name?

If he asked about Julian, should she lie that he was a nobody, or tell him a semi-truth?

When sleep finally came, Logan didn't take long to appear.

"I've been waiting for you," he said. "What time is it where you are?"

They were once again on her favorite beach, walking along the water line. She didn't know whether it was her imagination supplying the details or Logan's, but the setting was perfect for an evening stroll on the shore. The sun was setting, and the sky was gray with a light cloud cover.

There were no other people on the boardwalk that was normally pretty crowded, but there were plenty of sounds and smells to make the setting feel real. Waves crashing to shore, seagulls' cries, and even the smell of hot dogs coming from a nearby stand.

She smiled. "I have no idea. It was a little before midnight when I got in bed, but it took me a long time to fall asleep."

And how was that for an evasive answer? She was quite proud of herself for coming up with that.

"Is there something troubling you?"

As if he cared. She saw right through his fake concern. "Do you have to ask? I have a shitload of bad memories that haunt me at night. I'm afraid to fall asleep."

He stopped and faced her. "Am I one of those bad dreams you dread?"

She could've said yes. Especially after his dark promise from the other night. But when not trying to intimidate her with a harsh expression, his face was so handsome that it was hard to look away from it.

The term 'handsome devil' had never suited anyone better.

A beautiful, dangerous predator.

Waving a dismissive hand, she kept on walking. "I got used to you. Or maybe you are nicer now than you were before."

Logan followed, arching one perfectly shaped dark brow. "How so?"

"You're no longer acting like a brute, and when you're not trying to look scary, you're quite handsome."

"What about that Julian guy? Is he behaving?"

It was good that she was ready for that question and had prepared an answer. "Yeah, he is. He's a nice guy, but it's not serious." Not at the moment, so she wasn't lying.

"On his part, or yours?"

Ella sighed. "Mine. I would like to blame Gorchenco for that, but the truth is that there is something missing. Julian doesn't have the *it* factor."

Logan's nearly black eyes sparkled red, which she now knew was the color of his inner glow. "And may I ask what that mysterious ingredient is?"

Hesitating, Ella went with the closest thing to the truth. "He's sweet, mellow, and way too nice. Apparently, you were right about me, and I do have a thing for bad boys."

Taking her hand, Logan turned her around to face him. "I am a very bad boy, Ella."

As he hooked a finger under her chin and tilted her head up, his lean body was so close to hers that she could feel the heat rolling off him. Was he putting that sensation in her head, or was she supplying the extrasensory input?

Dipping his head, he didn't attack her mouth like he'd done in their first shared dream. Instead, his lips hovered a fraction of an inch away from hers, giving her the option to back away.

Ella closed her eyes and forced a small smile, bracing for the kiss.

As his lips touched hers, Logan wrapped his arm around her waist and pulled her against his hard body. Gently, his tongue flicked against the seam of her lips, coaxing her to open for him instead of invading her forcefully.

Nevertheless, she reacted to his subdued dominance, her arousal flaring hot and quick, so different to her reaction to Julian.

The hand on the small of her back slid down, cupping her bottom and lifting her a little, so her mound was pressed against his hard shaft.

Again, Logan wasn't forcing anything. If she wanted to back away, she could. But she didn't.

Instead, she moaned into his mouth and wrapped her arms around his neck. Suspecting Logan had fangs even in his dream version, she submitted to his kiss instead of kissing him back.

It felt so right even though it definitely wasn't.

Crap. Why did she have to be attracted to the wrong guy?

Way to go, Ella.

She had the best man possible fawning over her, and instead of falling head over heels in love with him, she had the hots for the worst man possible.

Except, for now she wasn't going to fight her inappropriate reaction to Logan, she was going to embrace it.

It was, after all, for a good cause. Any information she could get out of him would greatly benefit the clan.

She was a spy, which should allow her some moral wiggle room, right?

JULIAN

*A*fter the kiss last night, a heavy weight took residence in Julian's gut and refused to move out no matter what excuses he threw at it.

Logically, he understood that Ella was still traumatized even though she wasn't admitting it. Not only that, she was dealing with Lokan's compulsion and his dream visits, which must be extremely upsetting to her.

Was it a wonder that romance was the furthest thing from her mind?

But the annoying voice in the back of his head was whispering that none of that would have mattered if she was his true-love match, and that the force of that should've overcome everything else.

But those nasty whispers were lies. Had Kian and Syssi fallen into each other's arms right away, declaring their love?

Or why go that far? Had Magnus and Vivian?

They'd all struggled with some kinds of issues that had prevented the bond from snapping into place immediately.

What about Carol and Robert? the annoying voice whispered.

They'd tried to make it work, but it hadn't, and they'd separated. Robert had found his true-love match with Sharon, but Carol was still alone.

"Why the long face, my young friend?" Yamanu wrapped his arm around Julian's shoulders, his frying-pan-size hand hanging loosely over Julian's chest.

"Just thinking where we can cut costs. The glazing contractor has been measuring these windows for over an hour and shaking his head. I have a feeling we are not going to like his bid."

This was just the first of a long lineup of contractors Julian had arranged meetings with for today. The last one was scheduled for seven in the evening, so basically, he and Yamanu were going to spend the entire day there.

At least he wasn't missing out on time with Ella.

She'd gone to the sanctuary with Vivian, using her mother's sewing class as a pretext to be there. The real reason behind it was getting to know the girls and gaining their trust.

It was good thinking on her part. She couldn't just drop the filming on them without preamble. A lot of preparation work was needed.

"It is what it is, my friend. This is an old building, and those windows are not standard sizes. They will have to be custom ordered."

Julian cast the Guardian a questioning glance. "How do you know so much about construction?"

Yamanu shrugged. "A long time ago, I decided that I needed a break from the clan. I found a job as a construction worker. The human contractor was a swell fellow who loved what he was doing. He would go into a dump like this one and see potential no one else did. I learned a lot from him."

"I don't get it. You hate leaving the village and interacting with humans. How come you decided to live and work with them?"

The big guy sighed. "It's a long story."

After that evasive answer, Julian didn't expect him to continue, but Yamanu surprised him.

"I thought that since we were safe here in Los Angeles, the clan could do without me. There is no worse feeling than not being needed. Naturally, Onegus and Kian tried to convince me to stay, but I was itching to do something different."

"How long did it last?"

"Not long. I was back after five months."

"What happened?"

"Nothing major. I didn't like the stares. Even when I put sunglasses on, people still stared because I'm so tall and beautiful." He flipped his long hair back.

"I get stared at too. But so what? Why do you care?"

"Because I'm not just a pretty boy like you. I'm strange looking. When among humans, it's never good to be too different."

That was true, but Yamanu was strange looking in a good way.

"So that's why you offered to help? You miss your construction days?"

"Yeah, I do. I like working with my hands. Creating nice things. But I'm no good with the paint brushes like Dalhu."

"Did you know that he donated half of the proceeds from the exhibition to this project? That's where the money to start the remodeling came from."

"That ex-Doomer is a decent guy. Full of surprises."

Julian shook his head. "I don't think he likes being referred to as an ex-Doomer."

"You might be right. What should we call him then? Amanda's mate?"

"I'm sure he wouldn't mind that."

"It's a shame he didn't join the Guardian force. The guy is even better with the sword than he is with the brushes."

Julian had heard all about Dalhu's epic battle with the

Doomers' commander. Rumor said that he'd had an old grudge against the guy, but it wasn't clear about what. As much as people liked to gossip in the village, some things still remained a mystery.

Like Yamanu. There was more to the story about his construction stint, but the guy was as elusive as ever. Seemingly open and charming, but keeping everything about himself close to his chest.

That didn't mean, though, that Julian couldn't poke around some more. "Dalhu got a second chance and took full advantage of it. He doesn't miss his fighting days. Lately, I've been thinking of changing direction as well. Doing something different. How about you? The village could use an in-house contractor."

Yamanu laughed. "I don't know enough to be the boss. And besides, who will join my crew? I don't see any clan members jumping at construction jobs."

"I see your point. It's a shame, though. You should do what brings you joy."

The smile that was almost a permanent feature on Yamanu's face melted away. "Being needed is no less important. And it is fulfilling, just in a different way. Besides, I'm stuck in what I'm doing because I'm irreplaceable."

That was an unexpected revelation, and Julian was starting to get an inkling about what made the Guardian tick. He was one of a kind, and his talent was essential. The problem was that there was limited use for it, and most of the time Yamanu had nothing to do.

Then again, it was his choice. He didn't go on missions unless his special talent was needed or there was a shortage of Guardians, and he had to help. He could've easily joined the ranks and done some good with his regular fighting skills.

Perhaps he didn't like to fight. Being capable of it didn't mean he enjoyed it. But the man had to fill his days with something. Julian would hate sitting around and doing nothing. It would drive him insane.

As far as he was aware, the halfway house was the only project Yamanu had actually volunteered to help out with.

"You are irreplaceable, that's true. But you have plenty of spare time to dedicate to whatever you want. Like this project. I really appreciate your help, and I'm glad you have some construction background because I don't know what I'm doing here. These contractors could've robbed me blind, and I would have thanked them for it."

That brought the smile back to Yamanu's face. "I like hanging out with you. And I want to help these girls in any way I can."

"That's good." Julian clapped the guy's wide back. "I can't wait for your first karaoke night."

He wondered if that was what Yamanu was doing with all his spare time.

"Do you practice singing in your house?"

Yamanu lifted a brow. "I sing when I'm in the mood. Why do you ask?"

Not wanting to offend the guy, Julian scratched his short beard as he thought of a plausible answer. "No reason. It's just that it takes practice to sing as well as you do."

"I'm a natural."

As the glazing contractor waved them over, Yamanu headed his way, and Julian followed behind, pondering the Yamanu mystery.

The Guardian was rooming with Arwel, who was a powerful telepath. He should have more insight than anyone else.

Perhaps chatting with Arwel could provide more clues to the mystery. Provided that the guy was willing to talk.

Damn, he was turning into a busybody like the rest of the village occupants. Julian had never thought it would happen to him. Except, anything that could take his mind off Ella was a welcome distraction.

Obsessing about her twenty-four-seven was not good for him.

"Tell me, Yamanu. Do you and Arwel have a karaoke machine in your house?"

"Naturally."

"Would it be okay if I came over and gave it a try?"

A wide grin spread over Yamanu's face. "Not only okay, it would be fantastic. You can come over any time you want, but check with me at least two hours in advance. I might be busy."

Doing what?

Could it be that Yamanu spent his days in the gym? He wasn't big like a weightlifter, but his lean physique was perfectly sculpted. Perhaps that was his gig?

12

ELLA

he first thing Ella did as she got comfortable in her mother's car was to text Kian an update about her dream. She'd tested her phone this morning, and apparently texting was the same as typing on her laptop, which made life much easier. She could text what she wanted to say instead of passing her laptop to Julian or whoever else was going to read her messages out loud.

Mr. D visited me last night. I made him think that I'm into him and it looked like he bought the act. The only thing he tried to get out of me was my time zone, but I managed to avoid answering him.

She didn't mention the kiss. First of all, because it was embarrassing, and secondly because it was nobody's business how she went about her new spying job.

Kian's return text came a few moments later. *Next dream visit try to find out his time zone.*

Will do.

When they got to the sanctuary, Ella spotted the tall redheaded Guardian doing a walkabout.

"Mom, what's the name of Wonder's fiancé? I forgot."

"Anandur."

"Right. Anyway, I'm going to ask him to help us carry the supplies inside."

"Good idea. It will save us from having to make multiple trips."

It had taken Vivian over a week just to collect everything she needed for her sewing class. That included two sewing machines, two big trash bags filled with donated old clothes that she'd laundered and folded, two boxes full of miscellaneous craft and sewing supplies, one two-pound box of rhinestones, and twelve new Bedazzlers.

She should change the class name from 'sewing with Vivian' to 'rhinestone mania.'

It was going to be fun.

Ella still remembered bedazzling with her mom and the many pleasant evenings they'd spent embellishing old shirts, refreshing old dirty sneakers, backpacks, hats, and jeans pockets. Among other things, it was the perfect way to cover stains that wouldn't come out. Saved them from having to throw away clothes that were otherwise still serviceable. Money had always been tight, but she and Parker had never felt like they were missing out on anything.

So yeah, they hadn't worn the most fashionable labels, and eating out had been reserved for special occasions, but that hadn't been much different from what their friends had. Her mother had worked so hard to provide for them and take care of them, never taking time off for herself or splurging on anything that hadn't been an absolute necessity. Ella was so glad that she could finally take it easy. Her mother definitely deserved a break.

For some reason, the nostalgic memories brought with them a sense of tranquility Ella hadn't felt in a long time. Mother and daughter doing fun things together while the rest of the world was forgotten.

Despite the tragedy of losing their father, which had always loomed heavily in the background, and despite their modest means, those had been the good times.

Before her innocence had been lost.

With a sigh, Ella got out of the car and walked over to the tall Guardian. "Hi, Anandur. My mom and I could use your help. We have tons of things that need to go inside."

"I'll gladly carry everything up to the front door for you, but I'm forbidden from entering." He grimaced. "Vanessa thinks my hulking size will scare the girls."

As Ella looked up at his smiling eyes, she couldn't imagine any woman thinking of him as threatening. He had 'protector' written all over him. In a way, he reminded her of Misha. Anandur was much better-looking, and his smile showed a row of perfectly straight white teeth, not yellowing ones with gold crowns thrown in for embellishment. But he had that aura of a man that a woman could feel safe with, protected, and it was priceless, especially for someone who'd experienced the opposite.

Misha's company had made Ella's stay with Gorchenco tolerable.

Then again, she wasn't the best judge of character, and even if she was, traumatized girls might not see anything beyond his height and bulging muscles.

Stretching up on the very tips of her toes, she put a hand on his shoulder for balance and whispered in his ear, "I don't think you are scary at all. And to prove it, I'm going to have girls peeking at you from the second-floor window. So, if you hear giggling, smile and wave. I'm willing to bet that after seeing you, most will have no problem with you coming inside."

He scratched his red curls and smirked. "I hope Wonder won't mind. I love having girls peek at me, especially when they giggle because they think I'm such an irresistible hunk, but my mate might get jealous."

Ella patted his massive shoulder. "It's for a good cause."

Following her to the car, the Guardian hefted most of what they'd brought. "Make sure to tell her that. She's in there with Kri, helping out with the self-defense class."

He walked over to the front door and deposited the packages there. "That's why I'm here. I'm usually assigned to Kian, but since he's not leaving the village today, he okayed for me to accompany my girl here."

Ella chuckled. "I know your girl, and I doubt she needs you to hover over her. She can take care of herself."

His bushy brows drew tightly together. "Why, what have you heard?"

"Should I have heard something?"

"Never mind. Let me get the rest of the stuff."

There was a story there that Ella intended to pry out of Wonder the next time she came to study with Parker.

"Thank you so much, Anandur," Vivian said when all their packages were stacked by the front door.

"It was my pleasure, ladies." He bowed his head and walked over to his station at the building's corner.

"Do you think he is here because of you know who?" Ella asked. "Increased security?"

Vivian lifted one of the trash bags. "I didn't see any guards the other times I've been here. But that doesn't mean there weren't any."

Ella took the other bag and followed her mother inside. "Where to now?"

Vivian glanced around, but the receptionist wasn't there. "I don't know where Linda is. I'll get Vanessa to show us where to set up shop."

"I'm coming!" Vanessa called out from her office.

A moment later, she and the missing receptionist rushed out. "Let me help you." She grabbed one of the two boxes. "Follow me."

It didn't escape Ella's notice that Vanessa was hiding her superior strength. She could've easily taken a heavier load.

Linda, the receptionist, who like the rest of the sanctuary's staff was human, lifted four Bedazzlers and trailed behind them.

"This is our crafts room," Vanessa said. "We don't have enough classrooms to dedicate one to just sewing. After your class is over, you will have to store your things in the closet to make room for the next one."

"No problem." Vivian put the trash bag on the floor. "Ella will help me organize it so everything will fit."

Doubtful.

The closet barely had any shelf space left, but then her mother was an expert at stuffing as much as possible into closets and refrigerators alike. She didn't really need Ella's help.

"I was hoping to take a look at Kri and Wonder's class."

"Then go." Her mother shooed her away. "I can set up everything by myself."

Ella felt guilty about leaving. "I'll be back in time for the class."

"Don't worry about it, sweetie. Go have fun with the girls."

Vanessa smiled. "Let me take you there."

"Thanks."

When they were out in the corridor, the therapist gave her a once over. "I love your new look. It's edgy."

Ella had the torn jeans and monster boots on, but she had gone easier on the makeup.

"You should've seen me with the fake piercings and the brown contact lenses. They look awesome, but they irritate my eyes, and I figured sunglasses would do for this trip."

"Indeed. The sanctuary is safe."

"About that. I met Anandur outside. Is this something new, or did you always have Guardians patrolling the sanctuary?"

"We have two stationed here during the night and one during the day. Security was beefed up, but Anandur is here because of Wonder. Usually, we don't get the senior Guardians."

"He told me that you didn't allow him inside because you thought he would scare the girls."

Vanessa arched a brow. "Do you question my assessment?"

"I do. And I'm going to prove it to you."

"How?"

"You'll see. I bet you five bucks that at lunch at least half of the girls are going to take their plates outside to keep Anandur company."

Chuckling, Vanessa wrapped her arm around Ella's shoulders. "You are a rebel at heart, aren't you? You like to challenge authority."

"A very astute observation, madam therapist."

13

KIAN

*E*lla's text from earlier that morning kept bugging Kian throughout the day.

She was playing a dangerous game with Lokan, one a young girl like her was ill-suited for. This was a job for Carol, who could have run circles around the Doomer, ensnaring him without breaking a sweat.

Except, Lokan wasn't dream sharing with Carol.

Fuck. Kian threw his pen on his desk. As the Montblanc bounced off the surface and landed on the floor without falling apart, he released a relieved breath. The pen was a present from Syssi, engraved with a sweet love message. He would've hated to have broken it.

His volatile temper was hard to control on a good day, and this wasn't one of those. Sometimes doing the right thing wasn't as clear cut as he would like it to be.

On the one hand, it was low of him to use Ella for what he had in mind, but not to do so was just plain stupid.

This was most likely the only opportunity he would ever get to capture a high-ranking Doomer. And Lokan was nearly

69

as high as they got. Navuh's sons ran the entire Doomer operation.

Kian wasn't sure about their hierarchy. According to Dalhu, Navuh kept it fluid, promoting one son over the other and ensuring that none of them gained too much power.

At this moment in time, Lokan could be the least important or the most, but it didn't really matter. Capturing him and getting him to reveal the island's location would be invaluable. Any other information they could get out of him would just be a bonus.

He needed to brainstorm this with Turner.

Funny how the guy had become so indispensable to him in such a short time. It was becoming a knee jerk reflex to call Turner up and get his advice on anything having to do with security. But the truth was that he trusted Turner's instincts and his insight more than he trusted his own.

Over the years, Kian had become more of a businessman than a commander. Turner, on the other hand, was an expert in modern warfare in general, and special ops in particular.

Then there was his famous temper. Kian was well aware of his shortcomings. He was impatient, and often too emotionally involved. Sometimes it was hard to shove all that aside and think clearly. That was where Turner came in. His cold, calculated and logical brain was the antidote to Kian's hotheadedness.

Picking up his desk phone, he punched in Turner's number and counted three rings. The guy never broke protocol and picked up the phone before that.

On the fourth, Turner answered. "What can I do for you, Kian?"

"I have an idea I want to run by you."

"Shoot."

"Lokan wants to get his hands on Ella. What if she can lure him into a trap?"

"The thought has crossed my mind once or twice. The problem is that she's not sophisticated enough to pull it off. What does an eighteen-year-old know about playing a game like this?"

"Not much, I agree. But she can get coaching from a pro. What if we get Carol to instruct her every step of the way?"

"Carol can't help Ella while she's dream-sharing with Lokan."

"That is true. But she can instruct her before and after."

"I think you've already made up your mind."

"Catching Lokan could be the biggest breakthrough we've had since this has started. If we know where the island is, we can revisit the idea of planting Carol there and letting her do her thing because we can get her out. I'm asking your opinion because right now I can't think of a downside. Lokan can't learn anything from Ella, and if we set a trap for him, we will make sure that she is not in any danger. I'll get the entire Guardian force to watch over her if needed. This is that important."

"What if after all this he doesn't talk?"

"Then we will hold him as a bargaining chip."

"In stasis?"

Kian hadn't thought that far. "We can decide what to do when we get there. But I'm inclined to keep him prisoner. The anticipation of torture can be worse than the torture itself, and we are in no hurry. We can wait long years for him to talk."

For a long moment, Turner remained quiet, and Kian imagined him staring into the distance while the cogs in his brain moved faster and faster, running through different scenarios and calculating the probabilities of success or failure for each.

"I agree. We need to seize this opportunity. If Lokan is the one doing the compulsion, then chances are that he is not under compulsion himself, which means that we can get him to talk one way or another."

Kian leaned back in his chair and swiveled it around to look out his window to the village square. "I'm not sure about that. Lokan can compel only humans. One of the other sons is rumored to be able to compel immortals as well. He might have done it to Lokan."

There was another long moment of silence. "What if it's Navuh himself who does the compelling?"

Kian frowned. It was possible, but it didn't make sense for the leader to bother with things like that. "I don't think Navuh would deal with such mundane matters. He is above that. But even if it is him, does it make a difference?"

"That depends on how he does it. I've given it some thought, and I suspect that he can do with compulsion what Yamanu can do with thralling. Think about it. He has an army of tens of thousands of warriors, loyal to him despite being treated like disposable trash. He is a demagogue, using propaganda to unite his people, but with a twist. How else is he keeping such tight control over his troops?"

"Fear can be a very effective motivator for loyalty. Any unrest is dealt with quickly and brutally." Kian swiveled back to face his desk. "With all due respect to your brilliant mind, Turner, I think you are jumping to conclusions. The propaganda and the iron-fist rule are the most logical explanations for his control. We don't need to look further than that."

"Perhaps. But you know me. I like solving mysteries, and things don't add up as neatly as you think."

Kian chuckled. "Then by all means, try to solve this one. But while you do that, can you come up with a plan for us to catch Lokan?"

"Shouldn't be too difficult."

"Maybe for you it isn't. I've already thought about and discarded several ideas."

"Let me hear them. Maybe I can use one and improve on it."

"I'd rather not. I don't want to contaminate your thinking process with my lousy suggestions."

14

ELLA

"I'm glad we don't have to schlep anything back home," Ella said as her mother parked the car in the village's underground.

"Did you have fun?"

"Yeah, I did. The best part was getting the girls to come out and eat lunch with Anandur on the front lawn." Ella smirked. "I proved the hoity-toity therapist wrong."

Tucking her new bedazzled T-shirt under her arm, she closed the door and headed for the elevators. Vivian had left hers as a sample for the girls to copy, which was a shame because it came out beautifully.

The purple T-shirt had been donated by Amanda, so of course it was top quality and as good as new, and the huge butterfly her mother had added to the front had turned it into something that could've been displayed proudly in a boutique.

"I wondered about that," her mother said. "I saw the lunch exodus, but I thought you'd convinced them it would be fun to eat out in the sun. I didn't know they were going to hang out with Anandur. How did you manage that?"

Ella shrugged. "Easy. I convinced the two queen bees to

come with me to the second floor and peek at him from a window. He did his thing, winking and waving and looking charming. Then I told them that he was Wonder's fiancé and that was it. They were convinced he was a harmless teddy bear. When the other girls saw them picking up their plates and going outside, many followed."

"Queen bees, eh? Even in the sanctuary?"

"Of course. They have cliques like any other bunch of girls stuck in the same place. High schools, women's prisons, sanctuaries, it doesn't matter. I figured that if I got the queens to tell their stories first, it would be easier to convince the others."

"Did you ask them?"

"Not yet. I'm building up a rapport first."

Ella was starting to realize that it was going to be harder than she'd imagined. The girls were suspicious and skittish, and she braced for weeks of coaxing instead of days.

Her mother smiled. "Do you have a plan?"

"The stunt with Anandur was great for that, and also joining your bedazzling class and the self-defense training that Kri is teaching. I'm making friends. But this is going to take much longer than I anticipated. Those girls have been through a lot, and asking them to do something as emotionally draining as telling their story in front of a camera is not going to be easy."

Vivian leaned and kissed her cheek. "I'm so proud of you."

"It's nothing. It's just common sense."

"Still. You've taken on this difficult project, and you're pushing hard to make it happen."

By the time they reached the house, it was starting to get dark, and Ella's stomach was rumbling. "I'm hungry. Do we have any leftovers from yesterday?"

Vivian chuckled. "The guys probably finished them off. But we can make some sandwiches and a salad for dinner."

"Sounds like a plan." Ella opened the door and was hit by aromas that made her salivate. "What smells so good?"

"Barbecue," Parker said. "Magnus has ribs and steaks on the grill."

"And how are you going to eat them?" Vivian asked.

"I took four Motrin's, and I'm going to chew even if my gums bleed."

Shaking her head, Ella patted his shoulder. "Good luck with that."

"Your timing is impeccable." Magnus walked in with a loaded platter. "You are just in time for dinner."

Vivian smiled and gave him a quick peck on his cheek. "You are the best."

Ella eyed the table. "Should I cut up some veggies for a salad?" Other than meat and more meat, the only side dish was corn on the cob.

"Why spoil the taste?" Parker said. "Forget the salad, Ella. Sit down and let's eat before all of this amazing beef gets cold."

As she pulled out a chair and sat down, Ella had that same weird feeling she'd experienced when Parker had told her to do the model walk. She'd really wanted some fresh veggies, and yet she'd done what the little dweeb had told her to do.

"Anything wrong, Ella?" Her mother looked at her with concern in her eyes. "Suddenly, you seem troubled."

She smiled and waved a dismissive hand. "It's nothing. I'm just hungry."

Magnus forked a juicy steak and dropped it on her plate. "Do you want some ribs too?"

"Sure. And also corn."

How was Parker doing that? Was he doing anything? Or was it her?

The thing was, the sensation was familiar, just in reverse. Logan's compulsion prevented her from talking about him, and

Parker's commands were making her do things she didn't want.

Could Logan messing with her head have opened her up for manipulation by others?

Or just by Parker?

"You're not eating, sweetie." Her mother pointed at her full plate. "Is it not well done enough for you?"

"I can put it back on the grill," Magnus offered.

Ella shook her head. "Mom, tell me that I have to eat."

Vivian looked at her with worry written all over her face. "Why?"

"Just do it."

"Okay. You have to eat, Ella."

Perhaps a direct command was needed? Or maybe it had to be issued by an immortal?

"Magnus, please tell me to cut a piece of steak and put it in my mouth. Just humor me."

Thankfully, Magnus just did what she'd asked without demanding an explanation. "Ella, cut a piece of the steak, put it in your mouth, and tell me if you like it."

Nothing.

"Parker, ask me to pass the salt."

Her brother rolled his eyes. "Is it a game?"

'Yes. Now say it."

"Please, pass the salt, Ella."

Nothing again.

But then Parker didn't care whether she did as he asked. Maybe he had to put some conviction behind it?

Rising to her feet, Ella lifted the platter. "There is too much meat on the table. I'm taking this back to the kitchen."

As she'd expected, Parker responded. "Put it down! I'm not done yet."

The moment he said to put it down, she almost dropped the

platter, barely managing to hold on to it in order to lower it to the table without incident.

Letting out a breath, Ella slumped back in her chair. "I guess we've just found out what Parker's talent is. He can compel."

15

KIAN

*A*s Kian hung up the phone with Magnus, he lifted his eyes to the ceiling and offered a prayer of thanks to the Fates. The last time he'd felt so grateful and so elated was when Syssi had come into his life.

The stars seemed to be aligning in his favor.

It had started with the very tangible possibility of capturing Navuh's son and finally discovering where the Doomers' fucking island was.

That in itself was a cause for celebration.

But if what Magnus had reported was true, then they finally had a compeller in the clan. Having an asset like that opened up a host of possibilities, and that was true even if the kid could only compel humans. But since Parker was exhibiting this talent so soon after his transition, he might grow up into a powerhouse.

Heck, the boy hadn't even transitioned fully yet, and already he could compel his sister without even meaning to do it.

"Is Amanda coming?" Syssi came out of the closet, dressed and ready to go.

The only downside of that phone call had been interrupting

their making out session in the Jacuzzi that he'd planned on continuing in bed. But the news he'd gotten from Magnus was well worth the sacrifice. Besides, they could continue when they came back home.

After all, they were on a mission. Almost as much as Kian wanted to give Syssi the baby she craved, he wanted to be done with drinking Merlin's foul-tasting potion.

"Amanda is just as excited as I am. Probably more. So, of course, she is coming. I wouldn't be surprised if she's already there. Do you know how long we've been waiting for this?" She had no way of knowing, so he told her. "Since we discovered that someone in Navuh's camp could compel. If they have an immortal who can do it, then we should too. And here he is."

Kian shook his head. "Little Parker. Who would have thought."

Stretching up on her toes, Syssi wrapped her arms around his neck and kissed his lips. "We don't know that for sure yet. Ella might be imagining it. I don't want you to get your hopes up and then get disappointed."

"I won't. The girl knows what compulsion feels like. If anyone would know, it's her."

Syssi smiled sadly. "Parker could be inadvertently pushing a thrall on her. I don't think she can tell the difference. Heck, I don't know if I can tell a thrall from a compulsion."

She was right, of course. As always, Syssi was the voice of reason.

He stroked her cheek. "I know. And I have some doubts too. But on the other hand, I have a good feeling about this. Things are going our way for a change. First with Ella and Lokan, and now this. I sense a shift coming up in this conflict. We are finally getting a break."

"Did we switch places? Are you the seer now?"

Kian laughed. "I don't know about that. First, you will have to start barking orders at everyone and cussing up a storm. Then I'll consider us switched."

"Oh, no." She pretended horror. "I can't do that. If I start cussing, you're going to spank me."

Chuckling, he cupped her butt cheeks and lifted her up. "That should be an incentive, not a deterrent." He pressed his erection against her mound.

"Indeed." Syssi's cheeks pinked as they usually did when she was thinking naughty thoughts. "People are waiting for us. We'd better get moving."

He nuzzled her neck and then let her slide down his body. "I want you to think up some creative cuss words for later tonight."

Syssi was funny that way. Even though cussing was their agreed-upon invitation to playtime, she had a hard time saying anything harsher than shit or crap. Instead, she invented cusses that were often too cute or just plain hilarious. Like Wooly Wanker, or Jerkemaia Johnson. That one had another variation —Jerkorama Douchensky.

Her blush deepened. "It's a deal."

16

JULIAN

*B*y the time Julian was done with the last contractor, the sun had set, and he was more than ready to call it a day. Or rather call Ella and ask her how her day at the sanctuary had gone and see if she wasn't too tired to see him.

Even though it was torture to hold her in his arms and wait for her to make each move, it was a sweet torment.

Yeah, he must be a closet masochist. No one should look forward to a case of blue balls. But he did.

Perhaps it was the novelty of it. After years of having girls practically dropping their panties for him without him having to even ask, the old-fashioned courtship dance was refreshing.

"Do you mind driving?" he asked Yamanu. "I want to make a phone call."

"No problem, buddy." He smirked. "I know you're missing your girl."

As Yamanu got in the driver's seat, Julian got in on the other side and pulled out his phone.

Ella answered right away. "Julian, I'm so glad you called. Are you back home?"

"I'm on my way. What's up?"

"Come straight to my house."

He frowned. "Why? Not that I need a second invitation. But did something happen?"

"Maybe. We are not sure yet. But you will want to be here. Heck, I want you here."

"Can you give me a clue?"

She hesitated for a moment. "It has to do with Parker and his special talent. But that's all I'm going to say."

Julian let out a relieved breath. As long as it wasn't more bad news about Ella, he was good. "I can be there in about twenty-five minutes."

"Perfect. Kian and Syssi are coming too. And so is Amanda."

"Now you've really got me curious."

She laughed. "See you here, Julian." The call ended.

"Little Parker has discovered his special talent?" Yamanu asked.

"It sounds like it's a big deal. Otherwise, Kian wouldn't have bothered coming over there to check it out."

Yamanu rubbed his hand over his clean-shaven jaw. "I wonder what it is. Probably telepathy, like his mother and sister."

"Not necessarily. Talents are kind of random. I'm surprised that Vivian and Ella share the same one. The commonality is usually in how powerful it is."

"Makes sense." Yamanu chuckled. "My mother can't thrall for shit. But she can do other things."

Julian's ears perked up. Any nugget of information about Yamanu could shed some light on the mystery he was. "What's her talent?"

"Nagging."

"Seriously."

"I am serious. She has everyone doing exactly what she wants just to stop the nagging. That's one hell of a power."

Julian sighed. Yamanu was pulling his chain. This mystery

wasn't going to get solved anytime soon, but at least he was going to find out what Parker could do.

The rest of the drive was spent with Yamanu telling him one anecdote after another about his mother's nagging and what she'd managed to achieve with it, and by the time the Guardian parked the car, Julian was inclined to believe him that it was a special talent.

"Is she very charming? Because I can't see people cooperating with a horrible nag unless she has some redeeming qualities."

Yamanu smiled wistfully. "My mother is one hell of a woman. She's always ready to help in any way she can, and she can do a lot. Many owe her favors, and she is not shy about collecting."

They parted at the village square, with Yamanu heading to his house and Julian turning toward Ella's.

He got there at the same time as Kian and Syssi did.

"Hello, Julian." Syssi gave him a quick one-armed hug.

Kian nodded in his direction and knocked on the door.

Amanda opened it. "Good, you are all here, so we can finally begin with the testing."

Given Amanda's excitement, Parker's talent must really be a big deal.

As soon as he entered, Ella ran up to him and took his hand. "Come sit with me. We are about to begin."

He let her pull him to an armchair. "Both of us can squeeze in here."

"Or you can sit on my lap."

She smiled. "I can do that."

"Okay, Master Parker. Let's start," Amanda said. "You've demonstrated that you can compel Ella to do what you want, now let's try your mother."

Julian's eyes widened. "Compulsion? That's his talent? It's impossible."

Ella patted his arm. "We will find out soon enough."

"Mom, give me ten dollars," Parker said.

Vivian shook her head. "I don't feel anything."

"You need to really want it," Ella said. "Ask for a steak dinner every night for the rest of the week."

Parker grimaced. "Right now I don't want any. My gums are hurting."

"So think about something else that you really want, and that Mom wouldn't normally agree to."

Parker scratched his head, crossed his legs, looked up at the ceiling, and then smirked. "I know the perfect thing." He looked at Vivian. "Sing me that lullaby you used to sing when I was little. The one about me being your sunshine."

Ella snorted. "That's a good one, Mom. I know how much you hate singing in public."

Vivian's cheeks turned red, and she shook her head, but she started singing. Very, very quietly.

"Louder, Mom. I can't hear you."

It was evident that Vivian was struggling against the compulsion. Nevertheless, her voice got louder.

She really was a lousy singer. Not tone deaf, she was on key, but her voice was cracking like a teenage boy's.

"Okay, Mom. That's enough. You can stop."

Vivian let out a breath and then looked at Ella. "Now I know how you feel. It's terrible."

Amanda clapped her hands. "Amazing demonstration, Master Parker. Now we need to try it on an immortal."

Sitting on a bar stool and facing a room full of adults, Parker was grinning from ear to ear. The kid was eating up the attention.

"Julian, come play video games with me."

Julian wasn't sure whether he felt something or not, but he found it easy to refuse. "Sorry, kid, I'd rather take your sister out for a walk."

"Try me," Magnus offered.

Parker smirked. "No problem. Just remember that I have a good excuse."

"Go ahead."

"Magnus, give me your beer. I want to taste that Snake Venom you guys keep chugging."

Magnus held out the bottle as if handing it to Parker, but then shook his head and laughed. "Not working, buddy."

"Bummer."

"Did you really want to taste that beer?" Ella asked.

"I did. And I tried really hard. But I guess it doesn't work on immortals."

Amanda walked up to him and kissed his cheek. "You did very well. Your powers are just starting to develop. I have no doubt that you'll become formidable."

Parker looked at her with hopeful eyes. "You really think so?"

"I'm positive. You just keep practicing and flexing those mental muscles of yours. Just make sure you don't do that on unsuspecting victims. You need to tell people before you try it on them. Compulsion is a very serious matter and doing it without getting permission is considered a crime. The only exceptions are the same as for thralling. If it's in self-defense or to defend others and to keep the secret of our immortality."

He nodded. "I get it."

"Good. Now I want you to try something that is most likely not going to work, but it's worth a try. Command Ella to talk about Mr. D."

Julian sucked in a breath, and so did Ella.

"I've got my fingers crossed." She lifted both hands to show everyone. "Go for it, Parker. Give it all you got."

The kid swallowed and nodded. "Ella, tell me who Mr. D is. Now!"

"Logan," Ella blurted out and then clapped her hands. "It worked! I can't believe that it did!"

She jumped off Julian's lap and ran up to her brother. "I love you." She wrapped her arms around him and tried to lift him off the stool, but he was too heavy for her. "Crap, you're getting big." She wiped her eyes.

"He calls himself Logan?" Kian asked.

Ella turned to him and nodded. "Not very imaginative, right?"

"Tell us a little more," Amanda prompted. "I want to make sure it worked."

"I met Logan when I was with Gorchenco. Then he started popping up in my dreams. At first, he was really creepy and scared the hell out of me, but then he learned to behave, and now he's okay. He even helped me out right after the rescue. When I was feeling down, he complimented me at a time when I really needed it."

Julian felt his fangs starting to elongate. The way Ella was talking about the Doomer, it sounded as if she was fond of him. He knew she was supposed to pretend when Lokan invaded her dreams, but there was no reason for her to pretend now.

Kian got up, walked over to Parker, and clapped him on the back. "Parker, my boy. You have no idea what a great asset you are to the clan. You're the first clan member with the power to compel, which in itself is a miracle. But that you can remove a compulsion, or rather overpower someone else's, is an even bigger one."

Embarrassed, Parker lowered his eyes. "Thank you." But his momentary shyness didn't last long. "So, does that mean that I can be a Guardian? You need me, right?"

Kian chuckled. "The clan needs you, Parker. And yes, you're welcome to join the Guardian training program once you reach majority. Which is seventeen in our culture."

Parker waved a dismissive hand. "That's silly. Why wait so long? I can be helpful right now."

Kian shook his head. "I know. But you're still a kid. We will see. The clan's needs will have to be balanced with yours. And naturally, your mother will need to approve every time we ask for your help." He glanced at Magnus. "And once the adoption is complete, your stepfather will have to approve too."

Parker squared his shoulders. "My mom and Magnus are both cool. You have nothing to worry about, Boss man. They will approve."

17

ELLA

"*I*t's such a relief to be out from under his control," Ella said, just to say something.

Walking hand in hand through the lush village grounds could've been pleasant if not for the big fat elephant lodged between her and Julian.

It used to be easy to talk to him, about anything, but that was when Ella hadn't felt like a cheater.

"I can imagine. Parker saved the day."

She chuckled. "Yeah, he did. From now on, it's going to be a nightmare living with him and his overblown ego. It's not good for a kid his age to have such power."

"Magnus should have the talk with him."

She lifted a brow. "About girls? I don't think it's necessary. Mom already did that, and I'm pretty sure Parker watches porn."

"Not that kind of talk." Julian spotted a bench and headed in its direction. Sitting down, he pulled Ella onto his lap. "It's the talk every newly turned boy gets. Mostly it is done by the mothers, but sometimes one of the male immortals gets involved. Especially if the boy gets in trouble."

Ella wished he hadn't done it. Sitting in such an intimate way after dream-kissing another guy felt wrong. Then again, refusing to sit in his lap would hurt Julian's feelings. Good thing that she'd become such an adept actress. If she played it right, Julian might not notice the change in her. And if he did, she could come up with plenty of excuses.

"What kind of trouble?"

"Let me put it this way. Being able to thrall and refraining from using it requires a strong moral code that many teenage boys don't have. You think being good-looking leads to feelings of entitlement? Imagine what being a powerful immortal among humans leads to."

"Dropped panties?"

He nodded. "But not for the right reason, and not voluntarily. That's why the talk is necessary. The penalty for abusing the thralling power is severe. I'm sure the same applies to compulsion."

It reminded her of Logan's behavior in the first dream they'd shared. Apparently, Doomers didn't get the same talk as the clan boys, and thralling an unsuspecting human female into having sex with them was the norm. That's why Logan had just gone for it and had forced a kiss on her without bothering to check if she was interested.

Entitlement.

He was the son of a powerful leader, which probably made him much worse than the average Doomer in that respect. Heck, the human sons of politicians and rich people weren't much better.

She'd read about that. The son of a well-known CEO had raped a girl in his Ivy League college, and it had been covered up.

Power and money were morally corrupting. Or maybe it was simply that some people were naturally moral or amoral, and the amoral ones acted upon their urges when they were guaranteed immunity.

What she wondered, though, was whether Logan's behavior had improved because of her influence, or just because he knew he needed to do better in order to entrap her.

Most likely, it was the second one. But then again, maybe not. People could change, right?

"What are you thinking about that makes you frown like this?" Using his forefinger, Julian massaged the crease between her eyebrows.

Crap. She didn't want to talk to him about Logan.

What she was doing was already bad enough. She didn't need to hurt his feelings too. But what about honesty?

Looking at her hands instead of his face, she shrugged. "I was thinking about my dream encounters. Doomers don't get the talk you mentioned. They think that they can take what they want either by physical or mental force."

Julian's entire body stiffened. "Did he force you to do anything in the dreams?"

She nodded. "The first time he invaded my dreams, he kissed me against my will. But, later on, he mellowed down. I don't know if it's because he wants me to like him, or because he's realized the error of his ways."

His eyes blazing blue fire, Julian snorted. "He's trying to play you. Don't fall for that."

"Yeah, that was what I thought too. But the joke is on him, since I'm playing him back." With that admission, Ella looked away once more.

She hadn't disclosed any details, but Julian was a smart enough guy to figure it out.

When a long moment passed, and he didn't respond, Ella chanced a glance at his face and wished she hadn't.

Not because of the glowing eyes or the pointy fangs that had punched out over his lower lip, she was no longer scared of those, but because of the inner emotional battle that was raging on his handsome face.

"I don't want you to do that."

Ella sighed. "I know. And I don't want to do it either. Even though it's happening in dreamland, it feels real, and it's like a replay of what I had to do with the Russian. But this is too important an opportunity." She looked up at him. "You must realize that."

"Did Kian ask you to do it?"

She shrugged. "You were there with me, so you know what he asked for. But I have a feeling he is going to ask for more. Kian doesn't want to involve me in this either, but guess what? I'm in it whether I want to be or not, so I'd better make the best of it and get something valuable for the clan."

Julian nodded. "Logically, I get it. Emotionally, every cell in my body rebels against it. I can't stand the thought of you smiling at the Doomer, let alone doing more than that."

Ella tilted her head. "Is it because you are jealous, or because you are afraid for me?"

"Both. But mostly I'm jealous."

She liked that he was honest with her. Two points for Julian.

"Don't be. I only pretend to like him, but you I like for real." It was the truth, just not the whole truth. She wasn't going to fess up to her annoying attraction to the bad boy.

Letting out a breath, Julian rubbed a hand over his jaw. "Perhaps it would not be so bad if you weren't distancing yourself from me. I can feel you pulling away."

She was, so there was no denying it.

"I'm afraid my feelings for you will seep through into the dreams. He can't know that I'm serious about you."

Julian arched a brow. "You are?"

"Of course, I am, you silly."

"Then prove it. Kiss me."

Ella preferred for Julian to do the kissing. "Why don't you kiss me?"

He shook his head. "I told you. All the power is yours. I'm not going to pressure you into anything."

"You are not pressuring me if I'm asking you to kiss me."

Letting out an exasperated sigh, Julian cupped the back of her head. "But I did. I've already broken my own rules. I asked you to prove that you like me by kissing me."

"Semantics. Just kiss me, Julian."

His lips were soft on hers, gentle. Julian wasn't demanding anything, he was coaxing.

It wasn't what she wanted, and for some reason she felt annoyed, which made her feel like a jerk. But even though Julian was pouring his heart into his gentle kiss, it wasn't doing anything for her, and Ella hated the lukewarm response his kiss was eliciting.

Why wasn't this enough to ignite her passion?

Frustrated, she threaded her fingers through his hair and pulled him down to her, kissing him the way she wanted to be kissed.

With a tortured groan, Julian's hand tightened on her nape, his fingers digging into her flesh for a brief moment before he loosened his grip.

"I'm sorry," he murmured into her mouth. "I got carried away."

18

MAGNUS

*A*s Magnus collected the empty coffee mugs and carried them to the sink, he thought about the talk he had to have with Parker.

The one every immortal boy got.

The difference was that Parker was much younger than the average age that it was usually done at, and if not for his newly discovered talent, it could have waited for at least a couple of years.

By then Vivian would have been familiar with clan laws and could have done it herself.

Unfortunately, though, the task fell to him, and it was not going to be easy to explain to both mother and son the consequences of using compulsion or thralling on unsuspecting victims to one's advantage.

Cleaning the mugs by hand, Magnus took his time at the sink while planning his speech.

If only he didn't suck at things like that. Maybe it would be better to send Parker to Kian for the talk? If anyone was going to instill fear in the kid, it was him.

But that was a cowardly move.

If he hoped to be a father to Parker in more than just name, Magnus had no choice but to step up to the plate and give the kid the talk himself.

Wiping his hands on a dishrag, he glanced at the living room. Parker was already gone, probably in his room gaming, and Vivian was wiping the dining table clean.

When she was done, he walked up to her and pulled her into his arms. "One hell of a night, eh?"

"Yeah, you could say so. I'm still trying to wrap my head around it. How come my kids' talents are so powerful? My mother, who we obviously inherited the genes from, never exhibited anything out of the ordinary."

"How about her family? Any weird aunts or uncles? Eccentric grandparents?"

Vivian shook her head. "I was a miracle baby who came when my parents were in their mid-forties. I had one grandmother who lived in Florida and died when I was ten, and she had no siblings."

"It's a shame." He leaned and kissed her lips. "Now you have an entire clan of relatives."

She smiled. "I love it. It's so nice to have a big family."

"I agree." He leaned his forehead against hers. "I have to talk to Parker about his new powers, and I need you to be there when I do it."

"Why?"

"Clan law is very specific about the use of thralling, and the same rules apply to compulsion even though it's not specified. But since both can be used to gain an unfair advantage over humans, I'm sure the punishment for using either in an unlawful way is the same."

She frowned. "What's the punishment?"

"It'd be better if I explained it to Parker and you at the same time. You know how bad I am at things like that."

"You'll do fine."

He definitely hoped so. "Do you want to call him out here, or should we go to his room? I don't know what the protocol is for having a talk with a kid."

"I'll get him."

"Thank you."

Without thinking, Magnus headed back to the kitchen, opened the fridge, and pulled out another bottle of Snake Venom.

Like that was a good example to give the kid.

Was that the message he wanted to impart on an impressionable boy? That when a tough talk was coming the way to go was to reach for liquid courage?

Vivian expected him to be a positive role model for her kids.

Magnus put the beer back and pulled out a water bottle instead.

"You wanted to talk to me?" Parker asked as he sat on one of the barstools.

"Yes. But let's take it to the living room couch."

When Parker and Vivian were seated, Magnus sat on the coffee table facing them. "Remember what Amanda told you about asking permission before practicing your talent?"

"What about it?"

"I want to explain what she meant so there will be no misunderstandings."

"I got it. She said not to do it without asking permission first. What else?"

"You shouldn't use it on humans either. At times, you'll be tempted to, and other times you might not even realize that you're pushing compulsion on them. You need to pay attention and make sure that you don't do it unintentionally."

Parker nodded. "I didn't know I was compelling Ella to do the model walk. I just asked her to do it, and she did."

"Do you remember how you felt when you asked her? What tone of voice you used?"

"I didn't feel anything different, if that's what you mean. I wanted her to do it and thought that she was being stubborn, or shy."

"Did you get angry?"

"Maybe a little bit."

"When you practice on Ella and your mom, pay attention to how it feels."

"I will."

"You can also practice on me. But every time you do, you need to give us a warning."

"Okay."

Magnus smoothed his hand over his goatee. "Right now it's not a problem yet, but when you get a little older, you might get tempted to use your power on girls."

Parker's eyes widened. "What do you mean? Like to get a kiss or something?"

It was endearing that he was still so innocent despite his secret forays into anime porn.

"Yeah, like that. Always ask permission first. You might think that the girl wants a kiss, but don't kiss her unless you're sure she does."

Parker frowned. "Should I just ask, can I kiss you?"

"That's one way, and it's a very good one. But if you're embarrassed about asking, you can also stop a moment before your lips touch and let her close the distance."

Blushing all shades of red, Parker shrugged, pretending nonchalance. "I'm not going to kiss anyone for years. And besides, what does it have to do with my talent? This is basic stuff every guy should know."

Magnus felt his chest swell with pride even though Parker's attitude wasn't his doing. It was Vivian's.

"You are absolutely right. But when you can thrall or

compel, it is easy to get consent that otherwise would not have been granted."

"I will never do that."

"I believe you. Nevertheless, I have to tell you what the consequences of breaking this most important law are." He took a deep breath. "It might seem barbaric to you, but you have to remember that teenage boys are usually not as mature and level-headed as you are, and when they have supernatural powers, it's even worse."

"You're scaring me with all this pep talk, Magnus. Just say it."

"Whipping. The penalty is whipping."

Vivian sucked in a breath. "That really is barbaric. Tell me that it hasn't been done in ages."

Magnus grimaced. "Unfortunately, I can't. It wasn't a boy, though. The offender knew what he was doing and was willing to suffer the consequences. I don't want to say too much, but he had a good reason for what he did. The judge wanted to reduce his sentence to a short prison stay, but he preferred to get it over with."

She shook her head. "Is he a masochist?"

"I don't think so. You forget how quickly we heal. He was fine the next day and could go back to work."

Parker hadn't said a word and was still staring wide-eyed at Magnus.

"Are you okay, buddy?"

Parker shook his head. "I'm just not going to do it. At all. I'm going to always ask nicely and say please, so no one can accuse me of compelling anyone."

"Don't be scared. As long as you ask permission, it'll be okay. And anyway, you are only going to practice on your family. We are not going to judge you too harshly if you slip up here and there."

19

ELLA

*W*ith thoughts of Julian filling her mind, Ella was afraid to go to sleep. If Logan entered her dream, she couldn't afford to be consumed by thoughts about another man.

Except, things were not working between them, and even though she'd told herself to wait until the thing with Logan was over, it bothered her.

Julian was the one for her. Ella knew it like she knew her own face in the mirror, before and after the makeover. They were destined to be together, and she had to fix what was broken.

Was it her?

Yeah, it definitely was. How could she be falling in love with one man while feeling attracted to another?

Julian was the one she wanted to spend her nights with, sleeping in the safety of his arms, listening to his heart beating against her chest, looking into his eyes first thing when she opened hers in the morning.

This was her future, the one that gave her hope and made her heavy heart feel lighter.

Until she remembered the dark one, with his semi-evil smirk, his condescending attitude, and the dark eyes that emitted a red demonic glow whenever he got excited.

Then her heart would get heavy again, and the hope for a better future would seem distant and unachievable.

If only the clan didn't need her help, and if she could find a way to banish Logan from her dreams, she might be able to forget him and concentrate on building her relationship with Julian.

Except, indulging in what ifs was not going to solve those problems for her. The clan needed her, and she had no way of getting rid of Logan.

With an exasperated sigh, Ella opened her laptop and searched the internet for her old high school's site. If her login credentials still worked, she could download pictures from the recent yearbooks which, thankfully, had all been digital to save on printing costs.

It was a small security breach, but she was sure Gorchenco's people wouldn't go as far as checking that. Entering her user name and password, she had little hope of getting in, but apparently her school hadn't revoked her user credentials yet.

First, she copied and pasted Maddie's picture, then enlarged it until it filled an entire page. Next, went Mr. Panties Fetish, Jim. A best friend and a pretend boyfriend would be enough to fill her head.

After printing out both, she taped them to the bathroom mirror next to hers.

Jim even had the same coloring as Julian, though his hair was short, his face was clean-shaven, and he wasn't nearly as handsome. But he would do. As far as Logan was concerned, that was the guy she was dating.

Lying in bed, Ella closed her eyes and replayed old memories in her head. Hanging out with Maddie, Jim's smiling face, sleeping over at Maddie's, laughing her ass off as she'd told her best friend about Jim's panties obsession.

She hadn't realized it back then, but those were the good times. That Ella no longer existed, but the new Ella could still enjoy those memories and fall asleep smiling.

"Come on, Ella, what's the big deal? I'll pay you for the fucking panties. How much did they cost? Five bucks?" Bracing his beefy arm on the lockers, Jim smirked and leaned over her. "Or are you hiding something sexy under those jeans?"

Laughing, she pushed on his chest. "Give it up, Jim. You're not adding mine to your collection."

He didn't resist, letting her push him off. "To be included in my collection is an honor, Ella."

Walking away, she flipped him the bird. He was such an asshole, but she liked him anyway. The good thing about Jim was that he didn't take himself too seriously.

"Is that the guy you're seeing?" Logan asked.

Suddenly, she was not walking down the wide corridor of her high school, but a fancy shopping mall's.

"Where are we?"

"Paris. I got sick of your beach. I hope you don't mind the change in scenery."

Wow, that was progress for Logan. He was actually interested in her opinion.

To reward him, Ella threaded her arm through his. "Not at all. I've always wanted to see Paris. Although the inside of a mall doesn't count as sightseeing."

He grinned at her. "Where would you like to go?"

"The Champs-Élysées."

He snapped his fingers. "Voilà."

"Awesome." She leaned her head against his bicep. "You're learning. Taking a girl to Paris is so romantic."

He chuckled. "No one has ever accused me of being romantic. I've never even taken a woman on a date."

Ella faked surprise. "A handsome guy like you? You must be joking. I'm sure it was not for lack of candidates."

"No, of course not. I just don't date." He winked. "I take them straight to my bed."

Ella huffed. "Well, I'm not that sort of girl. If you want a chance with me, you'll have to behave like a gentleman and take me all over the world." She waved a hand at the street. "Or just to Paris. It's such a beautiful city."

"I can take you wherever you want to go. The one caveat is that it has to be a place I've been to before. Otherwise, I can't create it in my mind."

"Have you been to many places?"

"I've traveled all over the world." He looked down at her. "But most of it is not as pretty as this."

"Then take me only to the nice parts. Which city is your favorite?"

"St. Petersburg is beautiful."

That reminded Ella of the Russian. "How is Gorchenco doing?"

"Recuperating. He's a stubborn human. He'll be fine. Physically."

Ella ignored the 'human' slip up, pretending not to notice. "Maybe you should suggest a visit to that vacation spot you guys were talking about at that lunch meeting. Something to take his mind off his loss. In fact, I'm curious about that place. Can you take me there?"

Logan laughed. "It's beautiful, but I don't think you're going to like it there. It's where rich men go to indulge, if you catch my drift."

"Wow, Logan, you've changed so much since our first meeting. Back then you would've just said that it was a sex resort."

Wrapping his arm around her shoulders, he tucked her closer against his side. "I want you, Ella, you know that, and it gives you power over me. In the past, I would've resented you for it, but I find myself enjoying being different with you. It's a new experience for me, and I didn't think there were any left for me to try."

She smiled at him sweetly. "That's nonsense, Logan, you are talking like an old man. There is plenty you haven't experienced yet. And if you play your cards right, and by that I mean keep being nice and not acting like a jerk, you might enjoy those experiences with me."

2 0

KIAN

"*H*ave a great day at work." Kian pulled Syssi into his arms for one last kiss before they had to part for the day.

He hated letting her go and kept on kissing her until she pushed on his chest. "I'm already late, my love. I have to go."

He nodded, handing her the coffee thermos Okidu had prepared for her. "Don't drink and drive." He winked.

She popped the lid and took a sip. "Only when I'm waiting for the lights to change. Don't work too hard."

"I'll try." Kian closed her door and then watched her drive away.

On his way to the office, he stopped by the row of vending machines and bought a pastry, popping it into his mouth as he moved over to the coffee machine and ordered a double cappuccino.

Usually he and Syssi had breakfast together, and that included at least two cups of her unrivaled cappuccinos, but this morning's romp had taken a little longer, and they'd had to rush out without eating.

Cappuccino cup in hand and his laptop tucked under his

104

arm, Kian took the stairs to his office two at a time. With as little time as he was spending in the gym lately, he needed to take every opportunity to do at least something.

Regrettably, frequent sex with his wife didn't count as exercise.

Kian smiled. If it did, his quota would have been covered.

Ah, the good life.

As he reached the top of the stairs and turned into the corridor, he found Turner waiting for him outside his office.

If it were anyone else, Kian would have sensed his presence as he was coming up, but with Turner's lack of emotional scents, he had no forewarning. It was disconcerting to an immortal who relied on his sense of smell to detect unexpected visitors.

The guy should at least put some cologne on to announce his presence, but he was probably avoiding it purposely so he could sneak up on people.

"Good morning, Turner. What brings you here so early?"

"I wanted to talk to you before I left for the office. I have an idea I want to run by you."

"You could've waited inside. My door isn't locked." Kian opened the way.

Following, Turner closed the door and then pulled out one of the visitors' chairs. "After our talk yesterday, I spent some time thinking about a safe way for Ella to lure Lokan into a trap."

Putting his coffee cup and laptop down, Kian sat behind his desk. "Go on."

"Ella is eighteen and a recent graduate from high school. Before she was taken, she had plans to go to college. I think she should start looking into that again."

"That is a good excuse to get her out in the open. But if she lives on campus, it's going to be difficult to guard her."

Turner shook his head. "That's not what I'm suggesting. All

she needs to do for now is start thinking about colleges and talk about it with Lokan. Let him suggest one. If he takes the bait, he will probably choose one that's near him, and reveal his general location. Not that it's necessary for my plan to work. But if she schedules a visit to the college he suggested, he's not going to be overly suspicious about her decision to check it out."

"We lure him during her visit."

"Precisely. And that also solves another variable that kept bothering me. What if Lokan is interested in Ella because of the telepathy, and he uses seduction as a way to lure her to him?"

"That's a possibility, but I don't see how it affects our plans for capturing him."

Turner smirked. "Since Ella and Vivian can only communicate with each other, their talents are useless unless he has both of them. If Lokan wants to use Ella's telepathy, he would need Vivian too. We have to assume that he probed Ella's mind during their one face-to-face meeting and that he knows that."

Although by now Kian shouldn't have been surprised by Turner's smarts, he was nevertheless impressed. The idea that Lokan might be more interested in Ella for her ability than her looks hadn't even crossed Kian's mind. He'd been so focused on her uncommon beauty and what had happened to her before that he hadn't taken into consideration the most unique thing about her.

Unlike Kian, Turner was logical and methodical. Now that he'd brought it up, it seemed so obvious, but it had taken someone who thought with his brain and not his heart to consider all the variables.

"Brilliant as always, my friend. An eighteen-year-old girl wouldn't travel alone to tour a college. Her mother would go with her."

Turner nodded. "We can have Guardians stationed in the

same hotel Ella and Vivian are going to stay in, other Guardians posing as the taxi drivers taking them places, and we can have some posing as students who are giving them the college tour. They won't be without protection even for a moment."

Kian smirked. "I like it."

"I can see only one problem with my plan, but it's a major one. If Lokan can compel immortals, then this is out because we won't be able to keep Ella and Vivian safe. Not if he can compel a Guardian to let them go."

Kian rapped his fingers on the desk. "Dalhu doesn't think so. As far as he knows, Lokan can only compel humans."

"But he is not certain. I won't risk Ella and Vivian's safety unless I'm sure we can protect them and overpower Lokan."

Kian pulled out his phone. "Instead of speculating, we should talk to the man himself." He looked at Turner before pressing the call button. "Do you have time now, or should I tell Dalhu to come over this evening?"

Turner leaned back in the chair and crossed his arms over his chest. "I'll wait. Otherwise, the uncertainty is going to bug me all day long."

21

DALHU

*A*bsorbed in sketching the outline for a new painting, Dalhu ignored the phone ringing.

Whoever was calling was most likely looking for Amanda, not him, but she had left for the university already. The caller would either leave a message or try her cellphone number.

But when the ringing stopped and immediately started again, Dalhu got worried.

What if it was Amanda trying to reach him?

What if she had car trouble? Like a blown tire she needed him to change?

But why would she call the house phone instead of his cell?

In his rush to pick up, Dalhu didn't wipe his hands clean and cursed as his charcoal-covered fingers stained the white receiver.

"What?" he barked into the phone.

"Am I calling at a bad time?" Kian asked.

Fuck.

"No, it's nothing. I answered the phone with dirty hands. If you're looking for Amanda, call her cellphone. She already left."

"For a change, I don't need Amanda. I need you. How quickly can you get to my office?"

Dalhu tensed. "What's going on?"

"Relax. Everything is fine. I have Turner here, and we need to ask you a few questions about Navuh and his sons."

"I'll be there in ten minutes."

"We are waiting."

Dalhu would rather not talk about the fucking island and its leaders. The less he thought about it, the more he could forget. He would much rather focus on the blissful life he led with Amanda and his canvases.

But Kian needed his help, and he owed the guy.

Kian hadn't welcomed him into the clan with open arms, far from it, but he had been man enough to change his mind and accept a former enemy not only as his sister's mate, but as a full-fledged, trusted clan member.

In a hurry, he washed his hands and put on clean clothes that he double-checked for paint splashes. If he was being called in as a consultant, he'd better look the part.

When Dalhu knocked on Kian's door, it was precisely ten minutes after he hung up the phone.

"Come in!"

He walked in and pulled out a chair next to Turner. "Morning."

The guy nodded.

"How can I help you?" Dalhu asked Kian.

Turner answered, "Tell us everything you know about compulsion on the island. Who was doing it, when was it done, what were the effects, how long did it take you to shake it off, and how did you manage to do it?"

Dalhu rubbed a hand over the back of his neck. "That's a lot of questions, and the truth is that what I know is no more than speculation. It's not like we got lined up for compulsion before leaving the island. I didn't even know I was under one until over time it started to fade, and I realized that I could think more clearly."

The rage had subsided too. But that might have had nothing to do with the compulsion. He'd had a lot of baggage stored deep inside him, and it had simmered and festered for centuries. If not for Amanda and his love for her, that rage might have still ruled his life.

Kian waved a dismissive hand. "I told Turner that. Just tell us what you can. Figuring out Lokan's powers is most important to us. The more information you can provide, the more clues we will have to piece together and maybe get a better understanding as to who is doing what and how."

Dalhu nodded. "Two of Navuh's sons are rumored to have compulsion powers. One is Lokan, and I know for a fact that he is the one who's compelling the human pilots to never reveal the island's location. In his case, there is little or no doubt that he can do that. I don't think he can compel immortals because he is not in charge of debriefing the units going out. Although things could've changed since I left."

"Who is the other son?"

"Kolhud. But the thing is that he wasn't there to brief my team either. I never interacted with him. We got briefed by Hocken, who as far as I know has no special powers."

"Interesting." Turner rubbed his chin. "Are you sure you've been compelled at all?"

"I'm sure. The more time I was away from the island, the saner I got. It felt like a fog was lifting from my brain." He shook his head. "Not a fog, since fog is benign. It was more like a suffocating haze."

Kian and Turner exchanged glances. Did they doubt him? Were they thinking that he wasn't right in the head?

Pinning Dalhu with his pale blue eyes, Turner leaned closer. "What you've felt could have been psychosomatic. You weren't happy in the Brotherhood, and you were conflicted about what you were doing."

"I don't think so."

He hadn't been. Back then he hadn't cared one way or another. Not about the Brotherhood, and not about the clan, and certainly not about the humans.

He'd been filled with hate and loathing for everything and everyone.

Amanda had changed that. His love for her burned away all the sludge that had taken residence in his soul, or at least most of it. Her people had become his people, and that was why he cared. It was as simple as that.

"What about the others?" Kian asked. "Were you the only one under compulsion, or was the rest of your unit as well? It seems like a waste of resources to compel each soldier before sending him on a mission. If it were me, I would've bothered only with the commanders and left it up to them to control their men."

Dalhu shrugged. "Doomers never stay away from the island for more than a couple of months. Even those who are stationed abroad have to come back once a month and give a report in person. Two at the most. They usually stay for a few days and attend Navuh's propaganda sermons. And then there are the five daily mandatory adulations to reinforce the soldiers' devotion. Navuh personally leads the evening one. He is a very powerful demagogue."

Turner rubbed his chin again. "Maybe he is more than that. What if he is capable of mass compulsion? That would explain his tight hold on his people, and why there has been no rebellion against him yet. In fact, he must be controlling the sons too, since they are the most likely usurpers."

Kian shook his head. "It doesn't make sense. Navuh is vain. Why would he hide having such power and pretend that one of his sons has it instead?"

"Actually, it makes perfect sense," Dalhu said. "Compulsion is like thralling. A cheat. A hack. An ability that is inherited. What would gain Navuh more respect? This, or a belief that his success is the result of his charisma and unparalleled leadership skills?"

Kian still didn't look convinced. "So let me get this straight. What you and Turner are saying is that through his propaganda sermons, Navuh compels his entire force to believe in his lies and stay loyal to him and the cause, and then reinforces it every evening through the mandatory devotions?"

Turner nodded. "We are speculating here. But it is the only logical conclusion I can make. If Dalhu and his team didn't get briefed by either of the two sons suspected of having the ability, then who could've put the compulsion on Dalhu? On the other hand, they all attended the sermons and the devotions on a regular basis. If Navuh's compulsion works the way we think, then there is no need to do anything special before sending the soldiers on a mission."

Staring at Turner, Kian rapped his fingers on his desk. "None of the Doomers we captured in the past talked. Most because they didn't know anything, but some must have known something but were under compulsion not to talk. How was that command delivered?" He turned to Dalhu. "Does Navuh repeat a silencing order in each of his sermons?"

Dalhu shook his head. "Not directly, but he repeated the word secret a lot. He would talk about our secret mission to one day rule the world, and that it would no longer be a secret once the clan was obliterated and all of humanity trembled before us. Or he would talk about the secret island paradise he'd created for the Brotherhood and how grateful we all needed to be to him for that. I've never thought much of it, regarding it as propaganda and self-aggrandizing, but maybe there was more to it."

22

JULIAN

*H*is eyes getting blurry from all the reading he had done, Julian closed his laptop and glanced at Merlin. "Can you make love potions?"

"Maybe." Merlin arched one white eyebrow. "Why would a handsome guy like you require a love potion?"

"Who said it was for me? You left a book about love potions in the bathroom, so I flipped through it."

It was a bunch of nonsense, but Julian was tired of the dense research material he'd been reading all day, and discussing love potions seemed like a topic that didn't require a lot of brain bandwidth.

Merlin swiveled his chair around, turning his back on the open monitor and the paper he'd been reading. "I can make it. But using it would be unethical. There is not much difference between this and compulsion."

Julian's interest was piqued. "How so?"

"Pheromones, my boy. Consumption of certain compounds can increase their production, and these can be found in nature as well as chemically produced. The thing is, when you emit an unnaturally high concentration of pheromones, the females around you can't resist the spike in desire. So, in a way it's the same as compulsion. Just instead of brain waves, you'd be using chemicals."

Julian pretended disappointment. "So, it's not like you can give a girl a potion and make her fall in love with you. It's like broadcasting to every female in the area."

"You got it. And it's not about love. It's about sex."

"Did you find the recipe for this in that old book?"

"Not everything in these ancient scripts is a fable or a myth. In fact, a lot of it isn't. These books are the result of centuries of experiments, of trial and error. When something finally worked, it was recorded in a book."

"Good to know. Next time I try to find a cure for cancer, I'll consult your ancient books."

Merlin wagged a finger at him. "You can mock it all you want, but you'll be ignoring a fount of information."

"Is that where the idea for the fertility potion came from?"

"In part. Gertrude and I have been working on improving it and adapting it for immortals." He turned back to the monitor.

"I have another question."

"Yes?" Merlin looked at him over his shoulder.

"Why do all your potions taste so horrible? It shouldn't be too difficult to add strong syrup to sweeten them."

"I don't want to. If the potion tastes bad, there is less chance of overzealous patients overdosing on it."

There was some convoluted logic to that. But then the flip side was often the more problematic one. Making sure patients actually took the medicines prescribed to them was difficult enough when all they had to do was swallow pills.

"I need coffee to go back to those research papers." Julian pushed to his feet. "Do you want me to get you some?"

"I'll make it." Merlin got up.

Looking at the sink full of dishes, Julian doubted there was a clean cup left in Merlin's house. "I was thinking of jogging to the café and bringing coffee from there. Maybe a couple of Danishes?"

Merlin shuffled to the kitchen. "That would take too long. I can have coffee ready in five minutes." He pointed at the sink. "And in the meantime, you can wash a couple of mugs."

With a sigh, Julian pushed his sleeves up and got to work on the pile of dishes. "You should have a housekeeper, Merlin."

"I know. And I had one in Scotland. But over there I lived among humans, and it wasn't a problem to find domestic help." He sighed. "I miss Maggie. She kept my house clean and cooked my meals, and sometimes she even stayed to eat dinner with me." He chuckled. "Her husband got so jealous. I think she did it just to get a rise out of him."

"Was she pretty?"

"Beautiful, for a sixty-four-year-old grandmother, that is. But you know how love is. Her husband saw her with the same eyes as when he'd fallen in love with her forty-some years earlier. To him, she was still a bonnie lass."

"How long did she work for you?"

"About five years. She lasted longer than most. Dealing with me and my mess isn't easy."

"William should invent a housecleaning robot."

"I have the one for floors. But using it requires lifting stuff, so I don't. But maybe now that we have a compeller in our midst, we can hire some human help out here."

The plate Julian had been washing slipped from his hands, but he caught it before it hit the sink.

"What are you talking about?"

Merlin shrugged. "Do you have two clean mugs over there?"

"Here." He put them next to the coffee maker. "Now explain what Parker has to do with bringing humans to the village."

"When the kid gets good, we can hire a cleaning crew and have him compel them not to reveal our location or even that they work here. We can have one of the Odus pick the crew up with the bus and bring them here, then at the end of the workday drive them back. And the same goes for all the other projects we need to be done here. Like gardening and remodeling." He waved a hand around his messy kitchen. "Not everything can be solved with automation."

Well, that wasn't exactly true, and the Odus were proof of that. The technology that had created them had been lost, but new advances in artificial intelligence were promising thinking machines in the not so distant future.

23

ELLA

"*I* love bedazzling." Tessa tucked her new and improved wallet into her back pocket. "Thanks for inviting me, Vivian."

After the success of the day before, Ella had thought it would be a good idea for her future production assistant to mingle with the girls as well, and what better way to start than in her mother's sewing class. Not that any sewing had been done.

It really should be renamed the bedazzling workshop.

"You're welcome to join every class. It's become so popular that Vanessa asked me to come every day this week." Vivian closed the closet with her craft supplies.

"I wish I could, but I also need to work sometimes." Tessa followed them out into the corridor. "By the way, Eva sent me a message that she's coming to visit during lunch today, and she's bringing Ethan with her."

"Did she check with Vanessa if it's okay? I'm sure it's not a problem, but still."

"I assume she did."

As they headed toward the dining room, Ella told Tessa

about organizing the little riot the day before. "You have no idea how good it felt to prove Vanessa wrong. I knew the girls weren't going to be afraid of Anandur."

Tessa nodded. "He is such a nice guy. One look at him and anyone can see that."

"Not everyone," Vivian said. "Magnus told me that Anandur and his brother are called the undefeated duo because they are so deadly together."

Tessa giggled and then lifted her hand to cover her mouth. "I'm sorry."

"What's so funny?" Ella asked.

"I'm not one to gossip, but this is a story everyone in the village knows, so it's not fair to keep it from you. The undefeated duo got their asses handed to them by Wonder."

Ella's eyes widened. "Get out of here. She is a big girl, and I can see her overpowering a guy, but two Guardians? And why?"

Tessa leaned closer to whisper in her ear. "The why is a story for another time. But the how is easier to explain. Wonder's special talent is physical strength. And she has killer fighting instincts too. Unfortunately for the rest of us, she doesn't want to be a Guardian. Wonder likes being a girly girl."

"Good for her," Vivian said. "The fact that she is capable of fighting doesn't mean that she is obligated to do it."

Ella wasn't so sure. Weren't people supposed to utilize their God-given gifts, or Fate-given as the immortals liked to say, for the greater good?

At least Wonder had been given a choice, though. Ella hadn't. No one believed she could be a badass, but she was going to prove them wrong. When they entered the dining hall, Eva was already surrounded by a bunch of girls fawning over Ethan and pleading with her to let them hold him.

"Okay, girls. One at a time. Ethan is a friendly baby, but you

118

need to give him some space. Back off, you all." Eva pointed to one of the girls. "What's your name?"

"Sarah."

"Did you ever hold a baby before?"

"Yes, I did, ma'am."

"Sit down next to me."

"Yes, ma'am."

"Here." Eva handed her the baby. "You can hold him for five minutes."

Ella stifled a chuckle. Eva sounded like a drill sergeant, and the girls were responding to her commanding attitude with the right mixture of respect and fear.

"Thank you!" Sarah cradled Ethan close to her chest. "Aren't you a cutie?"

Eva lifted her head and winked at the three of them. "Come and sit with me." She waved them over, while at the same time shooing the girls sitting at her table away. "Make room. Everyone except for Sarah move to the next table."

No one argued.

"I see that you are making friends." Vanessa joined them at the table.

Eva arched a brow. "Do you have a problem with how I go about it?"

"I wouldn't dare. What brings you here? You said that you wanted to check out the place, but knowing you, this visit wasn't born of just curiosity. You're too pragmatic for that."

"True. I want to help out."

Vanessa smiled. "That's wonderful. We always need more help around here. Do you have something specific in mind?"

"I can do makeovers. It's a great way to boost a girl's morale. It did wonders for Tessa, am I right?"

Tessa nodded. "I felt like a different person. From a mouse who looked like a twelve-year-old, Eva turned into a sophisticated, confident woman. At first, it was just skin deep, but some of it got internalized. Naturally, Jackson helped too, and so did the Krav Maga training." She lifted her arm and flexed her muscle. "Strong and confident."

Stretching, Eva sighed. "I'm bored. And I need something to do besides being a full-time mom. Makeovers are fun, and they will generate positive energy rather than the negative one I deal with in my regular line of work."

"I bet." Ella snorted.

A kick under the table reminded her that what Eva had shared with her and Tessa was a secret between the three of them.

Except, killing scumbags hadn't been all that Eva had been doing before taking a break to be a full-time mom, and Ella knew how to fix her slip up.

"It must be difficult to spy on cheating spouses and not bring it home with you." Ella sighed. "Witnessing it must leave a bad taste and make you doubt your own husband. I know it would have affected me."

Eva waved a dismissive hand. "I don't doubt Bhathian. But you are right about the taste. And the same goes for the industrial espionage. Getting exposed to the rotten underside of things is contaminating, and I don't want it anywhere near my baby. That's why I stopped writing the book too. I got carried away and made it into a thriller, and the more I wrote, the darker it became. I had to stop."

"That's a shame," Vivian said. "It was very interesting."

"Maybe I'll pick it up again when Ethan is older. For now, I'm only engaging in positive activities." She glanced at Vanessa. "Like makeovers."

"I think it's a wonderful idea," Vivian said. "As one very smart woman once told me, some demons can be exorcized with a witchy ritual, while others can be exorcized with a box of hair-dye and makeup."

Ella pointed to her pink, spiky hair. "Exhibit two."

"How soon can you start?" Vanessa asked.

"Today." Eva bent down and lifted a case from the bottom compartment of Ethan's stroller. "I brought my equipment. I can come twice a week and do two or three makeovers at a time."

"What about clothes?" Tessa asked. "Those are an important part of a makeover."

Vanessa chuckled. "If everyone was tall and skinny, we could've done it with Amanda's discards alone. The woman doesn't wear anything more than twice, and she buys new stuff all of the time."

That gave Ella an idea. "We can post a request for female clothing donations on our bulletin board." She glanced at Sarah.

The girl was listening intently but not taking part in the conversation.

Nothing Ella had said sounded out of the ordinary, so she continued. "I'll put a big box for the donated clothing in the mail center."

"What do you think, Sarah?" Vanessa asked. "Does that sound like a good idea to you?"

The girl nodded enthusiastically. "I volunteer to babysit the baby while Ms. Eva is doing the makeovers."

Ella smiled. Eva's visits were going to be popular not just because of the makeovers. There would be a line of girls waiting to entertain Ethan while she was at it.

24

MAGNUS

"*I*'m going to Merlin's." Ella wiped her hands on the dish towel. "Julian is there, and he said I can come over."

"Merlin or Julian?" Vivian asked.

"Julian. But Merlin said it's okay. They are having a marathon of reading research papers about fertility. I offered to help."

"Doing what?"

"I don't know. Maybe Merlin can tell me what they are looking for and I can read some too."

Vivian huffed. "Good luck with that. All that medical jargon is going to be like reading Chinese."

Ella shrugged. "Then I'll just sit next to Julian and read something on my phone. See you later." She headed for the door.

"I'm going out too," Parker said. "Wonder invited me to her house to study math." He sounded smug.

Magnus wondered how Anandur was taking that. Parker was just a kid, and his infatuation was harmless, but it probably didn't escape the Guardian's notice that Wonder's study buddy was drooling all over her.

"Have fun, kids." Vivian waved.

As soon as the door closed behind Parker, she sighed and plopped on the couch. "It was a long and tiring day, especially because of the drive. But I'm really enjoying helping out in the sanctuary. Who knew that my bedazzling skills could bring so much joy to a bunch of traumatized girls?"

Sitting next to her, Magnus wrapped his arm around her shoulders. "You bring bling into their lives."

She laughed. "Almost as good as the real thing."

"We have the house to ourselves for the evening. That doesn't happen often." He nuzzled her neck.

"For the next couple of hours. Any ideas for how we should fill those?" She waggled her brows.

"Several, and all of them involve you getting naked. We can grab a bottle of wine and get into the Jacuzzi. Or I can give you a massage first and then we can shower together."

"After the sex, or before?"

"Maybe after. So we don't have to shower twice."

"Hmm. Let me think. We have two hours, which is enough to do all three. We can make out in the Jacuzzi, after that you can give me a massage, and after that, we can hop into the shower."

"You forgot the sex."

She laughed. "I didn't. We can have sex in the Jacuzzi, then again after the massage, and again in the shower."

Pulling her closer against him, Magnus hooked a finger under her chin and planted a soft kiss on her lush lips. "I like the way you think. But two hours are not enough for all that."

"We don't have to come out of the bedroom. The kids will think that we are sleeping."

"True." He rose to his feet and offered her a hand up. "To the Jacuzzi."

As the big tub filled up, Magnus went back to the kitchen and grabbed a wine bottle and two glasses.

Wearing her fluffy white bathrobe, Vivian sat on the tub's lip and checked the water's temperature. "This thing is so big that it takes forever to fill up."

"That's plenty for me." He put down the wine and the glasses on the ledge, and then took his clothes off.

"I'm getting in." He liked the way Vivian's eyes followed his nude body.

Lying in the half-full tub, he patted his chest. "Come on, love. Get in here. I'll keep you warm."

"You seem in a hurry." Vivian reached for the robe's belt. "How about I add another feature to tonight's entertainment." She waggled her brows. "A striptease."

"A lovely suggestion." He waved a hand. "Please proceed. But don't take too long. As much as I like watching, I like touching more."

Turning around so her back was to him, she shrugged the sleeve off one shoulder, then peeked at him over it with a sultry smile. Satisfied with the effect her teasing had on him, she repeated the same with the other shoulder. Not letting the robe drop all the way down, she tempted him with just the top part of her rounded bottom exposed.

Focused on her slow reveal, Magnus didn't notice that the tub was full until water splashed over the rim. "Now, look what you made me do, lass." He opened the drain to let some of it out.

Laughing, Vivian tossed the robe on the vanity counter. "Can I come in? Or is the water too high still?"

He reached for her hand, pulled her closer, put his hands on her waist and lifted her off the floor. "Come here, you minx." He lowered her down to lie between his outstretched legs, her back to his chest. Some water splashed out, but as long as it wasn't a flood, Magnus didn't care.

Vivian sighed contentedly and let her head drop back against his shoulder. "This could have been very comfortable if not for that thing poking me in the butt."

"What thing?" He swiveled his hips, grinding his shaft into her soft ass cheeks. "I don't know what you're talking about."

She giggled. "I just hope the kids are not going to come back early and look for us. Did you lock the bedroom door?"

"I forgot. But don't worry, they are not going to come in without knocking first. They know I can hear it."

"Yeah, but I don't want to go into a mad scramble. Parker sometimes knocks and then just walks in."

"When they get back, I'm going to hear them coming in."

She turned around in his arms, her hard nipples poking at his chest. "How? There are two soundproof doors between us and the living room."

He motioned with his head toward the slightly open window. "If anyone comes up the walkway, I'll hear it."

"I'm at such a disadvantage here. It's like being hard of hearing in the outside world. Perhaps I should get a hearing aid."

"A simpler solution would be for you to transition. I think it's time."

She shook her head. "I can't. Not until this latest crisis with Ella is over."

"There will always be something, Viv."

"After this situation is resolved, I promise no more stalling."

Cupping her cheek, Magnus kissed her softly. "I'm going to remind you that you said that when you come up with the next excuse."

"No more excuses. A promise is a promise."

25

ELLA

"*I*'m sorry." Exasperated, Ella closed her laptop. "I can't understand any of it."

When her mother had told her that it would be like reading Chinese, Ella had thought she was exaggerating. But it seemed these research papers were purposely written so that no layman could understand them.

It just confirmed her opinion about most doctors being pompous asses.

Present company excluded, of course. Julian was the most unassuming guy ever, and Merlin was eccentric, but in a nice way.

"It's not as difficult as it seems at first glance," Merlin said. "You're just not familiar with the jargon yet."

She waved a hand. "I'm not going to keep on trying. I give up. You guys will have to do without me."

Glancing at Merlin's cluttered and dirty living area, Ella decided she could be useful in a different way. "How about I clean up and organize a little while you two finish up with those papers?"

Merlin smoothed his hand over his long beard. "You are my guest, Ella. I don't feel right about you cleaning up my mess."

"Don't be silly. First of all, I'm not a guest, I'm a neighbor. And neighbors help each other out. You made that paste for Parker to ease his fangs-growing pains, and you also made that tongue relaxer for me. The least I can do is help you with something you're apparently not good at, but I am. I'm the queen of cleaning hacks."

Merlin cast Julian an amused glance. "You're going to have your hands full with this one. When Ella sets her mind to something, she doesn't let anyone or anything stand in her way."

"That is one of the many things I like about her." Julian winked. "My girl is a fighter."

She rolled her eyes. "Come on, guys. I'm only going to clean up, not solve world hunger. Now, enough with the chitchat. You have work to do, and so do I."

Less than an hour later, the place was unrecognizable. The stacks of books were dust free and piled high against one wall, the lab equipment was stowed in the kitchen cabinets, the floor was vacuumed, and the tables and counters wiped. The fridge still needed cleaning. The moldy leftovers were not going to get up and walk out on their own. But she would do it next time.

"Do you want a cup of coffee?" Ella asked, mainly to get their attention so they would notice how nice everything looked.

They'd been so focused on reading and taking notes.

Merlin looked up. "You're a miracle worker, but I feel bad about you doing this for me. Let me at least treat you to some coffee and Godiva."

As Ella's mouth watered, she put her hand over her chest. "You know the way to a girl's heart."

"Just don't show her where you hide them." Julian leaned

back against the couch cushions and stretched his arms over his head. "She'll sneak in here in the middle of the night and raid your stash."

"You're welcome to raid it anytime." Merlin pushed to his feet and headed for the kitchen.

He stopped by the dining room table that was now clear of equipment. "Where is my stuff?"

"In the kitchen cabinets. You should order some bookcases. If you have a place for everything, it's not going to get as messy in here."

He pulled out a coffee can from the fridge. "I was just telling Julian before you came in that Parker opens up new possibilities for us. When he gets the hang of his ability, we can hire human crews to do cleaning and maintenance, or even put up bookcases. He can compel them to keep this place a secret."

Ella took the carafe and filled it up with water. "It's something to think about, but I'm afraid the village will lose its charm if we bring outsiders here. I like it that it's isolated from the world. It feels safe."

Merlin eyed her as she measured out the coffee for the machine. "What about when you go to the sanctuary? Do you feel unsafe?"

"No. Well, maybe a little. I look at it as going to work, and at the end of the day, I come home. But home is not just my house where my family lives, it's the entire village. And just as I don't want strangers hanging around my house, I don't want them hanging around the village. Does that make sense?"

"It does." Julian walked up behind Ella and wrapped his arm around her middle, pulling her against him. "We are like one big family who lives together."

Merlin opened a cabinet, pulled out a box of chocolates, and offered it first to Ella and then to Julian. "And just like with any family, little birdies need to spread their wings and fly away. At least for a little while. Don't you want to go to college, Ella?"

With everything that had been going on lately, she hadn't thought about her education, but it didn't mean that she'd given up on going to college. She just hadn't decided what she wanted to do with the rest of her life.

"I always wanted to be a nurse, but now I need to rethink it. There are already two nurses in the village, and there is no need for a third one."

Merlin arched a brow. "How about a doctor? Nowadays it takes almost as long to get a nursing degree. So why not take the extra step?"

Behind her, Julian groaned. "As if we need any more doctors in the village."

As the coffee maker was done spewing, Merlin lifted the carafe off and filled the three lined-up cups. "If we continue with the humanitarian effort, we will need more therapists. Vanessa is already stretched to the max."

Ella added cream and sugar to her mug. "But she can use humans. Why doesn't she hire a couple of full-time assistants?"

Merlin shrugged. "I guess part of it is monetary constraints, and part of it not wanting non-clan people in the thick of things. People are nosey."

Taking a sip, Ella tried to imagine herself as a therapist and cringed. "I can't be a psychologist. It's too emotional. Especially what Vanessa deals with. I don't want to hear stories like mine all day long. I want to forget."

Julian kissed the top of her head. "I can help with that. If you want, I can thrall you to suppress those memories."

She shook her head. "No offense, Julian, but that sounds creepy. I don't want to forget it completely. What happened to me didn't destroy me, it made me stronger. I just don't want to swim in that emotional cesspool on a regular basis. Do you get what I'm trying to say?"

"I guess so." He leaned his chin on her head. "Besides, it's not over yet. Even if you wanted to forget, you can't because of your dream visitor."

"Yeah, talk about creepy. But I'm dealing with him too." She chuckled. "It amazes me how easy to manipulate men are. I got a badass mafia boss wrapped around my finger, and now I'm doing the same to a big-shot Doomer. If I'm not careful, it will go to my head."

"By the way, Ella," Merlin said. "I was wondering about something. From what I understand, you could talk about Lokan with Kian and then suddenly you could no longer do that. Am I right?"

"Yeah. When he confessed to being a dream walker, Mr. D made me promise that I wouldn't talk about him. I thought nothing of it, and I had no intention of keeping that promise, but that was when he must have compelled me."

Merlin nodded. "That's what I've been afraid of. If the Doomer can compel you in the dreams, he is much more dangerous to you than you think. He can make you do things you don't want to."

"Then I guess Parker will have to release me. Just as a precaution, I'll have him do it every day."

"That's a very good solution. And also make sure to report everything to Kian."

"I will."

As Ella reached for another chocolate, a hopeful thought flitted through her mind. What if Logan was compelling her to be attracted to him, and not feel attracted to anyone else?

He'd said something to that effect several times. She'd dismissed it, thinking of it as nothing more than harmless flirting and boasting, but it might have been more sinister than that.

If that was true, it was a huge relief.

There was a logical explanation for why she craved a man she shouldn't want, while being indifferent to the man she should. The problem was that even if that was the case, Parker couldn't help her get rid of that particular compulsion. First of all, because she wasn't going to explain what was going on to her twelve-year-old kid brother, and secondly, if he commanded her to want Julian, that would be a compulsion too.

But what if that wasn't the reason after all, and there was something wrong with her?

That made sense too. She was damaged goods, with hidden emotional scars that she was trying to ignore. Julian was like a pristine-white glove she wouldn't put over dirty hands, but Logan was already dirty, so her soiled hands fit right in.

Crap, she needed to talk to someone, and it wasn't Vanessa. Perhaps Carol would have some words of wisdom to help her sort it out.

26

JULIAN

"Well, I think that's enough." Merlin turned his computer off. "Let's call it a day."

Julian offered a quick thanks to the Fates. "You mean call it a night." He pushed to his feet and offered Ella a hand up. "Are we meeting up in the clinic tomorrow, or here?"

"I like working in my pajamas." Merlin smirked. "Come here when you're up."

"I'll see you tomorrow morning."

"Good night, Merlin." Ella kissed their host on the cheek. "Are you going to monopolize Julian's entire day tomorrow too?"

"I'm afraid so. I want us to be done with those papers, making sure that I'm not missing out on any new developments. Sometimes a small detail that no one thinks much of is a pointer in the right direction and leads to a new breakthrough. Especially anomalies." He smirked. "If not for those pesky discrepancies that kept popping up, we wouldn't have discovered quantum physics."

"In that case, I'll come over when I'm back from the sanctuary."

He wagged his finger at her face. "Just don't think about cleaning anything else!"

"We will see about that. That fridge of yours needs cleaning. You have leftovers there that are ready to walk out on their own."

"Now you're forcing my hand. I'll have to clean it, so you don't."

She shrugged. "Whatever works. Good night, Merlin."

Once outside, Julian wrapped his arm around Ella's waist, and as soon as they were a few feet away from Merlin's front door, he turned her around and pulled her against his chest.

"I've been wanting to kiss you for hours." He took her lips, trying to be gentle but failing miserably.

The entire time she'd been bending to lift books off the floor or stretching on her toes to reach the top kitchen cabinets, Julian had been struggling to keep his focus on the reading material.

That curvy, compact body of hers had been very distracting.

He threaded his fingers into her hair, gripping fistfuls of the pink tufts as his tongue teased her lips, urging them to open for him.

When he delved into her mouth, her long lashes fluttered down and her soft body melted against him.

Surprisingly, Ella didn't seem overwhelmed or frightened by his sudden attack. The scent of her arousal flaring, she clung to him instead of pulling away, her fingers digging into his shoulders as she kissed him back with just as much urgency.

Well, almost as much. He was damn sure she didn't have the urge to bite him.

The need to claim her, to have his shaft deep inside her while his fangs sank into the creamy skin of her neck, was overpowering.

He should disengage before doing something he was going to regret.

Ella wasn't ready for an immortal male's intensity. She needed patience and gentle coaxing, neither of which he was capable of at the moment. Except his arms refused to obey, and instead of pushing her away he clutched her to him even harder.

Slanting his mouth over hers, he lifted her up and deepened the kiss, devouring her. But that wasn't going to cut it. There no way he was going to sate his hunger like that.

With a monumental effort, he let go of her mouth and put her down.

Looking dazed, Ella touched a trembling finger to her swollen lower lip.

"I'm sorry. Did I scare you?"

She lifted a pair of confused eyes to him. "What?"

Damn. She was in shock, and it was his fault.

"I got carried away, I should've been more gentle."

Shaking her head, Ella patted her lip again. "You didn't scare me. I was surprised, that's all." She put a hand on her hip and struck a pose. "Tell me the truth, Julian. Were you just pretending to read fertility research papers and were watching porn instead? Because you seemed awfully excited all of a sudden."

For a moment, he thought she was serious, but then her lip started twitching. "Or maybe you're just weird this way, and research papers make you horny."

Grabbing her arm, he pulled her against him, his erection prodding her belly through his jeans and her shirt. "It was you. Watching you from the corner of my eye was very distracting."

Ella chuckled. "I didn't know cleaning could be sexy." As she wrapped her arms around his neck, her eyes were hooded with desire. "Kiss me again, and don't hold back. I loved the kiss."

He was tempted, but in his current state, it was too dangerous. "I'd better not. I promised you that I would let you dictate the pace, but I'm barely in control right now, and I don't want to push you to do things you're not ready for."

As a long moment of indecision passed, he could see several emotions drift through Ella's eyes. Because of the strong mental blocks that she'd erected to guard against telepathic intrusions, she wasn't broadcasting her feelings as loudly as most humans, and even with his empathic sensitivity, Julian had to rely on other clues to guess her moods.

The good thing was that Ella's face was very expressive. The bad news was that she'd proven to be an excellent actress. To fool someone like Gorchenco, she had to be.

Finally, she nodded and pushed away from him. "Can we still go for a walk, or do you have to rush home and take care of business?"

Damn, she was blunt. Or was it sarcasm?

Again, it was hard to tell with Ella.

"Let's talk about something else." He took her hand and started walking.

"Like what?"

"College. I think you should rethink medical school. Merlin is right about nursing taking almost as long and being nearly as difficult. Why limit yourself? And you don't have to work in the village once you get your license. You can work in a human hospital or open your own practice."

"Same goes for you."

He waved a dismissive hand. "Ignore me. I'm suffering a midlife crisis at twenty-six."

Resting her head against his arm, Ella looked up at the sky. "During my hibernation period, I looked into some schools. Columbia seems awesome, but it's very hard to get into. I have a high GPA, and I've done some extracurriculars, but that's not enough to get me in."

"You know that it doesn't matter, right? You can't use your

real transcripts anyway. We will have to supply fake ones for you. Might as well give you amazing grades."

She cast him a sidelong glance. "People go to jail for stunts like that, Julian. I hope that's not how you got into medical school."

"I worked my ass off. That's how I got in. And we don't falsify records for clan members just because they want to get into good universities. This is reserved only for extreme cases. Like you needing a new identity after faking your death, or a clan member who finished high school fifty years ago and now wants to go to college."

"Do you fix their grades as well?"

"We use professionals to do those things, so I wouldn't know, but it makes sense that we can make your application look a little better. I would not have suggested it if you were a lousy student, but you said that your grades were good."

For some reason, Ella seemed disappointed. What did she want to hear? That he would cheat for her? Because he would.

"I'll think about it." She threaded her arm through his. "Right now I'm not ready to make any more big changes. I've had enough for a while. But I do need a job that pays. What I do at the sanctuary keeps me busy, and I love the chance to make a difference, but I need money too."

Hmm, that was a problem.

Ella didn't have a share in the clan's profits, and even after Magnus officially adopted her, she wouldn't qualify for one until she was twenty-five or went to college, whichever came first.

"I have an idea. It won't get you money right away, but once the charity starts bringing in donations, it will. Kian can nominate you as the charity director, and you'll get paid a salary from the proceeds. Every non-profit organization has paid employees, and the director is usually paid well."

Smiling, she lifted her chin. "Ella Takala, Director of Save

the Girls. Sounds important. Maybe I should go study chari-
table organization management."

"Sounds like a plan, but then who is going to run it while
you're away at college?"

"Good point. And I forgot that Ella Takala is supposedly
dead. The director's name is going to be Kelly Rubinstein."

"That's a shame." He chuckled. "I think another makeover is
needed. Somehow I can't picture Kelly Rubinstein, director of
Save the Girls, with spiky pink hair and fake piercings. I like
the name you gave it, though. We should keep it."

27

ELLA

"*I* wish the sanctuary was closer to the village," Ella said as the car switched to self-driving, which meant that they were almost home.

Her mother nodded. "I hate driving so long. It's the most exhausting part of this volunteering gig."

As the windows turned opaque, Ella removed her sunglasses and put them in her purse. They were such a convenient solution to the whole contact lenses and eye makeup routine. As long as she wasn't going out shopping or on a date, Ella wasn't going to bother. The sanctuary was safe enough, and the glasses were specially designed to fool facial recognition software.

The car entered the tunnel, and several minutes later parked itself in the underground garage.

"Did you make any progress in regard to the videos?" Vivian asked as they headed for the elevators.

"I didn't bring it up yet. I'm rethinking my approach."

Her mother cast her a sidelong glance. "Care to elaborate, or is it still in the thinking stage?"

"I haven't made up my mind yet. The thing is, even though

I'm making friends, it will take weeks or even months until the girls are comfortable enough with me to entrust me with their stories."

"There is no rush, you know." Vivian threaded her arm through Ella's. "Kian donated the building for the halfway house, and your engagement ring will provide the money to run it."

Leaning against her mother's shoulder, Ella sighed. "I don't have the patience to wait. I want it up and running, and then I want Kian to nominate me as the charity's director so I can get paid for running it. I need money, Mom, and don't tell me that all I need to do is ask. I don't want to ask. I want to earn my own."

Vivian laughed. "I stopped listening after I heard the word director. Are you serious?"

"It was Julian's idea, but yeah. Why not?"

"Indeed. Don't you need to go to school for that, though?"

"That's what I said. But then Julian pointed out that if I go to school someone else is going to have to run the charity. I doubt anyone would volunteer for that, and besides, it's my baby. I'm not willing to give it up."

Narrowing her eyes, Vivian attempted a stern look. "You are going to college, Ella. I don't care if your charity is successful or not. I want you to get an education."

"Yeah, yeah. I know. But before I go to college, you have to transition. I'm not going to leave Parker and Magnus with no emotional support."

"Blackmailer."

"No, I'm not." Ella lifted a brow. "You made me a promise that if I started dating Julian, you'd do it."

"It hasn't been two weeks yet. Heck, it hasn't been even one. And anyway, that was before I knew about your dream visitor. I can't check out while this is going on."

Ella had no answer for that. Especially after what she'd said before. If she wasn't willing to leave Parker and Magnus to deal with her mother's transition without her, she could understand Vivian not wanting to leave her while she was dealing with Logan.

"That's a problem, Mom. I don't know how to get rid of him. Thank God for Parker, though. With his help, I can at least manage it."

It reminded her that she wanted to speak to Carol about what was going on with Julian.

"I'm heading to Carol's," she said when they reached a fork in the pathway.

"Don't you want to come home first and eat dinner?"

"I can't. I promised her I'd come to see her as soon as I was back. And then I'm going to Merlin's."

"What about food?"

"I'll grab something from the vending machines."

Vivian didn't look happy about it, but her mother was cool, and she wasn't going to make a big deal out of a missed meal.

"Have fun, sweetie." She kissed Ella's cheek. "And say hi to Carol and the guys from me."

"I will." Ella gave her a quick hug. "You're the best, Mom. Thanks for schlepping me to and from the sanctuary every day."

The drive took over an hour in each direction, and Vivian wouldn't have done it more than once or twice a week if not for Ella. Instead, she'd agreed to do the class every day that week.

"It's my pleasure. Seeing the girls' smiling faces as they bedazzle their outfits and their accessories gives me great satisfaction, and so does helping you with your project."

Ella kissed her cheek. "As I said, you're the best."

Heading toward Carol's house, Ella regretted not wearing something warmer. As usually happened at that hour of the evening, the temperature was dropping fast. Hopefully, the immortal would offer her some nosh because Ella didn't feel like making a detour to the café for a sandwich.

By the time she knocked on Carol's door, her arms were prickling with goosebumps.

"Oh, dear," Carol said as she opened the door. "I don't know what was louder, your knock or your chattering teeth." She pulled her into her arms. "Come on. I'll lend you a sweater."

Passing through the living room on the way to Carol's bedroom, Ella glanced at the vacant couch. "Where is Ben?"

"Went out. We have the house to ourselves." Carol walked into her closet and a moment later came out with a pink sweater. "Here, it matches your hair."

"Thanks." Ella pulled it over her head. "I'm glad that Ben isn't here, so we don't need to go outside to have a private conversation. What's the deal with this weather? Hot during the day and freezing at night."

"This is normal for here. I guess San Diego is more temperate?" Carol headed back to the living room.

"It is." Ella sat on the couch. "The differences in temperatures between day and night are not as crazy."

"Did you have dinner already?"

Ella shook her head. "I came here straight from the sanctuary."

"Good, then you can join me." Carol motioned to a barstool. "I love cooking, and I don't like eating alone. Usually, I have Ben to feed, but since he's not here, I'm glad that you haven't eaten so I can feed you instead."

She pulled out two plates and ladled a pile of spaghetti on each. "My spaghetti bolognese is to die for, if I may say so myself."

"It smells amazing." Ella wanted to attack the thing like a hungry wolf, but she was wearing a pink angora sweater that wasn't hers. "Do you have a napkin I can stick in the collar? I don't want to put stains on your sweater."

"Good thinking." Carol got up and pulled out two aprons from the broom closet. "I'm a messy eater too." She handed one to Ella.

"Thanks."

For several moments, Ella just chewed, pausing only to utter the occasional moan. "This is so good."

Carol chuckled. "If you're making so much noise when enjoying food, I can only imagine what you sound like during sex."

"You mean good sex, the kind I haven't had yet."

Momentarily embarrassed, Carol pushed a lock of hair behind her tiny ear. That probably didn't happen often. The woman could talk about the most intimate of subjects without breaking a sweat.

"Yeah, I forgot. Sorry about that. Except, if you're here, that's probably what you want to talk to me about." She narrowed her eyes at Ella. "I hope you are not still thinking about the island."

"I can't," Ella said over a mouthful of spaghetti. "Mr. D will recognize me."

"Mr. D?"

Ella had been sure that by now the entire village knew about her dream visitor and her compulsion problem.

Finishing chewing, she put the fork down and wiped her mouth with a napkin. "Did you hear about what happened to me at the exhibition?"

"Someone said something about Julian carrying you home. I assumed you either didn't feel well or were swept off your feet." She winked.

"I had a bad headache."

When Ella was done telling her story, Carol frowned. "You think that he's compelling your attraction to him?"

"How else can you explain it? Navuh's son is handsome, and he can even be charming when he wants to, but he is so bad it

142

practically radiates from him. I don't want him. He is not the one for me. Julian is."

"But you said that you're not attracted to Julian. That's not a good sign."

"I didn't say that. Julian is gorgeous, and smart, and kind, and everything a girl could ever want in a guy. He just doesn't excite me as much as Mr. D does. So, it's either because the Doomer is messing with my head or because of what I've been through."

"Meaning?"

Ella sighed. "To put it in the simplest terms, Julian is pure, and I'm not. I don't feel worthy of him, but before you give me a speech about how wonderful I am, it has nothing to do with me as a person not being good enough, well, maybe a little. But the main problem is that I feel kind of dirty."

Carol took her hand and clasped it between hers. "It's all in your head, Ella. You have this scratchy recording playing on a loop in there. Get rid of it and put on some good music. Imagine that you are made of a special kind of Teflon. Nothing bad can ever stick to it. It will just wash off. Good things, on the other hand, stick to you like paperclips to a magnet."

"Is that what you do?"

"I don't need to. I've never felt dirtied by sex. I could not have been a courtesan if I did. For me, sex was always a game, one that I was very good at, could use to my advantage, and enjoyed immensely at the same time."

"What about when you were captured?"

Carol's expression darkened. "That's complicated. The cruelty was much worse than the sex. For me, anyway. But I got over it. My tormenter paying for it with his head helped."

"Yay for Dalhu!" Ella pumped her fist. "I forgot to thank him for it."

Carol chuckled. "You were kind of busy trying to break through a compulsion."

"Yeah. About that. So, what do you think? What should I do about my wayward hormones misfiring? Or is it firing in the wrong direction?"

"You need to figure out what excites you and why. I'm not discounting the possibility that the Doomer is compelling your attraction to him and at the same time blocking you from being attracted to anyone else, but there might be a simpler explanation. Women are complicated creatures, and we each have our preferences and triggers and so on." She smiled. "Sometimes I feel sorry for the men. Figuring out what makes a woman tick is not easy. They have to work hard at it."

Running her fingers through her spiky hair, Ella scrunched her nose. "I have to be honest with you. If Mr. D was blocking me, it would make sense for me to feel nothing at all. But that's not the case. Last night, Julian and I kissed, and it was exhilarating, but then Julian pulled away because he was afraid of pushing me into doing things that I was not ready for."

"Was he right?"

Ella nodded. "We both got carried away by the intensity of the kiss, and for a moment there I wished he would do more, but then I got scared. Not of Julian, because it would be insane to be afraid of a sweet guy like him, but of my own response. What if he touched me intimately and it brought back bad memories? I don't want to associate any of that with him."

Carol smiled sadly. "At some point, you'll have to take a risk and try. Don't let fear stop you from having the life that you deserve."

"I want a clean start with Julian. I don't want any contaminants from before crossing over to my relationship with him."

"I can't tell you what to do, but I can share a little secret with you." Carol took her hand and gave it a squeeze. "Life is full of compromises, and we don't always get what we want. Still, it's better to get some of it than none at all."

28

JULIAN

"Okay, kids. Time to go home." Merlin got up and stretched his long limbs. "We've made good progress."

Regrettably, they weren't done, but it was time to call it a night. Ella had been yawning for the past hour, and Julian felt guilty for keeping her up. But when he'd suggested taking her home, she'd refused to leave unless he was ready to head home as well.

"Did you find anything useful?" Ella asked.

"I hope so. We will see. Thank you for cleaning up my fridge." He lifted a finger. "Wait here."

Rushing into the kitchen with his purple bathrobe flying behind him like a cape, Merlin pulled out a big box of Godiva chocolates from the pantry cabinet and then rushed back.

"A small token of my gratitude." He bowed and offered her the box with both hands.

For a split second, Ella looked at the box as if she wasn't sure whether to accept the gift or not, but Julian had a feeling she couldn't say no to the chocolates any more than she could say no to Merlin. Besides, the guy would be offended if she refused.

Instead, she curtsied. "Thank you. Your gift is much appreciated and will be consumed promptly."

Julian groaned. "Please don't tell me you're going to finish it all tonight. You'll be sick."

Eyeing the box wistfully, she handed it to him. "Save it for me and don't let me have any more than four at a time." She eyed it again. "Maybe six."

Laughing, Merlin patted her back. "Another benefit of turning immortal will be eating as many chocolates as you want and not getting a tummy ache."

"What about gaining weight? Are immortals immune to that?"

"Unfortunately, we are not. But it takes a lot of overindulgence for us to gain excess weight." He glanced down at his thin frame. "Although in my case, it seems like I can eat and eat and not gain an ounce even though I would like to."

Julian chuckled. "You only think that you eat a lot. I think you often forget to eat because your head is somewhere else."

"You might be right, my boy. I get distracted by my work, and I don't have Maggie here to remind me to eat."

"Who is Maggie?" Ella asked.

"His old housekeeper." Julian took her hand and led her toward the front door. "Good night, Merlin."

Hopefully, it would be the last day of that. He had a project to run, which in his absence had fallen on Yamanu's capable shoulders.

He was curious to see what progress had been made. Not that much could've been accomplished over three days, but this was his baby, and he didn't like not being on top of that.

"Would you like to go see the halfway house?" he asked Ella as they took the steps down to the walkway.

"When?"

"Right now."

"It's after ten at night."

"Are you tired?"

"A little. But what the heck. Let's go. Do you have your car keys with you?"

He patted his pocket. "I do."

"Then we have all we need." Ella took his hand. "I didn't go home yet, so I have my purse and my sunglasses with me."

"I've been meaning to ask you about it. I've noticed that you no longer wear the contact lenses or eye makeup. Are you sure the glasses are enough?"

"I'm only going to the sanctuary and back. It's not like I'm going out." She looked up at him. "Do you realize that we haven't gone out on a date since the one time I asked you to take me to the mall?"

Damn. Way to make him feel like an ass.

Then again, he really was an ass. Instead of having her come see him at Merlin's, he should've taken her out to a nice restaurant, or to a club. The poor girl had kept herself from getting bored by cleaning the guy's house.

"I'm sorry. Let me make it up to you. How about tomorrow night we do something nice together? Would you like to go dancing? Or maybe to the movies?"

"What's the point? You have all the new releases right here. We can watch a movie in your theater again. And you have the best popcorn too."

Ella was confusing him. "One moment you're complaining about us not going out, and the next you want to spend Friday night in the village?"

"I wasn't complaining. I was just stating a fact."

"Are you sure? Because if I'm supposed to get some hidden messages, I can admit right now that I'm clueless."

Threading her arm through his, she put her hand in his back pocket. "You are so cute, Julian."

Cute was not a term he wanted her associating with him.

Women were not attracted to cute. Hot, sexy, manly, brave, those were heat inspiring, not cute.

As they reached his car, he opened the passenger door for her, but she didn't get in. "Can I ask you a favor? Can I drive? I haven't driven a car in so long that I'm afraid that I've forgotten how."

It was going to be nerve-wracking to let a human drive his car. Ella's responses were nowhere near as fast as his, and Julian was not looking forward to the trip. But saying no was out of the question.

His track record as her boyfriend couldn't count even as decent. This was the least he could do.

"No problem." He walked to the driver side and opened the door for her. "I'll put the address into the GPS, but it will not engage until after the self-driving mechanism disengages."

"That's fine. Until it does, all I have to do is just keep my hands on the steering wheel, right?"

"That's correct."

29

ELLA

"It's so dark in here," Ella whispered. "Can you see anything?"

The old hotel reminded her of every creepy horror movie she'd seen, and she'd only watched parodies of them because real horror was too scary.

She and Julian were like the stupid teenagers who on a dare enter a deserted building at night.

"Perfectly." He held her to him tightly. "Let me find the light switch."

Clinging to Julian, Ella was very glad that he was a big guy. Potential attackers wouldn't know that he was the gentlest soul. All they would see was a tall, muscular guy and, hopefully, it would be enough of a deterrent.

Did he even know how to fight?

Ella doubted it was included in his medical training, but he had to work out to look so good.

When Julian found the light switch, Ella let out a relieved breath. All the scary shadows that had looked like crouching monsters or potential robbers were nothing more than piles of either construction material or debris.

"That's the lobby, right?"

He nodded as they walked deeper inside. "We are going to build a wall right there." He pointed. "That will create a separate entry, where a guard station can be put, or a receptionist's desk. The area behind the wall is going to be the communal living room where people can hang out together and where the different activities are going to take place."

"Like what?"

He chuckled. "Right now we have only one idea. Yamanu wants to organize a karaoke night."

"Sounds like fun. And my mom can have a bedazzling evening. The girls are loving it."

He arched a brow. "Is that some make-believe magic?"

That was funny, and not entirely out of left field. Bedazzling sounded like something similar to thralling.

"It's make-believe alright, just not magic. It's about decorating clothes and accessories with rhinestones. Fake bling. My mother's original idea was to have an arts and crafts sewing class about refreshing old things in all kinds of creative ways. She started with the rhinestones and got stuck there. That's all the girls want to do."

"Fascinating. I would've never guessed that would be a popular activity."

She patted his bicep. "That's because you are a guy."

Suddenly, the muscle under her hand tensed, and Julian's head tilted up.

"What's the matter?"

He put his finger to his lips and then pointed up. "Someone is upstairs," he whispered. "I'm taking you back to the car." He started to back away with her clutched tightly against his side.

Ella had no idea what he'd heard, but she trusted his superior hearing. Except, the place was probably infested with rats and that was what he'd heard.

"Maybe you heard a rat?" She whispered so quietly that no one other than an immortal could've heard her.

"Yeah, rats who walk on two."

They were almost back to the front door when the sound of several footfalls running down the stairs confirmed Julian's assessment.

It seemed like there was more than one two-legged rat in the building.

As one of those rats jumped down from the half-story landing, Julian pushed her behind his back.

"What do we have here?" one of them said.

Hiding behind Julian, she couldn't see the guy, but he sounded either drunk or high.

There was another thud, which she guessed was one more junkie jumping off the landing.

"A pretty boy." This was a different voice than the first. "What are you hiding there, pretty boy? A pretty girl?"

"I'll take either. I don't care which," the first one said.

The low growl that started deep in Julian's stomach didn't sound human, and if those guys weren't so shit-faced, they would have scurried away.

"Look, Vince. Pretty boy is baring his teeth at us. Do you think he'll bite?"

"Not if one of us holds a knife to his girlfriend's throat while the other shoves his cock deep down pretty boy's."

As the guy talked, the growl intensified until there was no way the idiots didn't hear it.

"Stay back," was the only warning she got before Julian turned into a blur.

If Ella had any doubts about his ability to fight, they were gone now.

Closing the distance in one giant leap, Julian caught both guys by their throats and lifted them up, each dangling from a hand.

One of them had a knife, and Ella screamed as he jabbed at Julian with it, but Julian saw it coming and flung the guy away before he had a chance to stab him.

Sailing through the air, the guy landed at least thirty feet away in a pile of debris, the impact sending it flying every which way.

He didn't get up.

And the one still dangling from Julian's hand wasn't moving either.

"Are they dead?" Ella whispered.

Her hands were shaking, and she was cold despite Carol's warm sweater, but she couldn't fall apart yet. Julian had enough to deal with without a panicky girl making a scene.

"Not yet," he hissed.

His fangs were fully descended and dripping venom.

"Don't kill them."

"Why not?"

She came up to him and put a hand on his back. "Because you're a doctor. You save lives, not take them."

Releasing his grip, he let the one he'd been choking drop down to the floor.

Julian was in a weird state, looking dazed as if shocked by the violence that had exploded out of him. He needed her help.

Letting out a breath, Ella collected her wits about her and forced her hands to stop shaking. There was a situation she needed to defuse, and a boyfriend who looked as if he was suffering from a post-traumatic stress disorder.

"Can you thrall them to forget what happened here?"

He nodded.

"Then do that, and then call the police."

"I'm still not sure I want to let them live."

She wasn't sure either. If left alive, those two would attack someone else. But Julian wasn't a killer, and this wasn't the Wild West. The police should handle it.

First, though, she had to talk Julian down from his murderous rage.

"Have you ever killed anyone before, Julian?"

He shook his head.

"Then you don't want to start tonight with these rats. They are not worth the stain it will leave on your soul. Let the police deal with the trash collection."

30

JULIAN

*W*ith the haze of rage receding, Julian looked at what he'd done and prepared to feel contempt for himself and the violence he'd committed, but all he felt was satisfaction.

Up until tonight, he'd believed himself to be a nonviolent man, but apparently his inner beast had just lain dormant, waiting to emerge when it was needed.

At first, Julian had been ready to deal with the vagabonds rationally and defuse the situation, but they'd made the mistake of threatening Ella. The thought of one of those junkies holding a knife to her throat had flipped a switch inside his head. It had brought out the savage he hadn't known existed inside him, shutting off everything else.

Julian the scholar had turned into Julian the barbarian, and the worst part was that it had felt damn good to annihilate the threat.

If not for Ella's gentle touch and calm voice, he would've finished what he'd started and killed the scum, ridding the world of the two maggots. With their ugly words still reverberating in his head, Julian wasn't sure he'd done the right thing by not finishing them off.

Except, he was dimly aware that he wasn't thinking straight because his rage was still at a near-boiling point.

"Come on, Julian. You need to thrall them before they wake up and start screaming murder, or worse, pull out a phone and send a picture of you with your fangs showing to all of their friends."

He shook his head to clear the haze. "Yeah, you're right."

First, though, he had to arrange them in a way that would make his thrall plausible. He was going to make them think that they'd knocked each other out, and that wouldn't make sense if they were thirty feet apart when they woke up.

Grabbing the leg of the one he'd choked, Julian started dragging him closer to the other one.

"What are you doing?" Ella asked.

"I'm staging them to look like they've gotten into a fight and knocked each other out."

"Don't. Drop him where he is."

"Why?"

"Because we want them to get arrested and locked up."

He arched a brow. "Trespassing is an offense, but I don't think it's serious enough to serve time for."

"Exactly. But rape is. Put it in their heads that they raped me. After all, if you weren't who you are, they would have done it, so it's not as if they're innocent and we are framing them for a crime they didn't commit. In this case, the line between their intentions and what actually happened is very thin."

That was a crazy idea, but he was curious to hear the rest. "And in this scenario, who knocked them out?"

"A bunch of my friends showed up and beat them up. I'm going to call the police, crying hysterically, but refuse to give my name or give a statement in person. But that won't be necessary because you will thrall them to confess to the rape."

Ella didn't understand what she was asking of him. But what he found amazing was how calmly she was approaching this after the scare she'd had. The poor girl had grown accustomed to dealing with intense situations.

"I can't do that."

She grimaced. "The thrall is too complicated?"

"It's not that. In order to put these images in their heads, I need to create them in mine first. I can't do that without killing them." He rubbed a hand over his jaw. "And going crazy while I'm at it."

She nodded. "Okay, I get it. What about drugs? I'm sure they were high, and we can probably find their stash upstairs. We'll call in the trespassing, and when the police find the drugs, they will arrest them."

"That's better."

He picked up the leg he'd dropped and dragged the junkie over to join his friend. Thralling them to forget what had happened required much less effort than planting new memories in their ugly brains. He also added a command to keep sleeping.

"All done. Let's see what's going on upstairs." He took her hand. "Stay close to me. There might be more of them."

"I don't think so. With all the ruckus, they would have either showed up or run away."

"Normally yes, but what if whoever is up there is stoned out of his mind?"

She got closer to him. "That's possible."

They found where the scumbags had been staying after opening the first door.

Ella pinched her nose with her fingers. "You'll have to burn everything in this room."

"I just hope that it's the only one they infested. Let's check."

They went from room to room, but fortunately found the rest of them intact.

When they went back to the contaminated room, Ella glanced at the contents. "Do you think these drugs are enough to get them arrested?"

"I hope so."

"Should we drop a few syringes next to them? Just to make sure the police search for the rest?"

"Good idea. Do you have tissues in your purse? I don't want to touch anything with my hands."

"I have a fabric swatch." She pulled out a folded piece of blue fabric. "Here you go."

It had a small flower design made from rhinestones.

"Are you sure you don't need it?"

She waved a dismissive hand. "There are plenty more where that one came from."

When they were done staging the scene, Julian regarded it for a moment. Would a cop buy that?

He didn't know, but Turner would.

Pulling out his phone, Julian shook his head. "I'm an idiot. I should've called Turner right away. He would know what to do."

Turner listened to the story with his usual stoic detachment. "I'll take care of it, Julian. You and Ella can go home."

Julian raked his fingers through his hair. "Did I mess things up? I shouldn't have staged anything."

"Don't worry about it. As far as you and Ella are concerned this is over. Go home."

"Thanks."

"Anytime."

Julian returned the phone to his back pocket. "We can go. He's going to take care of everything." He took Ella's hand and headed toward the front door.

"How?"

"He didn't elaborate."

Leaning against him, Ella sighed. "It was cool what you did

in there." She lifted up on her toes and kissed his cheek. "My hero."

31

ELLA

*J*ulian was a badass.

Was it wrong to think even more highly of him because he'd almost killed two druggies?

Maybe the old Ella would've thought so, but the new Ella, the one who'd been touched by evil, appreciated having a strong protector at her side.

But that wasn't the only reason she was feeling a weird happy feeling deep down in her stomach. To do what he had done, Julian couldn't be as pure as she'd built him up to be.

She'd seen the savage hiding just under the surface of the civilized, well-mannered doctor, and he'd excited her.

Not that she wanted him to be like that all the time. Cavemen were not her style, but Guardians and warriors were. Men who fought not for the sake of fighting, but to protect what they held dear. She had a feeling that Julian could have made an excellent Guardian.

Perhaps it was the career change he should look into?

Should she suggest it?

He had been deep in thought throughout the short drive from the hotel to the village. Figuring he needed time to process what had happened, Ella hadn't interrupted, but now that they were walking toward her house, the silence stretching between them felt awkward despite the closeness of having their arms wrapped around each other.

Especially since Julian hadn't calmed down yet. He was doing his best, and if not for his immortal tells she would have assumed he was fine. But his eyes were still glowing, and his back muscles were tight where she was touching them.

Maybe a little diversion was needed and talking about a career change might just be the thing.

"Have you ever considered becoming a Guardian?"

Julian chuckled. "When I was a kid, I hero-worshiped Kian. He was everything I wanted to be. A warrior who was also a great businessman and a respected leader. But then, I also worshiped my mother. It was a hard choice, but she convinced me that my talents were better suited to medicine than battle."

"Well, I think you could be an awesome Guardian. So, if you're still contemplating a career change, that's something you might want to consider."

"Thank you. That's a very nice compliment, but being a Guardian is not as glamorous as it seems. Most of the time what they do is kind of boring, which is good because no one can function at high levels of stress indefinitely."

Ella smiled. Her diversion tactic had worked. Julian's eyes were no longer glowing, and he was back to his old, calm and civilized self.

Now the question was how to get him to kiss her before they got to her house.

Strangely, the unpleasant incident had brought them closer. On top of everything else, now they were also partners in crime, and that new closeness had brought about an unexpected side effect.

A craving for more physical closeness.

Ella didn't want to go home. She wanted to spend the night

in Julian's arms and keep him safe from the bad dreams that were inevitably going to assail him after the violence he'd done.

The aggression had been so out of character for him, and it obviously bothered him.

Except, that would be unfair to Julian on several levels. As long as she wasn't ready to have sex with him, she shouldn't torment him like that. Maybe she should listen to Carol and just go for it?

What was the big deal? It wasn't as if it was going to be her first time. And she wanted Julian.

But then there was the issue of freaking Logan.

"What are you thinking about?" he asked. "I can feel your agitation rising by the minute."

She cast him a sidelong glance. "I thought you couldn't read my mind."

"I don't need to. It's enough that I look at your face. You're very expressive when your guard is lowered."

"That's your doing. You make me feel safe."

"That's a good thing, right?"

"Yeah, I guess so. I didn't do it consciously, though. I'm usually hyper-aware and careful about what I reveal with my facial expressions and body language."

"So, what's troubling you?"

She shrugged. "I want things that I cannot have."

"Like what?"

"Like going to sleep with you in your bed and holding you throughout the night because I know you're going to have bad dreams. But that's unfair to you because I'm not ready for more than kissing."

And then there was Logan and the game she was playing with him. She couldn't tell Julian about that.

Talk about hurting a guy.

Blue balls were easier to deal with than a blue mood. At

least in her opinion. A guy might have a different perspective on that.

"I don't want to go to sleep alone either. I won't lie to you, it's going to be hard to have you in my arms and not do anything, but I'd rather have that than not having you there at all. And don't worry about me starting something. You are in the driver's seat, Ella. Nothing happens unless you initiate it."

That shouldn't have brought tears to her eyes, but Julian's kindness and thoughtfulness were just too much. Even the old, naive Ella hadn't thought guys like that existed.

And yet, she couldn't help but feel a little disappointed too.

Damn, she was confusing herself. On the one hand were the cravings, and on the other were the fears, and she was continually teetering between them.

Hiding her little emotional meltdown, she looked away. "I need to tell my mom that I'm not coming home tonight."

32

KIAN

*U*sually, when the alarm went off at five in the morning, Kian was already awake. His body knew the rhythms of his days.

Not this morning, though.

When the annoying music started, he reached for his phone, turned it off, and went back to spooning his wife. Her naked body was so warm and soft, molding perfectly into his and robbing him of the willpower to get himself out of bed.

"Good morning," Syssi mumbled sleepily.

He nuzzled her neck. "I'm feeling lazy today. I think I'm going to skip the workout."

She turned in his arms and kissed his chin. "What's the matter, couldn't sleep?"

After they'd made love last night, twice, once in his home office and the second in the shower, Syssi had fallen asleep as soon as she'd gotten in bed.

He, on the other hand, couldn't fall asleep for hours. It wasn't often that he felt so conflicted about a decision, but using Ella to entrap Lokan made him uneasy. Not only that, both Ella and Vivian were still human and, therefore, more at risk of getting hurt.

And pushing Ella into having sex just so she could transition was even worse. Vivian could go for it, but then she might be out for a long time.

In short, Kian was stuck with using two fragile human females to entrap a very powerful and dangerous immortal.

He wasn't going to back away, though. The upside of capturing Lokan outweighed any misgivings he might have, but that didn't ease his conscience.

"I have a bad gut feeling about using Ella and Vivian to entrap Lokan, but at the same time, I can't afford not to use them. And the thing is, I don't know why I'm so worried. On the face of it, the plan seems foolproof."

Syssi sighed. "There is no such thing as guaranteed success. But Turner knows what he's doing. He proved that and then some with the rescue he orchestrated, and how well everything turned out. You can trust him to keep mother and daughter safe."

"That's what I've been telling myself last night. But it didn't help. It's just unconscionable to send Ella into danger so soon after what she's been through. She is just a kid. And sending her mother with her isn't making it any easier."

Cupping his cheek, Syssi gave him a closed-mouth kiss. "I know what will make you feel better. Let's get up and have breakfast together, and then go back to bed for a morning delight."

"Why get up?"

She chuckled. "Because your wife needs to brush her teeth and pee. And you should know by now that she can't make love in the morning before drinking at least two cups of coffee first. The other day was a one-time exception."

That was true, and the reason for a five o'clock wake up.

Syssi didn't want him leaving the bed while she was still

asleep, and she wanted them to have breakfast together before they left for work, which meant that his workout had gotten squeezed into a twenty-minute routine with free weights that he kept in their master closet.

A far cry from the full hour he used to spend at the gym, but it was a sacrifice well worth making.

"Then up with you, Mrs. Morning Coffee." Reaching down, he playfully smacked her bottom.

"I'm up!" She scooted off the bed and rushed into the bathroom.

He watched her cute little bottom swaying from side to side. Knowing that she wasn't doing it on purpose made it even sexier.

Kian's bathroom routine was much shorter than Syssi's, and when he was done, he put on a robe and went out to the kitchen where a tray was waiting for him.

"Good morning, Okidu. Thank you for breakfast."

His butler smiled and bowed. "It is my pleasure to serve, master."

Taking the tray back to the bedroom, Kian put it down on the table. He was pouring coffee into the two porcelain cups when Syssi came out of the bathroom wearing a silk kimono robe.

After watching an old rerun of *Shogun*, she'd decided that Kian would look even better than Richard Chamberlain in a kimono and had bought them a matching pair.

"Thank you," she said as she lifted her cup.

He watched her face as she took the first sip, waiting for the look of pure bliss that always followed.

Syssi didn't disappoint.

Sitting on the couch next to him, she leaned back with the cup in hand and kept on sipping slowly until it was all gone, and then handed it to him for a refill.

Other than lovemaking, their morning routine was the favorite part of his day.

He wondered how it would change when they had a child. Perhaps Syssi wouldn't mind handing the baby to Okidu so they could keep enjoying their mornings.

Yeah, he was a selfish bastard, already jealous of a child that hadn't even been conceived yet.

"I think the bad feeling in your gut has nothing to do with premonition. You just feel bad about using Ella and her mom. But you shouldn't."

"And why is that? I would love to hear a good excuse for exploiting a traumatized eighteen-year-old for my selfish needs."

Syssi waved a hand. "You see? You've just proved my point. It's that kind of thinking that keeps you up at night and gives you stomach aches. Eighteen is the age young men and women are drafted into the army, given machine guns, and asked to defend their country. It's not too young."

She handed him the cup for another refill. "Besides, I think it will be therapeutic for Ella. She hates feeling like a victim. She wants to feel like she can make a difference, and she wants to feel strong."

Kian added cream and sugar to the cup, stirred them in, and handed it back to Syssi. "She is already making a huge difference with the charity that she's organizing."

"It's not the same."

He arched a brow. "Did you talk with her? How do you know all that?"

"Observational skills." Syssi winked. "And Carol. Apparently, Ella, Carol, Eva, and Tessa have all become good friends. Do you see the pattern?"

"Not really."

She rolled her eyes. "It's so obvious. Carol and Tessa have both gone through similar experiences and managed to overcome them. Carol was always a badass, and Tessa learned how to be one. Eva, as we all know, is the baddest badass of them all. They are Ella's role models. That's who she wants to be."

"She's only eighteen, Syssi. I'm old, but I still remember myself at that age and how reckless I was. I can understand her wanting to prove herself, but I can't use it as an excuse to ease my conscience. Besides, what about Vivian? The poor woman might suffer a heart attack from stress."

"Vivian is only thirty-six, Kian. And if her heart survived the stress before, it's going to survive it now. Besides, can you afford not to use them?"

"Not really."

"Then stop tormenting yourself and just make sure that they have the necessary protection."

33

SYSSI

*K*ian nodded. "As a leader, I'm often forced to make hard decisions. I accept it, but it doesn't make me sleep any better."

Syssi put her cup down and lifted a piece of toast. "Speaking about hard decisions. What's going on with Perfect Match?"

"We are still negotiating. I did what you suggested and offered them full control over the development and design. That made them much more agreeable to selling me more shares and giving me a majority holding. They weren't cowed by me, though, which I respect."

"I'm so excited about this company. I wish it were mine." She regretted the words as soon as they left her mouth.

Thinking out loud about things she wished for usually meant Kian getting them for her right away.

She waved a dismissive hand. "I meant the clan's. It's not like I want to run a company."

Leaning, Kian whispered in her ear, "Liar. And you know what happens when you lie to me."

As a wave of intense heat washed over her, her nipples

tightened, and her core flushed with moisture in preparation for what his words had promised. Usually, games were reserved for the night, but the dice had been cast, and Syssi was more than ready to play.

As his hand snaked under the lapel of her robe, she sucked in a breath, then moaned when he pinched her nipple. Lightly, but the message was clear.

The game was on.

Letting out a whooshed breath, she closed her eyes and whispered, "Yes, sir."

Pushing the coffee table further away, Kian spread his thighs. "Stand right here and take your robe off."

His commanding voice alone was nearly enough for her to climax. Merlin's potion was indeed making her hornier, and it manifested in her arousal going from zero to one hundred in a nanosecond.

Releasing the tie, Syssi let the kimono slide down her arms and then fall to the floor.

The bright glow in Kian's eyes was a reminder that her husband was not human, and neither was she. Still, the games they played, although not mainstream, were not all that unusual.

Taking her hand, he guided her to lie down over his thighs.

As four smacks landed on her behind in quick succession, they weren't gentle.

"What did I say about you lying to me?"

"That you're going to spank me if I do."

"You're damn right. And especially when you want something and then deny it."

The next ten were none too gentle either, and Syssi bit on her lower lip to stifle a whimper. But even though he was harsher with her than usual, her arousal flared just as hot if not hotter.

Syssi wished she could blame it on Merlin's potion, but the truth was that she craved Kian's dominance, and from time to time she needed more than his playful warmup type of play.

When he stopped, she thought the punishment part was over and tried to push up, but he held her down with his hand on the small of her back.

"I'm not done."

She didn't know how much more she could take, not because it hurt too much, but because she needed him inside her like she needed to take her next breath.

"Do you want to own Perfect Match?"

"I want us to own it. But it's the same as the clan owning it. I don't know why I said that I wanted it to be mine."

"Tsk, tsk, sweet girl. I'm afraid you're going to have a very sore bottom if you keep lying to me like this."

"I didn't…"

"Ow! That hurt!"

It did, but instead of trying to get away or pleading with Kian to stop, which he would've immediately, she found herself pushing her bottom up for more.

It was true. She was certifiable, and it was time to embrace it and stop berating herself for it.

With another ten done, he rested his hot palm over her even hotter butt cheek. "Would you like to rethink your answer?"

For a long moment, she didn't respond.

"I'm waiting." He slid his finger down her wet folds but didn't push it inside her or touch her where she needed it most.

"You're playing unfairly. I can't think when you're doing that."

He chuckled. "I'm just giving you an incentive to hurry up and tell me the truth. What do you really want, my sweet girl?"

"The truth?"

"Yes, and nothing but the truth."

"Let me up."

Lifting her, he turned her around and seated her in his lap. "I'm listening."

She would have preferred to get on with the sex and talk later, but Kian wouldn't have it.

"I don't know why, but I have this silly wish to own that company. I want it to be mine, but it doesn't make any sense. I don't have time to get involved with it, and whatever is mine is yours anyway. And what belongs to the clan belongs to us too. It's not a dress or a pair of shoes, or even a crazy expensive diamond ring. Although to be frank, I would have rather owned that company than the ring."

He regarded her with a frown. "You are serious, aren't you? If you were free to sell your engagement ring, would you have done it to buy Perfect Match?"

Did he have to remind her that it was his engagement present to her?

"Ugh, now you're making me feel guilty. If it didn't have a sentimental value attached to it, then yes. I would have. But since it's my engagement ring from you, I can't part with it."

Her answer seemed to satisfy him, and his frown turned into a smile.

"I'll make you a deal."

She shook her head. "You and your deals. But okay, let's hear it."

"I'll buy Perfect Match's shares from the clan, and any further investment will come from our private funds. Not the clan's."

To her great embarrassment, Syssi hadn't been paying attention to their finances. "Do we have any left? I know you were funneling your own money into the clan."

"First of all, it's our money, not mine. Secondly, it was a loan, and the clan owes us the funds. I can sell one of the clan's holdings and pay us back."

She lifted her hand. "Deal accepted."

With a broad grin, he shook it. "Well, now that this is settled, let's move to the next item on our agenda."

KIAN

"*I* hope it's not more spanking."

Given Syssi's breathy voice, Kian wasn't sure that she'd meant it, but even if she hadn't, he had something else in mind. Now that she'd confessed her desire and agreed to the deal he'd proposed, she deserved a reward.

Lifting her off his lap, he set her on the couch and then kneeled in front of her. "Spread those lovely thighs, sweet girl, and show me what you've got for me."

Blushing crimson, Syssi inched her legs apart.

"I'll need a little more." He put his hands on her knees and spread them wider, until she was completely exposed to his hungry gaze. "That's better."

As he inhaled her aroma, filling his lungs with it, the effect was euphoric. He was like a drug addict who needed his daily dose to keep going, but he had no wish to ever get over his addiction.

Reaching his hands under Syssi's bottom, he pulled her closer to the edge of the couch, his nose almost touching her moist petals.

At first, Kian just blew a soft breath, cooling her a bit before extending his tongue and licking gently at her opening. Syssi moaned, involuntarily jerking in his hold. Clamping his hands on her thighs, he held her right where he wanted her and licked upward towards the top of her slit.

For a long moment, he just applied pressure, flattening his tongue over that most sensitive part of her and letting her get used to the sensation.

Syssi panted in anticipation, looking down at him with hooded eyes, then groaning when he flicked her clit with the tip, once, twice, thrice.

"Kian." She threaded her fingers through his hair. "More, please."

He nuzzled her opening, then murmured against it, "How can I not oblige you when you ask so nicely?"

Spearing his tongue inside her, he groaned in pleasure as her nectar leaked into his mouth.

"Oh, God." Her hips lifted off the couch.

For several moments, he pumped his tongue in and out of her while his hands kneaded her ass cheeks.

She was ready for more, though, and so was he.

Pulling his hand from under her, he withdrew his tongue and replaced it with a finger. As he screwed it inside her, he parted her petals with two others and flicked her swollen clit with the tip of his tongue.

Syssi's hips bucked up as he added a second finger, and as he curled them inside her, finding that sweet spot that drove her up the wall, she uttered that keening moan that was a prelude to her orgasm.

If they weren't in a time crunch, he would've slowed down and prolonged her buildup, but slow was reserved for the nights. Mornings were for quickies.

Closing his lips around her nub, he curled his fingers inside her and rubbed that inner patch of nerves that was sure to push her over the edge.

As her sheath convulsed, squeezing his fingers, Syssi threw her head back and called out his name. He kept pumping, prolonging her orgasm until her shudders subsided.

His sweet girl.

There was nothing Kian loved more than bringing her orgasmic pleasure and then watching her blissed-out expression. Knowing that he had put it there was more satisfying than closing the best business deal, and even more than his own climax.

After pressing a soft kiss to her lower lips, he lifted up and kissed her mouth.

She was still panting, her eyes glazed over, her eyelids heavy.

"Turn this way, baby." He motioned to the couch's arm.

There was a reason they'd ordered this particular model. It had tall, curving armrests, perfect for draping his lovely Syssi over one or the other, usually with her well-spanked bottom up in the air.

Unable to help himself, he slapped it lightly, first one cheek, then the other, and then pushed inside her, feeding his shaft into her wet heaven an inch at a time until he was seated all the way in.

They both groaned as the joining was complete. More than sex, it was a coming together, and despite the countless times they'd connected this way, that first moment always felt magical.

As Syssi arched up, offering him the perfect angle to capture her breasts, he pinched her nipples, adding to the volley of sensations assailing her.

His wife loved her pleasure spiced up with a bit of pain.

The harder he pinched, the higher she climbed, but even though they were pressed for time, he was not ready to let her orgasm yet. Releasing her stiff nubs, he cupped her breasts, keeping his touch gentle as he rammed into her from behind.

Going faster and harder, the couch groaning and screeching in protest at his relentless pounding, Kian felt his own climax bearing down on him.

Once again, he closed his fingers around Syssi's nipples, twisting and tugging. Her tortured moans made holding off his bite nearly impossible, but he didn't have to wait long.

As another orgasm exploded out of his mate, he released her breasts, clamped one arm around her torso, and grabbed a fistful of her hair. Tilting her head to the side, he forced himself to slow down and lick the spot before sinking his fangs deep inside her soft flesh.

Immediately, Syssi's body convulsed with another orgasm. Only then did Kian let his own climax erupt out of him.

35

ELLA

*E*lla woke up with a start.

Hand over her racing heart, she took several calming breaths. Her throat felt dry and itchy as if she'd been screaming for real and not just inside her head.

Maybe she had?

With the excellent soundproofing of the houses in the village, no one would have heard her, and judging by the pounding headache, she'd also been crying.

But where the hell was Julian? The one she'd been crying over so miserably in her dream?

Glancing at the nightstand, she picked up her phone to check if he'd left her a message.

There was one from ten minutes ago. *Gone to the café to get us breakfast.*

The question was whether Julian had sent her the text as soon as he'd left home or later when he'd arrived at the café.

In either case, he must have been with her in bed when she'd been gripped in the clutches of the nightmare because the freaking dream had lasted for hours. Which meant that she'd been screaming and crying inside her head and not out loud.

Unless only mere minutes had passed in the real world while hours passed in dreamland. She could've done all her yelling and sobbing after Julian had left.

"Wow, talk about messed up." Ella shook her head as she got out of bed and headed to the bathroom. "Thank God it wasn't real."

As she brushed her teeth, scenes from the nightmare replayed in her head.

Logan and Julian had been fighting over her, but it hadn't been one of the dream walker's visits. Those felt eerily realistic. It had been an ordinary dream, with hazy details and a scenario that didn't make sense.

Not that it felt any better. It had been more disturbing than Logan's dream intrusions, which in comparison were much less traumatic. During those, they walked on a beautiful beach and talked.

Or kissed.

But besides feeling like she was being unfaithful to Julian, it was peaceful. There was none of the heart-wrenching agony that she'd just experienced.

If she were a film producer, Ella would've named it *Clash of the Titans in King Arthur's Court.*

In her dream, Logan and Julian were both Knights of the Round Table, and she was Princess Guinevere. King Arthur was Magnus, but he was her father, not her husband, and thank God for that. Otherwise, it would have been super weird.

Her heart lodged in her throat, Ella, or rather Princess Guinevere, sat in the royal booth and watched the knights fighting for her hand.

The rules of engagement were that their battle wasn't going to end until one of them was dead.

Julian was holding his own against Logan, but Logan wasn't fighting fair, and Julian was bleeding profusely from several deep cuts.

Fearing for her beloved's life, she screamed every time Julian suffered another cut, and when it seemed like he was going to lose, those screams turned into sobs.

She'd cried so hard in the dream that her head was still pounding. Going on autopilot, Ella reached for the bottle of Motrin that had lately become a permanent feature on her bathroom counter.

Except, forcing herself to wake up could've been the culprit as well. Ella just couldn't stay and watch Logan deliver the death blow.

What the hell was that about, though? Was her intuition telling her that Julian was in danger from Logan?

Or maybe her mind had been sorting out her confused feelings and showing her who she really loved?

Not that it had ever been a question.

It also could have been triggered by what had happened last night, but Ella doubted it. If that was the impetus for the dream, Julian would have been the victor and Logan the loser. His impressive performance had proven to her that he could be a badass when the situation called for it.

Ella rubbed a hand over her face. It was so confusing. She needed to talk to Carol.

Snatching her phone off the nightstand, she texted Julian. *Are you still in the café?*

There is a long line. I'll be back as soon as I can.

Don't. I'm coming to you. We can have breakfast over there.

And after the morning rush was over, she could have a talk with Carol.

I'll try to get us a table.

At eleven, Tessa was picking her up, and they were going to the sanctuary together, but that was four hours away. Plenty of time to have breakfast with Julian, a talk with Carol, and go home to shower and change clothes.

Taking off Julian's T-shirt, Ella pulled on her own and

immediately followed with Carol's pink sweater. Mornings were cold in the village, and besides, she liked it. It made her boobs look larger than they actually were, and it matched the color of her hair.

Naturally, Carol would realize right away that Ella hadn't slept at home last night, but it didn't matter. After all, she was supposed to be Ella's confidant and privy to more embarrassing things than where Ella had spent the night.

Actually, sleeping over at Julian's wasn't embarrassing. The fact that once again they hadn't done anything was.

Rushing out, she waved hello at Ray without giving him a chance to leer or make annoying comments.

Ella didn't jog, but she walked fast, crossing the distance in less than ten minutes. And she didn't get lost, which she congratulated herself on.

Small victories counted for something, right?

At the café, Julian waved her over to where he was sitting. "I didn't pick up our order because I was afraid to lose the table." He rose to his feet. "Guard it with your life."

"Yes, sir." She saluted.

It was indeed crazy, with Carol and Wonder shouting orders to each other, and customers forming two long lines at the counter. On one side were those waiting for their order to be taken, and on the other those waiting to pick them up.

The girls definitely needed help. Perhaps she could convince Carol to hire her for two or three hours to help with the morning rush? And then again with the lunch one?

At least until her charity took off and Kian nominated her as its director.

Yeah, it sounded like a pipe dream and probably was. A girl with no education could only hope for waitressing jobs, not heading charities, even those she helped organize.

Julian came back with a tray and put it down on the table. "I got you a cappuccino, a sandwich, and a muffin. I hope that's okay."

"Perfect."

"Sugar?" He offered her a packet.

"Two, please."

He handed her his sugar packet as well. "I'll get another one."

"Thank you."

Ella waited for him to return before taking a sip. "What got you out of bed so early in the morning?"

Casting a nervous glance around, Julian leaned closer. "You need to keep your voice down here." He tapped his ear. "Immortal hearing, remember?"

She shrugged. "I don't care if people know. I have nothing to hide."

That brought a smile to his handsome face. "Does it mean I can start calling you my girlfriend in public?"

"Of course." She leaned too, almost touching her nose to his. "You can start referring to me as your mate if you like. Everyone assumes it anyway."

He didn't deny it. "I don't care what others assume or not. The only opinion I care about is yours."

"I would like that too."

Julian didn't seem as happy as she thought he would.

Raising a brow, he asked, "What brought that about?"

She didn't want to tell him about the dream because there was too much he could deduce from it. But that had been what had convinced her that she loved him, and that the obstacles she still had to overcome before they could have a real relationship were not insurmountable.

"It was a process. Why?"

"Does it have anything to do with what happened last night?"

She chuckled. "Maybe. You are my hero, Julian. And all girls want to marry a hero."

He eyed her from below lowered lashes. "You're joking, right? Because sometimes I'm not sure with you."

Glancing around, Ella took a fortifying breath and reached for his hand. "This is not the time or place for grand declarations, and even if it were, I wouldn't make any. But it is clear to me now that you were right and that we were fated for each other. The road to a happily ever after for us is still long, but I can see the neon sign flashing in the distance."

36

CAROL

*W*hen the morning rush was over, Carol poured herself a cup of coffee and took it to where Ella was sitting alone at a table.

The girl hadn't said anything about wanting to talk, probably because it had been so busy up until now, but it was quite obvious that she was waiting for her.

Julian had left more than half an hour ago, and the girl was still wearing the sweater that Carol had loaned her yesterday, which meant that she hadn't spent the night at home.

No more clues were needed.

"I see that you like my sweater," Carol said as she sat down, giving Ella an opening to talk about her nightly escapades.

Ella smirked but didn't take the bait. "It's cozy. Where did you get it?"

"Online. Where I get all my stuff. It's so convenient, especially now that I'm running around like a headless chicken." She sighed. "Life used to be so much more peaceful when I was a bimbette."

"I never understood that expression. A chicken with no

head can't run, and the visuals it brings are just gross." Ella shivered.

"You must have a very vivid imagination."

"I do. I immediately translate everything into pictures."

That was probably enough preamble before they got to the real reason that Ella had been waiting so patiently for her to come over and talk to her.

"So, what brings you here so early in the morning?"

Ella shifted in her chair and took a quick glance around. With everyone gone to work or back to their houses, the only ones left in the café were Wonder, who was in a cleaning frenzy behind the counter, and the two of them.

Satisfied that there were no eavesdroppers, Ella asked, "Remember our conversation from yesterday?"

"You weren't sure whether your lack of response to Julian was caused by Mr. D compelling you not to feel attracted to anyone but him, or by your unpleasant experience and your fear of it contaminating what you have with Julian."

"Yeah, that sums it up. But I've thought about one more possibility."

"Shoot."

Ella leaned closer and whispered, "I might be a thrill seeker. Danger excites me."

Carol arched a brow. "And you figured that out how?"

"Last night, Julian and I went to see the hotel he is turning into a halfway house for the rescued girls. We encountered two druggies who'd broken in and were using one of the bedrooms. They threatened to do nasty things to us, and Julian snapped. I've never seen him like that. The guy can fight like a freaking Guardian."

Carol had a feeling she knew where this was going. "You got excited."

"Well, not right away. While we were dealing with the situation, I had to somehow calm an immortal male's murderous rage, but after that, when we went home…"

Now it was getting interesting, and Carol leaned closer. "What?"

"I'm trying to articulate it, and it's not simple. So normally, or rather normal for the new me, my emotions are subdued. I try not to feel too much because I'm afraid that if I do, I'm going to break down into a thousand pieces. So, I numb myself."

Carol understood the need to seek emotional disassociation all too well. What surprised her, however, was that Ella was aware of doing that. The instinct to protect the fragile inner self was not readily apparent, and it took a lot of introspection to realize what was happening.

Pushing her fingers through her short hair, Ella continued, "When Julian seemed so shaken by what he had done, I felt an overwhelming need to protect him, to soothe him, and it loosened some of the emotional barriers I've kept up. Or at least I think that's what happened. Anyway, I felt closer to him than I ever did before, and with that came the desire to also get physically closer. But I chickened out. All I could offer Julian was to hold him while he slept because it seemed like he didn't want to be alone."

"And nothing happened? No smooching and no touching?"

Ella shook her head. "Julian decided that it was best if I was in the driver's seat. If I want to move to second base, I'll have to initiate."

"But you are too scared to do that."

"Exactly. And it's not only because of what happened to me. I have zero experience at initiating anything. I wouldn't know what to do."

"I think I know what's going on."

Ella arched a brow. "You do?"

"I might be wrong, but it makes sense given the fact that

you're so inexperienced. You are reacting to Mr. D because he's unapologetically dominant. Julian, on the other hand, is walking on eggshells around you, afraid to spook you with the tiniest show of assertiveness. That's why you're not reacting to him. He's not giving you what you need."

"But Julian isn't wrong. I am easily spooked. His restraint makes me feel safe. Otherwise, I don't think I could've slept in the same bed with him."

Carol leaned forward and took Ella's hand. "Poor baby. You are in a Catch 22. What excites you also scares you, so you can't have any. And poor Julian doesn't know what to do with you."

"Do you know?"

Ella looked at her with so much hope in her eyes that Carol felt terrible about having to disappoint her.

"I'm not the right person to give you advice. What's right for me is not necessarily right for you. But maybe it would help if you talked about it with Julian and explained your dilemma. You could start slow and go from there."

"I can't. What if I offend him?

"Why would he be offended? The problem is mainly yours. In order to get excited, you need to let go and have him drive the show, but you are too scared to do it."

"Yeah, but what if he is not assertive by nature?"

Carol waved a dismissive hand. "Almost all immortal males are dominant. I'm sure Julian is too, despite how sweet he seems."

"Almost is not all. What if he is like Robert?"

"Robert is a great guy. He just needed to find the right woman."

"Right, and apparently Sharon is that woman. But if you are right about me, and Julian happens to be an anomaly like your ex, he and I could end up like you and Robert. Incompatible."

Carol crossed her arms over her chest. "I don't think it's

likely, but I can't entirely discount it either. You won't know until you try."

Releasing an exasperated sigh, Ella slumped in her chair. "I'm no closer to a solution than I was before coming here." She lifted a hand. "I'm not blaming you. You did the best you could. It's just that this is so complicated, and it shouldn't be. I know that Julian and I are fated for each other." Ella patted her belly. "I know it in here, as well as in my heart. The only thing standing between us is all the crap that I'm carrying around with me. I wish I could just dump it down the toilet and flush the water."

Carol laughed. "I love your analogies. They are very visual."

Ella waved a hand. "I told you. That's how I think. Everything is a movie. You've said I have a broken record playing in my head, but it's more like a GIF."

37

MAGNUS

"*D*o you know what Kian wants to see us about?" Vivian closed the fridge. "We were supposed to go grocery shopping."

Magnus had been hoping to spend his day off alone with Vivian. Hopefully whatever Kian wanted wasn't going to take long.

Magnus put his hands on her waist and pulled her closer to him. "He didn't say. But we can still make it to the supermarket after the meeting. I also want to take you out for a nice dinner. We haven't been on a date in too long."

They'd settled into a routine of work and volunteering and taking care of two kids and a dog, and it was all great. Magnus was thanking the Fates every day for the family they'd given him. But a couple needed time for romance too.

Especially an immortal couple.

"In that case, I should put something nice on."

He waggled his brows. "Do you need help choosing?"

"If you 'help' me," she made air quotes, "we will never make it to Kian's on time."

Magnus glanced at his watch. "Regrettably, you're right."

"Give me five minutes." She kissed his cheek.

"While you're getting dressed, I'm going to check the pantry and make a list of what needs restocking."

"I already did that, but you can check the cleaning supplies. I think we are running low on laundry detergent."

When he was done, Magnus added to the list dryer sheets, glass-cleaning liquid, and toilet paper. Perhaps they should stop at the superstore and buy in bulk. It would save them some money.

He was about to suggest it but changed his mind when Vivian returned wearing a black wig, a silk blouse, a pair of tight pants, and spiky high heels.

Whistling, he walked up to her and pulled her into his arms. "Did I tell you lately how beautiful you are?"

She smirked. "This morning, when you groped my ass while I was brushing my teeth, and then after breakfast while I was loading the dishwasher and you were nuzzling my neck."

"Because you are always beautiful to me."

Pushing on his chest, she stepped out of her high heels, suddenly looking so much shorter. "I only put them on to make an entrance."

She pulled a pair of flats out of her satchel. "I'm going to leave the heels in the car and put them on when we are done shopping. They are good only for sitting in a restaurant, not for running around on errands."

"Smart. Walking through the village and then shopping in high heels would've hurt your feet. But then I would've massaged them." He winked.

Vivian loved his foot massages, and they usually ended in him massaging much more than her feet.

"We should go." She headed for the door.

When they arrived at Kian's office, his door was wide open, and he got up to greet them.

"Please, take a seat." He closed the door and motioned to the two guest chairs.

Magnus waited for Kian to sit behind his desk before asking, "What is this about?"

"Ella's dream visitor."

Next to Magnus, Vivian tensed. "Did something happen?"

Ella had left with Tessa for the sanctuary more than an hour ago. She should've arrived already.

Kian lifted his hand. "Nothing happened. You don't need to contact her."

"Thank God." Vivian slumped in her chair.

"I called you in here to tell you about my plan. I didn't discuss it with Ella yet. I thought that as her mother and future adoptive father, you should be informed first. Besides, it involves you too, Vivian."

Magnus had an inkling where this was going, and he didn't like it.

Kian hadn't invited them to his office to ask their permission to use Ella in whatever scheme he had in mind. He was informing them of it, mainly because he needed Vivian's cooperation with sending and receiving covert messages to and from Ella.

"Go on," Vivian said.

"Lokan's dream visits provide us with a unique opportunity. If we can lure him into a trap and capture him, we will finally have the island's location as well as a host of other information that Navuh's son no doubt has knowledge of."

As Magnus opened his mouth to protest, Kian lifted his palm. "Hear me out first. It wasn't an easy decision to involve an eighteen-year-old girl who has just been to hell and back, but I just can't let this opportunity slip away. Besides, if we don't capture him, she will never be safe from him. He can get to her no matter where she is. This is as much for her as it is for us. Once Lokan is in stasis, he will no longer have access to her."

Presented like that, Magnus couldn't argue with Kian's logic.

Vivian shook her head. "What if he can dream-walk even from there?"

"Stasis is a deeper state than a coma. He's not going to dream, let alone do any dream-walking."

"I hope you're right. So, what's the plan, Ella agrees to a date with him?"

Kian smiled. "Nothing that simple. First of all, he might get suspicious, and secondly, we don't want him to know where Ella is. Not even the general geographical area. So far, she's been very smart about it, not revealing even her time zone. The plan is for Ella to start looking into colleges."

That perked Vivian up. "I'm all for that. I told her she needed an education."

"Whether she actually chooses to go is up to her. My plan is for her to share her deliberations with Lokan and have him suggest a college. That will give us an idea where he is. Then she'll apply and schedule an appointment, which we will, of course, expedite, and tell Lokan about it."

Magnus smoothed his hand over his beard. "You think he'll try to capture her during the visit?"

Kian nodded. "She will tell him the date and time of the appointment. Not as a statement, that would make him suspicious too, but as an absentminded slip-up."

"I'll go with her," Vivian said.

Kian nodded. "Of course, and it's part of the plan. Turner suspects that Lokan might be more interested in capturing Ella's ability than her romantic interest, and if that's true, then she would be useless to him without you. The bait will be the two of you together, for which a campus visit is the perfect setting. Naturally, we will have you surrounded by Guardians posing as students, teachers, and taxi drivers, so there will be no single moment when you are unprotected."

Magnus shook his head. "I still don't like it. What if he can compel the Guardians to step aside?"

"According to Dalhu, Lokan can only compel humans. And don't forget that we know what he looks like. We can probably grab him before he gets anywhere near Ella and Vivian."

Magnus kept pressing. "As Navuh's son, he probably goes everywhere with a heavy guard of his own."

"I don't think so, but even if he does, there will be enough Guardians there to take care of him and his entourage. I'm not going to skimp on warriors. If needed, I'll have the entire fucking force guarding Ella and Vivian."

"I want to be there," Magnus said. "I assume Turner is planning this?"

Kian nodded. "He is."

"Then have him write me into the script. I want to be where I can see and hear Ella and Vivian at all times, and by that, I don't mean the surveillance van. If someone manages to grab either of them, I want to be close enough to intervene."

"I understand. It will be done."

38

ELLA

"Are you sure about this?" Tessa looked even paler than usual.

Ella sat in the interview chair. "No, I'm not. Record one minute. I want to make sure that only a silhouette is visible."

It was one of the hardest decisions Ella had to make, but it was necessary. If she wanted to convince the girls to record their stories, she had to walk the walk and not just talk the talk.

"Okay, go."

Ella cleared her throat. "You can call me Heather, but that's not my real name. I don't want you to know who I am, and most importantly, I don't want those who took me from my home and sold me to know that I'm doing this. My story is not the most terrible there is, but it is bad enough, and I'm telling it as a warning to girls everywhere." She motioned to Tessa to stop the recording.

"This will do for now." Getting up, she walked over to the camera and lifted it off the tripod.

"Crap, I need to wear a headscarf. My spikes are showing."

"So what? Many girls spike their hair."

"I don't want there to be any identifiable features."

Tessa waved a hand. "Where are you going to get a scarf from?"

"My mom's supplies. All I need is a long piece of fabric. Wait here."

She ran into the room where Vivian held her sewing class and rummaged through the box of swatches. Nothing was long enough to tie around her head, so she grabbed several safety-pins to hold three swatches together.

Tying it around her head, she took a peek in the window that reflected her blurry image. "Good enough."

It wasn't as if she was going on a date.

"Okay. Let's do it again. Ten seconds should do."

This time, Ella didn't say anything as Tessa shot the video. "Let's see." She rushed to the camera and checked the recording. "Good. That will do."

"How do you want to do it? Do you want to record it first and then show the recording to the girls, or do you want to record it with a live audience?"

That was a good question.

The upside of recording live was that they would see how it was done, and that Ella was for real, and not an actress reading from a script. The downside was that if they made any noise, the recording was going to be useless, and Ella doubted she could bring herself to do it again.

She still wasn't sure she had it in her to confess the entire ugly story on camera. Well, she actually wasn't going to reveal all the details, that would be stupid because those who knew her story would realize that it was her. She needed to change things around to obscure her identity in more than appearance.

"I still don't think you should do it," Tessa said. "I wouldn't want Jackson to see mine." She quickly lifted both hands. "Not that I'm going to make one. I'm not that brave."

"But if you and I are not willing to record our stories, how can we expect the others to do it?"

"It's not the same. Theirs will be truly anonymous. Ours will not. The entire village will watch them and know who we are, and that includes Julian."

"What if we camouflage our voices?"

"Jackson will recognize my story, and most clan members will recognize yours. So, unless you want to change the details so completely that it barely has any resemblance to what happened, or invent a whole new story, they will know it was you."

Ella shrugged. "If they know so much already, then what I say in that video is not going to be news to anyone."

Tessa shook her head. "You are a brave soul. I salute you."

She wasn't brave at all, but she was faking it well. This was going to be hell, and Ella wasn't even sure whether she was doing the right thing.

What if her story was too vanilla compared to what the other girls had gone through?

They might scoff at her, thinking that it was easy for her since there had been nothing truly horrific in what had happened to her.

From what Vanessa had told her, Ella had a clue as to how bad it had been for the others.

Compared to them, she'd been incredibly lucky.

But then Tessa's story was truly horrific, and if she thought that Ella was brave for telling hers, then maybe the others would think so too.

"I have a question for you, and I want you to answer me frankly."

Tessa's expression was guarded when she nodded.

"I need your perspective. I know that what happened to me is nothing compared to what you went through. Do you think the other girls will think that it was easier for me to go on video because of that?"

"Perhaps some will think that, but I don't. I admire your guts for doing it."

"Okay, good. Do you want to come with me to Vanessa? I need to run this by her if I want all the girls gathered for the recording."

Tessa pushed to her feet. "That's the least I can do."

As they headed to the therapist's office, Ella wrapped her arm around Tessa's slim shoulders. "I don't want you to feel bad. You have very legitimate reasons not to go on tape. First of all, because you want to forget, and I totally understand that, and secondly because you don't want Jackson to hear all the gory details, and I understand that too. I think you're incredibly brave for even being here. I'm sure it's no picnic for you to be surrounded by reminders."

"It's not. But again, that's the least I can do."

As usual, Vanessa's door was open, and she waved them in. "How is it going? Ready to start filming?"

"I am," Ella said. "But I decided to go first, and I want to do it with all the girls watching. I think this is the best way to present the idea to them, and to lead by example."

Vanessa looked impressed. "That's very brave of you. When do you want to do that and where?"

"The only place big enough for everyone to fit in is the dining hall. We will have to take the tables out and bring chairs from the classrooms. Tessa and I can set up the stage in the front of the room."

"The only problem I see with your plan is recording live. Are you going to prepare and rehearse what you're going to say?"

Ella had thought about it on the way and decided not to. If her delivery was too smooth, it might intimidate the other girls. She had to stumble and stutter and convince them that they could do a better job than her.

"Nope. Before I start, I'll explain that the video is going to get edited, so it's okay to stumble and repeat things or even tell the story out of order. I shouldn't even try to make it sound good. I don't want to add any unnecessary barriers like performance anxiety to what is already a tough gig."

Vanessa nodded. "You have good instincts."

"Thank you. What do you think about Monday after dinner?"

"Perfect. I'll put it on the schedule as a lecture."

Ella grimaced. No one wanted to listen to a lecture after dinner. "Instead of calling it a lecture, call it a presentation and add my name, so they will know who's doing it. Tessa's too. Several of the girls already know what we are planning, and they can spread the rumor, so it isn't going to be a complete surprise."

"No problem. Again, good instincts, Ella. You keep impressing me."

"Thank you."

Out in the corridor, Tessa let out a breath. "That went well. Things are moving along."

"Yes, they are."

"Are you nervous?"

"I'm shaking in my boots."

Ella was wearing the monster ones that added six inches to her height. Maybe that was why faking confidence had been so easy. They made her feel like a badass.

When her phone buzzed in her back pocket, Ella smiled and pulled it out, but the message wasn't from Julian. It was from Kian.

Come to my office as soon as you're back from the sanctuary. We have things to discuss.

"What is it?" Tessa asked. "You are frowning. Did anything happen?"

"Kian wants to see me this evening. I wonder what he wants."

39

KIAN

"Good evening, Kian." Turner walked into the office and put his briefcase on the conference table. "Other than Ella, did you invite anyone else?"

"Just you. I spoke with Vivian and Magnus earlier today. Naturally, they are not happy about the plan, but they understand that for Ella to be free of Lokan, we need to capture and neutralize him."

Turner pulled his laptop and yellow pad out of the briefcase. "By neutralizing you mean put in stasis."

"I'm not going to kill him, if that's what you're asking. That would be a waste."

"You shouldn't put him in stasis either. Just keep him locked up and well-guarded. There is a lot we can learn from him, and it will take time."

Kian waved a hand. "I'm not going to put him away until we learn all there is to learn from him."

"Even after we are done with the initial interrogation, I prefer to have him available for further questioning whenever needed. As I understand it, stasis is not a state one can go in and out of with ease."

"No, it is not. But as long as he is conscious, Lokan can enter Ella's dreams."

Turner chuckled. "You can tell the story to her parents, but we both know that once she transitions, Lokan's access to her mind will most likely end."

"We can't be sure of that. No one knows anything about dream-walking. It might not be limited to humans."

"But we can be quite sure that he won't be able to compel her."

Rapping his fingers on the conference table, Kian shook his head. "We don't have him yet, and once we do, we will decide what's the best way to handle him."

"Agreed. Now to the next item of concern. I think Julian needs to be here when we present the plan to Ella."

Kian had contemplated inviting the guy, but had decided against it. Just as with Vivian and Magnus, he wasn't looking for anyone's approval.

"He's not her mate. Not yet, anyway. And he has no say in this."

Pinning him with a hard stare, Turner lifted a brow. "Semantics, Kian. He is her mate, and we both know it. Besides, not having him here will just put the problem on Ella's shoulders. She is going to want to do this, and Julian is going to object. If he learns of it with us present, we can deal with him, making it easier for her."

"I can't argue with your logic. It is sound as usual."

After shooting a text to Julian, Kian got up and walked over to the bar. "Can I offer you something to drink?"

"What are you having?"

"Black Label."

"I'll take a shot."

After pouring the scotch, he handed Turner his glass and put his own down on the table, then walked back to the fridge and pulled out two water bottles and one of Snake Venom.

Perhaps Julian would want something to take the edge off, and as far as he remembered the young doctor hadn't developed a taste for whiskey yet.

When a few minutes later Julian walked in looking concerned, Kian motioned for him to join them.

"What's going on?" Julian asked as he took a seat across from Turner.

"Ella should be here any moment, and Turner thought you should be here when we tell her our plan."

"What plan?"

"Let's wait until she gets here, so I don't have to repeat myself."

The guy didn't look happy, but he knew better than to argue.

"How is the halfway house coming along?" Kian asked to pass the time.

For some reason, Julian exchanged looks with Turner before answering. "The work has started, and it's going well. I didn't know Yamanu had construction experience. He claims it's minimal, but at least he understands the contractors' jargon and sounds like he knows what he's talking about. If it had been left up to me, they would've known right away that they could tell me any story they want and I would buy it because I'm clueless."

"I'm glad Yamanu's found something to sink his teeth into. He spends too much time alone in his house."

Julian frowned. "I thought he lived with Arwel."

"He does, but Arwel is a busy guy. Most of the time Yamanu is alone."

As a light knock on the door announced Ella, Julian jumped to his feet and rushed to open it for her.

"Oh, hi, Julian. I didn't know you'd be here too." She glanced at Turner and then at Kian. "It seems like I'm playing with the big boys now."

Julian laughed, making Kian suspect that there was a double meaning to what she'd said, but the only one who'd gotten it was the young doctor.

"It's something from an animated movie," Julian said.

So, it was a generational thing. He really needed to brush up on the latest references. Syssi would probably know what it had meant. Remembering their morning fun time, he smiled. Perhaps he would find an excuse to play with her again tonight.

Pulling out a chair for Ella next to his, Julian waited for her to sit down and then took his seat and wrapped a protective arm around her shoulders.

Turner had been right about having him participate in the meeting.

No big surprise there.

By now, Turner probably knew Julian better than Kian knew the young man. In part because he was mated to Bridget, and in part because of the time the two had spent together in New York, preparing and executing Ella's rescue.

"I'm guessing that we are here to talk about Mr. D, right?" Ella said. "Or is it about the fundraiser?"

"Your first guess was right. What do you think about turning the tables on Lokan and setting a trap for him?"

Ella grinned from ear to ear. "I think it's a fabulous idea, and one I've been toying with ever since I discovered who he was."

40

ELLA

*T*alk about butterflies.

The swirling frenzy in Ella's belly should have made her float. They were actually going to let her do it, and she hadn't even suggested it.

Maybe that was the reason why. If she had offered to entrap Mr. D, Kian probably would have dismissed her idea and told her that she was a weak human that he wouldn't dare send into danger.

What had changed his mind though?

It hadn't been Julian, that was for sure. The guy's brooding expression made it clear that he didn't want Ella to do it.

"So here is what we propose you do," Kian said. "During his next visit, start talking about colleges and what you would like to study. Don't mention any specific institutions because I hope he will suggest one that is close to where he is staying in the States. Once he does, you will fill out an application and schedule a visit to the campus and perhaps a personal interview with the admissions person. The next dream visit, you're going to blurt the date and time of your interview excitedly, and that you and your mother are going to be there."

"Okay...but why make it so complicated? I can tell him that I want to meet him in a restaurant or something."

"He will get suspicious if you suddenly want to meet him."

"Probably, but he won't be able to help himself. He'd show up."

Julian's hand on her shoulder tightened. "Why?"

Crap, she'd almost said too much. "Because he wants me. Mostly for my telepathic ability."

"I'm glad you are aware of that. Turner brought up the possibility that Lokan is not interested in you romantically but thinks of you as an asset. He might be using seduction as a way to lure you to him."

Damn, she hadn't thought about that. Ella considered her telepathy as another attribute Mr. D desired, and not the only one he was after. If that was true, he was a better actor than she'd given him credit for.

Or maybe he regarded sex with her as a bonus.

In either case, it made perfect sense for him to compel her to want him and not want anyone else. Out of all the possibilities she and Carol had discussed, this one was emerging as the most likely.

Except, what about the times she'd gotten excited with Julian?

It was like the small discrepancies Merlin had talked about that had led to the discovery of quantum physics.

Ella stifled a chuckle.

Sometimes her reactions were just as impossible to understand, at least for her. But maybe the explanation was simple after all, and Logan's compulsion weakened in certain circumstances. Like the adrenaline rush that she'd experienced in the hotel. Perhaps it had burned through the compulsion, allowing her to feel attraction to Julian for a short time before snapping back into place.

The thing was, even the immortals didn't know much about compulsion and how it worked. They were all speculating.

As she thought about her little brother being the only one who could actually shed light on the subject, another chuckle almost escaped her throat.

What a shame that Parker wasn't a bit older. If he were at least sixteen, she would've explained the situation to him and asked him to override Logan's compulsion and order her not to feel attraction for the Doomer.

The way she understood it, Parker hadn't removed Logan's compulsion, he'd just given her a new one that had overridden the Doomer's. Which meant that the little guy was more powerful than Navuh's son, and that was beyond cool.

What was even cooler was that he was going to get stronger the older he got.

Next to her, Julian was sitting stiff as a broom, probably imagining what went on during those dream visits.

She had to say something to reassure him. "Well, Mr. D's not doing a very good job of it. If I didn't want to lure him so you could catch him, I would never agree to meet him face to face."

That wasn't entirely true. Logan was doing a great job with that freaking compulsion of his. If Julian weren't as perfect as he was, her lukewarm response to him might have convinced her that he wasn't the one for her, and that the Doomer was. In fact, the thought had crossed her mind, and if Logan weren't as dangerous and as scary as he was, she might have been tempted to meet him.

"Never is a strong word, and immortals have time," Kian said. "Eventually he would chip away at your defenses. All he needs is for you to accidentally reveal where he can find you, and most likely your mother too. If he is after your ability, you alone are useless to him. He needs you both. Unless he doesn't know that you can only communicate with your mother and no one else."

A chill ran down Ella's spine as she scanned her memory of their conversations. "I've never told him, but he knows. When he said that my mother and I are the only ones in the world with such a powerful ability, I didn't stop to think how he knew that."

"He probably got into your head during that one time you were face to face with him," Turner said. "And then he thralled you to forget it. Fortunately, you didn't know about us back then."

"Can he do that in my dreams?"

Kian shook his head. "Not likely. Thralling works differently than compulsion. He would need to be near you. Yamanu can thrall from a distance, but only when it's a blanket thrall. Everyone is affected. He cannot pick a specific person and thrall only him or her."

Ella raked her fingers through her short hair. "He said something about being able to dream share only with people who he'd met in person. Do you think he planted some kind of a mental tracker in my head?"

"He established a connection," Julian said. "But a tracker is an excellent idea. You and your mother should definitely wear one when you go."

Kian waved a hand. "They will be surrounded by Guardians at all times. I'll even send Kri with them so they will have a female Guardian to follow them into the bathroom."

"That's good. Nevertheless, it will make me feel better if they have another layer of protection."

"He is right," Turner said. "I can get tiny trackers they can easily hide. They can be hidden in a hairpin, or in a pair of sunglasses, or even sewn into underwear."

The idea of trackers helped with Ella's anxiety, lowering it to tolerable levels. As exciting as the prospect of entrapping Logan was, going against him scared the crap out of her.

Hopefully, the three immortals sitting at the conference table couldn't smell her fear. It was good that the whiskey Kian and Turner were sipping on had a potent aroma. Hopefully, it was masking whatever she was emitting.

"I didn't know they made them so small. It's so cool. It will make me feel safer knowing that in case something goes wrong, my mother and I can be located."

Pushing his chair even closer to her, Julian leaned and kissed her shoulder. "I'm coming with you too. Think of it as a third layer of protection."

"Thank you." She took his hand. "I want you to come."

Then again, maybe he shouldn't. What if her dream about him fighting with Logan and losing was prophetic?

She grimaced. "On second thought, maybe it's not such a great idea."

"Why? I'm sure Magnus will insist on going once he hears about this."

Kian cleared his throat. "I've already spoken to both Magnus and Vivian this morning, and you are right. Magnus demanded to go."

Thinking quickly, Ella waved a hand. "But Magnus is a Guardian." She turned to Julian. "I don't want you to be in danger."

He arched a brow. "You know that I'm not exactly helpless. Besides, I don't want you in danger either, and I'm not telling you not to go."

"You can't tell me anything. This is Kian and Turner's call."

Removing his arm from her shoulders, Julian looked down his nose at her. "And the same goes for you. It is not your call, it's Kian and Turner's."

Crap. They wouldn't tell him no.

41

JULIAN

*J*ulian was silently seething when he and Ella left Kian's office.

Why had she changed her mind about him accompanying her? He wasn't a weakling who was going to get himself in trouble.

He knew Turner would clear him to go, and Kian wouldn't oppose Turner, who he deferred to in these kinds of decisions. But Ella's lack of confidence in him was irritating.

Hell, it was offensive.

"Did Turner tell you what he did with the druggies?" Ella asked.

Shaking his head, Julian schooled his tone so she wouldn't detect his anger. "I haven't had the chance to talk to him yet. He went straight to Kian's office when he got back to the village, and Kian called me to join the meeting."

At least Kian and Turner thought that he had a say in what happened to Ella. Apparently, everyone was thinking of them as a mated couple except for her.

"Did he tell Kian?"

Julian shrugged. "Kian didn't comment on it, so I guess

Turner didn't share. Which is true to form for him. Everything is on a need to know basis."

"And he didn't think Kian should know? I would think that as the leader of this community, he needs to be told about anything important that happens to one of its members."

"But it wasn't important, and it was irrelevant to the clan."

He was well aware of what Ella was doing. She was very good at changing subjects and redirecting conversations. But it wasn't going to work with him.

"I don't get why one moment you wanted me to come, and then the next you changed your mind."

Scrunching her nose as she glanced up at him, Ella looked so cute that he had a hard time keeping up his anger. With her pink, spiked hair and innocent round eyes, she really looked like a life-sized Tinkerbell.

"Don't be mad at me. There was a good reason for why I changed my mind about you coming along."

He snorted. "There can be only one. You don't think I've got what it takes to defend you, and that I will get in the Guardians' way."

Letting out a breath, she shook her head. "I had a bad dream this morning. You and Mr. D were fighting over me in an Arthurian style tournament, and he was winning. What if it was a premonition?"

Casting her a sidelong glance, Julian frowned. "It could've been one of Lokan's tricks. He might have generated the scenario to scare you. Or maybe to check who you'd be rooting for?"

Hell, he would have loved to be a fly on the wall in that dream and see for himself.

Lokan was a handsome bastard, his looks reflecting how close to the godly source he was. The Doomer was a second generation immortal and the grandson of one of the most powerful gods. Mortdh might have been insane and delusional, but his power had rivaled that of Annani's father.

Perhaps Lokan had inherited his dream-walking ability from Mortdh, or from Mortdh's father, Ekin?

No one knew for sure what those gods could do. Some of them had kept their special abilities a secret.

So yeah, the Doomer was nearly as impressive as Kian, and a young girl like Ella could easily fall for his fake charm even without Lokan compelling her to want him.

Ella might naively think that she was toying with the Doomer, when, in fact, he was toying with her.

Even so, Julian couldn't imagine Ella rooting for the enemy.

She waved a dismissive hand. "It wasn't that kind of dream. It was just an ordinary one. Well, calling it ordinary is not right either. I was Princess Guinevere, and Arthur, who in the dream looked like Magnus, was my father."

He chuckled. "Did you tell Magnus about it?"

"I didn't see him today. When I got back to the house to get a change of clothes, he and my mom were out on a walk with Scarlet. He gets Fridays off."

"Magnus is going to love it. It will prove to him that you've accepted him as your stepdad."

Ella scrunched her nose again. "I accepted him as my mother's fiancé, and even as a stepdad to Parker, but the guy looks so young that I have trouble thinking of him as a father figure."

"Apparently not."

"Yeah, you're right. I guess dreams reveal deeper truths. It seems my subconscious is smarter than my mind, which is deceived by appearances. After all, Magnus is old enough to be my great-great-grandfather."

"I wonder how old Lokan is." Julian cast the bait, hoping Ella would reveal what she thought about the Doomer.

She shrugged. "I have no idea. He looks like all the other immortals. Late twenties or early thirties. I remember the

Russian commenting that Mr. D must have made a deal with the devil because he hadn't aged a bit in all the time Gorchenco had known him."

It seemed that a bigger bait was needed to loosen Ella's tongue. "In Dalhu's portrait of him, Lokan looks quite devilish. Does he look like that in real life?"

"Oh, he does. He has those intense dark eyes that are almost black, and when they glow, there is a reddish undertone in the light they emit. When he smiles, he looks charming, and he is a really good-looking guy. But when he is not happy about something, he looks a lot like what I imagine the devil would look like. If he were an actor, he would have been a shoo-in for the part of Lucifer. An evil fallen angel."

Nothing in what Ella had said indicated that she had feelings for the Doomer, but the excitement in her voice and the slight flare in her feminine aroma had told Julian a different story.

Ella was not only impressed with Lokan, but she was also attracted to him.

Julian felt like a boulder had settled in his gut.

If Ella was indeed his fated mate, she wouldn't have felt attraction toward another male.

Could he have been wrong about her? Had he convinced himself that she was the one for him only because he wanted her to be?

Since he'd seen her picture, Julian hadn't looked at or thought about another female. That was one of the best indicators that Ella was the one for him. And maybe she was, but he wasn't for her.

Was the fucking Doomer her fated mate?

That would explain her lack of arousal when they'd kissed.

It wasn't because of her traumatic experience, but because Julian wasn't the one for her.

42

ELLA

or some reason, Julian looked pissed.

Ella had tried to tone down her description of Logan. Calling him good-looking was a huge understatement. The guy was stunningly handsome. And most of what she'd said was her first impression when she'd still been scared of him.

What had gotten up Julian's ass? For sure it couldn't have been her calling Logan good-looking or charming.

Had he expected her to say that the guy was ugly? Anyone who'd seen Logan's portrait would have known that was a lie.

As she reached for Julian's hand, he didn't pull away, but he didn't give it the little squeeze he usually did. It felt like she was holding hands with a stranger.

He cast her an impassive glance. "You look tired. Let me take you home."

It had been a long day, and an emotionally draining one, but Ella didn't want to go home without fixing whatever had gone wrong between Julian and her.

She wouldn't be able to sleep, and thoughts of him and what had caused the change in his mood would permeate her mind.

And if Logan dream-shared with her, he was going to encounter Julian's manifestation because her head would be filled with him.

"I am tired. But I'm not going anywhere until you tell me what has gotten your panties in a twist." She pulled on Julian's hand and led him toward a bench. "Sit." She pointed at it.

That wrested a small smile out of him. "Yes, ma'am."

When Julian did as she'd asked, Ella climbed onto his lap and wrapped her arms around his neck. "Now tell me what's wrong."

"I'm worried. That's all. Lokan isn't stupid, and he is very powerful. I don't remember if I explained it to you, but the closer genetically an immortal is to the godly source, the more powerful he is. Lokan is a god's grandson. Not a great many generations removed grandson like most of us, but a direct one. And not just any god but one of the most powerful. You are no match for him."

She rolled her eyes. "Thanks a lot, Julian. Now I will be so scared of him that he'll know something is up. And since I can't stop him from entering my dreams, I'm screwed."

If she'd wanted Julian to feel guilty, she'd succeeded.

Raking his fingers through his gorgeous multi-colored hair, he sighed. "I'm sorry, but you should know who you're up against. You might think that Gorchenco was the big bad wolf, and that if you outsmarted him, you could outsmart Lokan. That's not the case. It's like with Magnus. Because he looks young, you regard him as you would a human that age. You're aware that he's intelligent and cunning, so you take it into account, but you think that your youth and beauty are enough to blindside him. They are not."

Ella shook her head. "I'm not that vain, Julian, and Mr. D was quite frank about what he sees in me. He told me point blank that it wasn't about my looks. He even said that he has had many girls who were prettier than me. He wants me for my ability, but I'm not sure Turner is right about him wanting to use my mom and me for what we can do. What would he do with us that he can't do with a satellite phone?"

"So why do you think he wants you?"

"Maybe he suspects that we are Dormants? Or maybe he wants me because I'm special. You know, like in rare. Because of my telepathy." She looked away.

Touting her own attributes wasn't something Ella was comfortable with. Heck, she had spent her life trying to act as modest as can be because people took one look at her and assumed that because she had a pretty face, she must be full of herself.

Hooking a finger under her chin, Julian turned her head, so she had to look at him. "You are special, Ella. And not just because of the telepathy. Why do you think I want you?"

"The face. It's always the face. I know you're going to deny it and list all the things you supposedly admire about me, but that is just the frosting on the cake. Maybe you're not even aware of doing it, but you're looking for justification."

"I don't need to justify myself to anyone. Besides, no one questions my reasons except for you."

"I wasn't talking about justifying it to others. I'm talking about justifying it to yourself."

He arched a brow. "Oh, really? And how do you know what's going on inside my head?"

Crap. They had been doing really well up until now, and then she had to go and ruin it because Julian's pissy mood had infected her.

Ella waved a dismissive hand. "People do it all the time, and especially guys. A man meets a beautiful woman who is up to no good, and he finds excuses for why she is marriage material. Women are a little better at this, but they do it too."

Julian's eyes softened, and he wrapped his arms around her, coaxing her to relax against him and put her head on his chest.

"I'm no expert, and I might be wrong, but I think everyone does it to some extent."

He kept rubbing his hand over her back in slow, soothing circles. "Falling in love with someone is not a logical process. I don't know if it's a chemical reaction, or if it's our subconscious collecting information lightning-speed fast and making an instantaneous decision for us, but the result is the same. We fall, and then we try to justify the why to ourselves."

Letting out a breath, Ella closed her eyes. "That's probably why it's called falling and not soaring or floating."

He chuckled. "That's such a clever observation. It had never crossed my mind, although it should have. Soaring in love sounds so much better than falling in love."

He was buttering her up, attempting to make up for his lousy attitude from before. "You're just trying to find ways to make me look smart."

43

JULIAN

*J*ulian stroked Ella's hair. "I don't have to. You are smart." It was spiked with a lot of gel and not pleasant to touch.

He wished she didn't have to do that, but on the other hand, he didn't want some random camera picking up her image and then someone running it through facial recognition software. Not that the different hairstyle could fool it, but it was part of her disguise, and an extra layer of security on top of the special glasses she wore every time she went out of the village.

"Sorry about the hair," Ella said. "I put in so much gel that it could qualify as a lethal weapon."

He chuckled, relieved that her sense of humor was back. His anger from before had made her anxious, and he didn't like seeing that look on her face. He'd much rather see the mischievous spark in her eyes and the sly smirk whenever she said something funny or sarcastic.

That was one of the reasons he hadn't answered her questions truthfully. The other was his stupid pride.

Admitting that he was jealous of her dream visitor would have made him seem petty and immature.

Besides, he hadn't lied.

Every word he'd said was true. Lokan was dangerous, Ella was no match for him, and Julian worried that this new plan Turner and Kian had hatched was going to misfire big time.

They'd put too much trust in Ella's ability to wrap Lokan around her little finger. Julian had a feeling Lokan was toying with Ella, letting her believe that she had him fooled, when, in fact, he was fooling her.

The thing was, while this was going on, Ella had to pretend that she was attracted to the Doomer, and it seemed to him that she didn't have to pretend too hard. Still, he had to remember that she was only doing what she thought was right for the clan, and what Kian and Turner wanted her to do.

Besides, it could very well be that Lokan was compelling her attraction to him while at the same time compelling her not to respond to any other male.

If the Doomer was playing a game of seduction to make a naive young girl believe that he was falling for her, it made perfect sense for the unscrupulous bastard to use every tool in his arsenal. And that included compulsion.

Julian let out a relieved breath.

Thinking of it that way made it much easier for him to deal with the situation. The attraction Ella felt for Lokan wasn't natural.

She was forced to feel it.

And the same argument held true for why his fated mate, his one and only, didn't find him irresistible.

"Speaking of weapons. Tell me about your dream."

When she scrunched her nose, he couldn't help but lean and kiss the tip. "You look so cute when you do that."

Shifting in his lap, she leaned against his arm and looked at him. "What do you want to know? The kind of weapons you and Mr. D used to hurt each other?"

"Among other things. You said that you were Princess

Guinevere and that Arthur was your father. I assume that I was fighting the Doomer for your hand in marriage?"

She nodded. "You each had a sword in one hand and a shorter dagger in the other. He wasn't better than you, but he didn't fight fair, so he was managing to wound you worse than you were wounding him."

Julian stifled a smirk. The dream was proving his hypothesis. On a subconscious level, Ella knew that both he and Lokan were trying to seduce her, but while Julian's intentions were pure, Lokan's were sinister. And on top of that, the Doomer was fighting dirty by using compulsion on her.

But there was one part that caused him to frown. "I was losing?"

Ella nodded. "You were losing so much blood. Every time he made an illegal move, I screamed to warn you, and every time he cut you, I cried. I sobbed so hard that my head started hurting in the waking world. Maybe the headache was what saved me from seeing him deliver the death blow because I woke up just as he was about to chop off your head."

Well, that answered the question of who she'd been rooting for.

Tears pooling in the corners of her eyes, Ella cupped his cheek. "I don't know what the dream meant, but it might have been a warning that you shouldn't come anywhere near Mr. D. I'm not willing to chance your life."

As the tears started sliding down her cheeks, making dirty tracks with her dissolved makeup, Julian's heart melted.

Could it be that Ella loved him?

If she was crying over him getting hurt in a dream, she must have feelings for him.

That didn't mean, however, that he was going to abide by her wishes and stay behind while she and her mother walked into the lions' den.

Using his thumbs, he wiped her tears away and then leaned and softly kissed her trembling lips.

"Don't cry, Ella. It was just a dream, a vivid representation of your fears. Have you ever had prophetic dreams before?"

She shook her head. "What if this is the first one?"

"Nice try. But I happen to know someone who has those, and she's been having them since she was a little girl."

"Who is it?"

"Kian's wife, Syssi."

Wiping her cheeks with the back of her hands, Ella just made a greater mess of things. "That's so cool. Did any of her premonitions come true?"

"They did, but because her premonitions are vague, they are not actionable. The when and the how are usually missing. I wasn't here when she had them, so I only know what my mother has told me."

"Maybe I should talk to her?"

"What for?"

"So that she can tell me whether my dream was a premonition or not. She would know the difference, right?"

"I'm not sure, and there is no point in your bothering her. Your dream reflected your thoughts and fears, nothing more. Besides, I'm not letting you go without me regardless."

Crossing her arms over her chest, Ella pushed her chin out. "You can't tell me what to do."

"And I'm not going to. But by the same token, you can't prevent me from going."

She laughed. "Are we back to that again?"

"You started it."

"True, which means that I have to end it. You can come, but you have to do exactly what whoever leads the Guardians tells you. No heroics, please."

44

ELLA

"Good night, Julian. I'll call you tomorrow morning, okay?"

He held on to her hand. "Are you sure you don't want to spend the night at my place?"

"I can't. I need to dream." She looked away, not wanting to see the anger bubble up from him again.

Except, he surprised her with a smile. "Can I at least get a kiss goodnight?"

"I would love a kiss."

Swooping her up, he crushed her to him and fused their mouths in a kiss that was all about possession.

Holy Thor and all of Asgard, that was hot.

No gentle coaxing, and no tentative sweetness. His hands cupping her butt cheeks, Julian pressed her against his hardness while ravaging her mouth with his tongue.

Needing to take a breath, she was loath to stop the mother of all kisses, but Julian sensed her need and let her come up for air.

His eyes glowing like two blue neon lights, he rested his

forehead against hers for a moment, and then let her down. "I'd better go. Good night, Ella."

Turning around, he jumped down the three steps separating the path from the front porch and broke into a jog.

Poor guy. Julian was probably suffering from the worst case of blue balls in the Northern Hemisphere.

The good news was that they had parted on a good note, so she knew they were okay as a couple and that Julian was no longer mad.

Which meant that she could go to sleep without worrying about that.

As much as she kept their relationship on a slow burner, Ella couldn't fathom not having Julian around. He'd become a vital part of her life.

Without him and his quiet and unwavering support, she wouldn't have been able to recover so quickly. Not that she was fully recovered, she would be deluding herself if she believed that, but she could function, and think, and come up with ideas, none of which would have been possible if she'd sunk into a depression.

It was still a daily struggle to keep it at bay, and from time to time disturbing thoughts managed to infiltrate the barricades she'd erected against them. But overall, she was doing better than she'd ever expected so soon after her rescue.

Julian was a godsend, and stubborn as a mule.

She didn't like that he'd refused to heed the dream's warning, or her asking him not to come. On the other hand, though, she liked that he'd stood his ground and didn't crumble under pressure.

Her guy was a fighter through and through.

Funny how her perspective had been completely changed by what had happened to her.

The old Ella had dreamt of marrying a nice guy who was fairly intelligent, motivated, and a hard worker, preferably tall because she was short and had a thing for tall men. Fighting skills hadn't been anywhere near the top of her list of desirable traits.

Quite the opposite.

She'd sworn that she would never marry a military man, no matter in what capacity he served. Her father had been a chopper mechanic, for God's sake, and he'd gotten killed, leaving a wife and two small kids to fend for themselves.

And the same went for cops, firemen, and any other dangerous profession.

But here she was, with a stepdad who was a combination cop and warrior, and a boyfriend who was a doctor, but a badass one who could fight.

Her mother would have scoffed at her, but Ella's priorities had shifted. She valued Julian's fighting ability more than his medical degree.

Knowing that he would defend her if necessary made her feel safe. Regrettably, though, he couldn't help her in her dreams, and she needed to make a mental shift in preparation for her encounter with Logan.

Which meant putting Julian out of her mind and filling it with information about colleges.

Getting inside, she tiptoed to her room, hoping Magnus and Parker wouldn't hear her through their soundproof doors.

It was late, and she still needed to spend a couple of hours on her laptop, researching colleges. Good thing tomorrow was Saturday, and she could sleep in.

Almost three hours later, Ella was still at it, but her eyes were getting tired, and although she was making notes of the information she was gathering, the details were all starting to blur together. She couldn't remember which of the colleges she'd checked out had a good nursing undergrad program and which had a good graduate program. Not to mention the different requirements each had for submitting an application.

Closing the laptop, she put it on the floor next to her bed and closed her eyes.

Sleep came almost instantaneously, and with it the dream.

"I've been waiting for you to start dreaming," Logan said. "I prepared this beautiful setting for you. And then you failed to show up."

They were lying on comfortable loungers on a sunny beach, the ocean in front of them lapping gently at the shore.

She was wearing a skimpy bikini, no doubt taken from Logan's imagination because she'd never owned anything like that. His muscular torso was bare, proudly displayed for her enjoyment, and he had on some sort of tight-fitting swimming trunks that left little to the imagination.

Did he think that was going to arouse her?

Well, it was quite impressive, and she took a quick glance before looking behind her to see where they were. Ella had been expecting a hotel, but the structure behind them was a private villa.

"Where are we?"

"In Hawaii." He motioned with his chin. "That's my house."

Was he telling her the truth?

This could have been the Doomers' island. It was hard to tell just by looking at the color of the sand and the ocean. Logan's house must sit on a big parcel of land because she couldn't see any other houses in either direction. Then again, this was dreamscape, and Logan could've created whatever he wanted.

"Very nice. I'm duly impressed."

Smirking, he flexed.

"I wasn't talking about you. I meant the house and the private beach."

"How disappointing." He looked at her stiff nipples that the bikini top was doing nothing to hide. "And untrue."

Ella crossed her arms over her chest. "I'm cold."

Leaning toward her, he whispered, "Liar."

"Think what you want."

Looking smug, he went back to reclining on his lounger. "Did you have trouble falling asleep?"

"No, I had trouble staying awake. I was researching colleges. My mother is pressuring me to get an education."

"Why? Don't you want one?"

"I do, of course. I'm just not ready to leave home. What if the Russian is still looking for me?"

"I don't think you have anything to worry about. Gorchenco's accepted that you are dead. Your mother's friends did a great job covering your tracks." He turned on his side and pinned her with his intense eyes. "I was wondering about that. How does a dental hygienist know people who can pull together an operation like that? Who are they?"

Crap, she should have known that he'd research her and her family.

Think fast, Ella!

"My father was in special forces. His old buddies helped my mother."

"Your father was a helicopter mechanic."

"For a special ops commando unit."

"I didn't find anything like that in his file."

Waving a dismissive hand, Ella snorted. "As if you would. Do you think information like that is accessible to just anyone?"

"I'm not just anyone."

"Right. You are a big-shot warlord. But guess what? This is the United States of America. I'm sure that if the military wants to keep some highly-classified information well protected, they can."

He smiled. "I'm actually glad to hear that. I was afraid that you and your mother were snatched by some secret organization that your government has for dealing with people like you, and that you were being kept locked in a research facility."

She arched a brow. "Why would you think that?"

"Governments love to get their hands on people with special abilities." His smile melted away. "Either to use them for secret missions or to experiment on them to find out what makes them special. I wouldn't want you suffering such a fate."

He sounded so sincere that Ella wondered if it was a superb act, or if he really did worry about her. Most likely, Logan was worried about someone else getting their hands on her and her mother first. It wasn't about her, but what he wanted from her.

"Yeah, I wouldn't want that either. But no one other than you knows about us. We were always very good at keeping our ability a secret."

"Very smart."

"Thank you. But it was actually my father who insisted on the secrecy."

"As I said, smart. The man protected his family."

"Yeah, he did. He was a good dad. I miss him."

Logan regarded her for a moment as if trying to decipher her meaning, but then he smiled and changed the subject. "So, Ella, what do you want to study?"

"Nursing. I've always wanted to be a nurse."

"Do you have a specific college you're interested in?"

"Not at the moment. I'm just collecting information and checking what the admissions requirements are, and how much it costs, and if they offer scholarships. I can't afford a fancy college."

Logan's eyes sparkled. "I have a friend in Georgetown. They have an excellent nursing program, and I can talk to him about arranging a scholarship for you."

Fortunately, Ella didn't need to stifle her excitement, just pretend that it was for a different reason. "That's awesome. Could you really do that for me?"

"I'll do my best. But if I get you an interview, can you get to Washington on your own?"

"Naturally, my mother would come with me."

"Of course." Logan smiled. "It's not safe for a beautiful young woman like you to travel alone. Big bad wolf might get you."

"Are you referring to yourself?"

He chuckled. "I'm big, and I'm bad, but I'm no wolf. A dragon maybe?"

Ella decided to play along. "I like dragons. But can you fly?"

"Regrettably, only on the wings of my imagination."

"That's a shame. I could have saved on airfare."

Crap, now she had given him an opening to ask where she was flying from. She needed to quickly redirect the conversation. "Joking aside, should I wait for you to talk to your friend or should I apply to Georgetown first?"

"I'll tell my friend to keep an eye open for your application. Fill it out as soon as you can. By the way, I assume you will not be using your real name, am I right?"

Crap, crappity, crap. What was she going to tell him?

She had no choice but to use the fake identity they'd given her and then make a new one.

What a mess.

Now she couldn't even buy an airplane ticket with that name because he would be able to find her before she reached the university. The clan would have to get her a new one.

"Tell your friend to look for an application from Kelly Rubinstein."

His eyes glowed demonic red as he smiled. "Oh, I will, lovely Ms. Kelly Rubinstein."

45

ELLA

*D*espite going to sleep as late as she had, Ella jumped out of bed and rushed to the bathroom as soon as she opened her eyes.

The net had been cast, and Logan had swallowed the bait, licking his lips and imagining how delicious it would taste. The red glow of his eyes had been so strong that Ella had had to bite her lip to stop herself from calling him a demon, or a devil.

Although knowing Logan, he would have loved it. Especially if she'd added sexy as a prefix.

In her closet, she reached for a pair of jeans, but then changed her mind. Something nicer was needed for when she delivered the news to Kian.

After all, she was a spy, a femme fatale so to speak, and this morning she felt like dressing the part. Maybe she should throw on the black wig and sunglasses for good measure?

Unfortunately, her closet offered a limited selection. Once she started earning some money, she could do something about it, but for now, she had to make do with what was there or borrow clothes from her mom.

A simple gray sweater matched her one long skirt, and the

black monster boots didn't look too bad with that ensemble. A little mascara and lip gloss, and she was ready to conquer the world.

Or maybe just stomp over it with her boots.

In the kitchen, she found her mom making pancakes for breakfast, and Magnus sitting at the counter with a coffee mug in one hand and his phone in the other, no doubt reading the news as he did every day.

"Good morning, family." She kissed Magnus's cheek and then walked up to her mother and kissed her too.

"Good morning," Magnus stammered a little.

It was the first time she'd given him a good morning kiss, and he still looked stunned.

Vivian smiled. "You are in a good mood. Did you have a good night's sleep?"

"It was too short, but I had a dream visitor. Mr. D took the bait. When I told him that I want to study nursing, and that I'm checking which colleges I can get into on a scholarship, he offered to speak with his friend at Georgetown University. Do you know what that means?"

Her mother's hand flew to her chest. "That my baby is going to be in danger again."

Ella rolled her eyes. "No. It means that Mr. D is in Washington D.C."

"You need to tell Kian," Magnus said.

"I'm going to text him. I just wanted to tell you first. I had to give him my fake name, which means I'll have to choose another for later. I know it's a hassle, but I didn't have a choice. Mr. D said that he was going to tell his so-called friend to look out for my application. I had to tell him what name to look for."

Magnus rubbed his jaw. "I wonder if he really has a friend there, or if he's going to thrall or compel everyone on the admissions board."

"Yeah, I had the same thought. I'm just sorry to give up that name. I kind of liked Kelly Rubinstein, age twenty-one. I'm so excited."

Her mother braced a hand on the counter. "I'm feeling faint."

In a blink of an eye, Magnus was next to her. "Let me help you to a chair."

Her mother was such a drama queen.

"You should be happy, Mom, not hyperventilating. Things are moving along according to plan, and this is going to be over soon. I can't wait to get rid of my dream visitor."

Plopping down on a chair next to her mother, Ella took her clammy hand and warmed it between both of hers. "I want to start my new life, Mom, and I can't do that as long as that Doomer is part of it. Everything is on hold until this is resolved. My education, my relationship with Julian, it all waits until I'm free of him."

Vivian nodded. "I understand. But that doesn't make me any less afraid."

"We are going to have plenty of Guardians with us, and Magnus and Julian are coming too. We are going to be safer than the President."

Snorting, Vivian waved a hand. "All those Secret Service guys, and still some assassination attempts were successful. The President is not a good example."

"How about when he is in the Oval Office. I'm sure nothing can touch him there."

"Let's hope so," Magnus said. "I can imagine several scenarios in which not even the Oval Office is safe."

She cast him a hard stare. "You are not helping, Magnus."

"I'm sorry." He sat across from Vivian and reached for her other hand. "I can promise you this, though. The two of you are going to be even safer than the President."

"What's going on?" Parker asked, coming into the living room. "Why are you holding Mom's hands?"

"She needed a little reassurance," Magnus said. "Come give her a hug. I'm sure that will help."

Parker smirked. "I can do better than that. I can compel her not to worry over whatever she is worried about."

"Don't you dare." Vivian pulled her hands out of theirs. "Come give your mother a hug. That's all I need to feel better."

Ella got up and wrapped her arms around her mother from one side, and Parker did the same from the other. "Then a group hug should be even better." She looked up at Magnus. "Come on, big guy, don't be shy. Join the hug and share the love."

46

ELLA

Come to my office in half an hour. Ella read the text and put the phone in her purse.

"What did Kian say?" her mother asked.

"He wants to see me in his office in half an hour."

"Just you?" Vivian turned to Magnus. "Shouldn't we be there with her?"

Magnus shook his head. "If Kian thought we should accompany Ella, he would have said so."

"Can we just show up? He's not going to kick us out, is he?"

Wrapping his arm around Vivian, Magnus kissed her forehead. "Patience, love. Ella will tell us all about it when she comes back."

Deflating, Vivian rested her cheek against his chest. "It's good that at some point I'm going to turn immortal because this stress is taking years off my life."

"I hope that point comes sooner rather than later."

Feeling like she was intruding on their moment, Ella grabbed her purse and headed toward the door. "I'm going to stop by Julian's first."

It sounded like a good excuse for why she was leaving so

early, but on second thought she decided it was a good idea. Julian had made such a big deal out of being involved that he would appreciate her keeping him in the loop.

She texted him while walking. *Put some pants on. I'm coming over.*

Ha, ha, was his answer.

Smiling, she dropped the phone back in her purse. The downside of wearing a skirt was having to schlep something extra just so she'd have somewhere to put her phone.

Perhaps after the talk with Kian, Julian could take her to the mall. She could get one of those cross-body wallets. That shouldn't cost too much, and she still had some cash left over from what Magnus had given her before.

Damn. She really needed to start earning some money.

Didn't spies get paid?

Julian opened the door wearing pants and a smirk and nothing else. "Good morning, beautiful."

Ella pretended to shield her eyes, admiring his muscular torso from between her spread fingers. "Cover it up. Your skin is so pale that it reflects the light and is shining it straight into my eyes. You are blinding me."

Looking down at his chest, he flexed, showing off impressive pectorals and abdominals. "I'm not that white."

She smiled. "I was joking, but really, Julian, cover it up." Walking by him to get into the house, Ella balled her hands to keep from reaching for that glorious chest and touching him all over.

"Am I distracting you?" He followed her inside.

"Terribly."

"Coffee?"

"Thanks, but I already had some, and I don't have time anyway. Kian wants me in his office in twenty minutes."

That got his attention. "Why?"

Ella smirked. "The dream-walker took the bait."

Reaching for her hand, Julian pulled her toward the couch. "Tell me everything."

She resisted. "Put on a shirt, and I'll tell you on the way. I want you to come with me to Kian's."

Heading to Julian's house she hadn't planned on asking him to accompany her, but now that she was here, it just seemed like the most natural thing to do.

"Thanks for asking me to join you."

"Yeah, I hope Kian doesn't mind. But since it involves filling in applications to universities, I can claim that I brought you along for your expert advice on the subject."

"That could work. Wait here. I'll be back in a minute."

He did it in less.

"I've just noticed that Ray isn't here," she said as Julian closed the front door. "Is he still sleeping?"

"Yeah. He partied until late last night."

"Oh, yeah? Where?"

Julian waved a dismissive hand. "Clubs, pubs, wherever the hunting grounds were good."

Right. She remembered Carol talking about it. Immortals prowled places like that for hookups. Did Julian?

She had no right demanding exclusivity from him, but she wanted it nonetheless.

"How come you didn't go with him?" she probed.

He cast her an incredulous look. "I haven't gone hunting since I saw your picture. Don't you get it? You are the one for me, and I don't want anyone else."

Ouch. He must have a really bad case of blue balls, and she couldn't help feeling a little guilty.

Taking his hand, she leaned against his bicep. "I'm sorry. It must be difficult for you."

He stopped and turned to her. "It's not your fault, so don't you dare blame yourself. It was my decision to wait. You were the one who was trying to rush things, remember?"

Ella felt her cheeks getting warm. She'd wanted to transition so badly that she'd convinced herself that she could go ahead with it, but Julian had seen right through her and had realized she wasn't ready.

With a sigh, she put her forehead on his chest. "I don't deserve you, Julian. How can you be so selfless?"

He kissed the top of her head. "I'm not selfless. I'm selfish. I want it to be perfect between us, and for that to happen, you need time to heal emotionally."

If only it were true.

Well, it was partially true. Just not entirely. But she couldn't tell Julian that she suspected Logan of compelling her attraction to him because then she would have to admit to what went on in their dream encounters.

Julian wasn't stupid, and he'd probably guessed it, but it wasn't the same as being told.

"Thank you. I appreciate it."

When they reached Kian's office, his door was open, and they walked right in.

"Good morning, Kian. I'm so sorry to drag you here on a Saturday."

He waved a dismissive hand. "I work on weekends anyway, and this is important. Tell me about your dream encounter and try not to skip over any details."

She nodded. "I'll do my best."

Neither Kian nor Julian interrupted her story, listening intently to every word until she was done.

"I'm sorry about the fake identity," she said preemptively. "I had no choice."

"Don't spare it another thought. We will get you another one. In fact, I don't want you leaving the village until you get it. From now until you leave for Georgetown, Kelly Rubinstein goes into hiding."

"I understand."

And just like that, gone were her plans to have Julian take her to the mall. Worse, Monday she was going to shoot a video, and Vanessa had already announced it to everyone.

"Don't worry about the plane tickets either," Kian said. "Kelly Rubinstein will buy airfare from Dallas to Washington, but she is going to miss her flight. Or something to that effect. We will fly you there in our private jet."

"I need to be in the sanctuary on Monday. Is there a chance those documents could be ready by then?"

"I will do my best, but I can't promise it."

"I have to be there. I have an event scheduled, and I would hate to postpone it."

For a long moment, Kian rapped his fingers on the table, but then he nodded. "As long as you are not driving and someone takes you to the sanctuary and back, I'll allow it even without the new papers. But nothing else. Don't use your credit card for anything."

He frowned. "Did you order anything online using it?"

Ella shook her head. "I didn't use it at all. The one time I went shopping I paid cash for everything."

"Excellent."

"Ella's travel arrangements to Georgetown should probably go through Turner," Julian said.

"Naturally, I just outlined the possibilities so she wouldn't worry needlessly. We will find a solution for everything." Kian turned to Ella. "Do you know what's involved in filling out a college application?"

"Not really. That's why I brought Julian along. To get into medical school, he must have submitted one hell of an application."

"My mother helped. But I know what's needed. What I don't know is how to get her fake transcripts. Unless the real Kelly Rubinstein had very good grades before dying prematurely, we will have to hack into her school records and do all kinds of illegal stuff."

"Roni will take care of that. All I need from you is a list of what's needed."

Julian chuckled. "Roni's mate is a perpetual student. I doubt he needs me to tell him what's involved in a college application."

"Nevertheless, I need you to prepare it. Sylvia didn't study nursing or anything related to it. I'm sure there is a difference and applying to study philosophy or some other nonsense like that is not the same as applying to medical or nursing school."

47

JULIAN

"I was hoping to go to the mall," Ella said as they left Kian's office. "But that is out now. I'm back to being stuck here until my new fake documents are ready."

Going down the stairs, he took her hand. "They might be ready by Monday. The forger is one of us."

"That would be awesome."

"How about I take you to the café instead?"

"Isn't it closed on Saturday?"

"It is, but Jackson keeps the vending machines stocked, and there are always people hanging out there on weekends. It's not like we have many options here." He opened the office building's front door for her.

Ella smiled up at him. "I could go for a pastry."

"Let's just hope we can find a table." He glanced in the café's direction. "Plenty to choose from."

"I see Wonder and Anandur, do you mind if we join them?"

"As long as they don't mind, I sure don't."

"Ella!" Wonder waved them over. "Come have coffee with us."

"Am I invited too?" Julian asked as he pulled out a chair for

Ella.

Wonder rolled her eyes. "Would you care to join us, Doctor Ward?"

"Thank you, I would." He bowed his head. "But first I need to get nourishment for my lady. What would you like, Ella?"

"What Wonder is having. A cappuccino and a Danish."

"Your wish is my command."

"I'll come with you." Anandur pushed away from the table. "I'm ready for the second round."

As they headed for the row of vending machines, Julian cast Anandur a sidelong glance. "How are things going?"

"That's what I wanted to ask you. Why were you and Ella meeting Kian in the office on a Saturday morning?"

He should have known the guy wanted to fish for gossip. There was no harm in telling him, though. Soon enough all the Guardians would know what was brewing.

Except, it wasn't his story to tell. It was Ella's, and it was up to her how much or how little she wanted people to know.

"You're asking the wrong person."

Anandur arched a brow. "Should I ask Ella?"

"It's her story. I'm just the…"

What the hell was he?

The boyfriend?

The confidant?

"I'm just the escort."

The Guardian gave him an amused look from head to toe. "I can see how you would be, but I was under the impression that only older ladies required escort services."

Julian flicked his hair back and looked down his nose at Anandur. "I don't discriminate based on age or ethnicity. Just gender. So you're out of luck, buddy."

Laughing, Anandur slapped his back. "Let's get back to our ladies. I can't wait to find out what this is all about. Seems big to me."

Julian handed Anandur one of the cappuccino cups. "Can you hold it for me? I need to get the pastries."

"I'll take it to the table." Anandur turned to go.

"Hold on. Before you ask Ella anything, I want to check with Kian if it's okay for her to tell you about it. He didn't give us any instructions, and I don't want her to mess up."

Looking disappointed, Anandur nodded. "Personally, I believe in doing first and if needed apologizing later, but it's your call."

Worried that Ella had already told Wonder, Julian rushed back to the table, but when he and Anandur got there, Wonder and Ella were talking about the sanctuary.

Thank the merciful Fates.

Putting the coffee and pastries down, he pulled out his phone and texted his question to Kian.

The answer was, *Use your discretion.*

Great. What was that supposed to mean?

"Well?" Anandur was looking at him with his bushy brows raised in a question.

"He said to use my discretion."

Turning toward him, Ella asked. "About what?"

"Anandur wants to know what we were meeting Kian about. So, I texted the boss to ask if it was okay to talk about it, and that was his answer."

"Use our discretion?"

"Yes."

Pursing her lips, she shrugged. "If Parker knows, I don't see the harm in telling Anandur and Wonder. But please don't spread it around. I know that you trust each and every clan member, especially those living with you in the village, but I come from the human world where anything can happen, including family selling each other out or even killing each other."

Anandur patted her back. "Not all of us are good. I'm well

aware of that. Whatever you tell Wonder and me will not leave this table."

When she was done, Anandur whistled. "This is huge. How come Kian didn't tell at least the head Guardians about it?"

"I guess because he didn't have a chance yet," Ella said. "Kian told me about his plan only yesterday, and I put it into action during the night. It worked like a charm. So, I texted him this morning to let him know, and he wanted to meet me. That's the whole story."

Pushing the fingers of both hands into his crinkly hair, Anandur stared at Ella with awe. "I can't believe it. I just can't. After all these years we finally have a chance to learn that bloody island's location, and it's thanks to an eighteen-year-old human girl. The Fates must be laughing their asses off."

Raising her palm in the air, Wonder grinned at Ella. "High five." They smacked hands. "And once again to girl power."

Smirking, Ella leveled her gaze at Anandur. "Speaking of girl power. I want to hear why and how Wonder kicked both your and your brother's asses. I told you mine, it's only fair that you tell me yours."

Anandur glanced at Wonder. "Do you want to tell the story?"

She blushed. "I should, shouldn't I? Ella was so honest about her dream encounters and the compulsion."

"Are you embarrassed about it?" Ella asked.

Wonder nodded. "I don't like flaunting my physical strength."

Taking her hand, Anandur brought it to his lips. "Your story is about much more than that. It's about courage, and about doing the right thing despite how difficult it was for you. You should be proud. And don't worry about my and Brundar's pride. I want everyone to know my mate is a hero and how proud I am of you."

48

ELLA

*a*s Wonder told her story, Ella's eyes widened with each new detail. She'd known the girl from the study sessions with Parker, and she'd heard about her defeating the undefeated duo, but she'd never heard about the Doomers she'd singlehandedly captured and kept imprisoned for months, probably saving countless women's lives. And she'd done all that while living in a refugee shelter and working as a bouncer in a night club.

Providing meals for her captive Doomers had been a financial struggle, but she'd done it nonetheless, showing them compassion they hadn't deserved.

Ella wondered if in Wonder's shoes she would've been as kind to the monsters. Probably not, but could she have allowed them to starve?

Eventually, they would've gone into stasis, but Wonder had no way of knowing that at the time. Because of her amnesia, she hadn't known who she was or where she'd come from, let alone who and what the Doomers were.

"That's the most amazing story I've ever heard." Ella put her hand over Wonder's. "Anandur is right. You are a real hero."

The girl blushed again. "I did what I had to under the circumstances. The Fates had put the right person in the right place at the right time. I was just a cog in their grand plan."

Ella shook her head. "You're too modest. Next time I'm in my mother's bedazzling class, which is going to be this Monday, I'm going to make you a badass badge from rhinestones. And they are going to be all pink to symbolize girl power."

"I love it," Anandur said. "Can you make me one too?"

She arched a brow. "You want me to make you a badass badge from rhinestones? I don't think it's going to work for you."

He put his arm around Wonder's shoulders and leaned to kiss the top of her head. "Mine is going to say, my mate is a badass. And I'm going to wear it proudly. Make one for Brundar too. His will say, my brother's mate is a badass."

Wonder laughed. "I don't think Callie would appreciate it. I think his should say my mate is an awesome chef."

"Yeah, you're right. Can you add a chef's hat to your design?"

"Sure thing." Ella pulled a pen out of her purse, took a napkin, and drew a quick mock-up of the badge she could make for Brundar. "How about that?"

"I love it. Can I show it to him?"

She handed the napkin to him. "Don't forget to mention that it's going to be made from rhinestones."

Wonder glanced at Julian. "What would yours say?"

Poor Julian, it wasn't fair of Wonder to put him on the spot like that.

Ella came to his rescue. "How about my mate is a dream-catcher?"

And wasn't that clever? She felt quite smug about coming up with that.

Wonder nodded. "I like it."

Julian didn't look happy, though, his brows dipping so low they formed an upside-down triangle between his eyes.

"I have a different idea. Ella's will say—Ella Takala, Director of Save the Girls. And mine will say Ella's deputy."

Was he the sweetest guy, or what? But way too modest.

She took his hand and gave it a little squeeze. "Let's wait with the badges until I actually accomplish something. I'm shooting the first video on Monday, and then Julian and I will probably have to edit the hell out of it before posting it on YouTube. Who knows if anything will come out of it? The idea seems good in theory, but there are no guarantees."

"Who did you convince to go first?" Wonder asked.

Ella grimaced. "Myself. I need to show the girls that I can walk the walk and not only talk the talk. That's the best way to encourage them to do it."

"That's very brave of you," Wonder said.

Anandur nodded in approval.

Julian shook his head. "I don't like it. That's too much exposure. Did you forget that you are hiding from Gorchenco and now also from a powerful Doomer?"

Crossing her arms over her chest, Ella lifted her chin. "I didn't forget a thing. We are shooting in silhouette, and we are going to distort my voice too. The whole point of me doing it is to show the girls that it's safe and that no one will be able to recognize them from the videos."

"What about the story itself? Gorchenco will recognize it. And once he has proof that you're not dead, he's going to hunt you down with every resource at his disposal. And those are vast."

She waved a dismissive hand. "I'm going to change the details. It's the gist of the story that counts, not the particulars. I want to emphasize that if it happened to me, it could happen to any girl."

From the corner of her eye, Ella could see Anandur and

Wonder's heads turning as if they were watching a tennis match.

Julian's eyes were glowing when he pinned her with a hard look. "Write the script of what you're going to say. I want to go over it."

Oof, he was so annoying.

She liked that Julian was protective of her, but she didn't appreciate that he didn't trust her to know what she was doing.

"I'm not stupid, Julian. I know what to say and what not to. I'm not going to write a script because if my story sounds rehearsed, it will lose its emotional impact."

His tortured expression softened Ella a little, and she decided to give him a break. "Don't forget that we are going to edit it later. We can argue about what to leave in and what to cut out then."

He still didn't look happy. "Every clan member in this village, and probably those in Scotland too will watch it. Do you really want everyone to know what you've been through? Unlike the other girls, you are not going to be anonymous. People are going to know it's you."

Stubborn man. Apparently, he didn't know her as well as he thought he did.

"I'm not going to provide any sordid details, if that's what you're worried about. As I said before, I want my video to serve as a warning to other girls and to their parents. I'm going to emphasize the methods traffickers use to lure unsuspecting girls away from their families, and the extortion tactics they use to make them cooperate. But instead of delivering it as a lecture, I'm going to tell a personal story, which is much more impactful."

"Nevertheless, it's still incredibly brave of you," Wonder said. "I think you're doing the right thing." She cast an apologetic glance at Julian. "As Ella's mate, it is natural for you to want to cocoon her in bubble wrap and prevent her from exposure to any danger. But you need to fight that instinct. It's always hard on the partners. I worry every time Anandur goes on a mission, but I know that I have to let him go. Being a Guardian is more than a job for him. It's who he is."

Wow, that was a good speech. Ella would be surprised if Julian had anything to say after that.

"Anandur can take care of himself. He's a huge male immortal with centuries of fighting experience. Ella is a human girl. The comparison is irrelevant."

Ouch. That was insulting to Wonder.

But the girl was a badass even though she tried to deny it.

Smiling shyly at Julian, Wonder nodded. "You are right. Physically there is no comparison between Anandur and Ella. But her spirit is just as big, and her need to protect and to contribute is just as all-consuming as Anandur's. This is who she is, not what she does. Do you really want to try stifling that?"

Touché, Wonder.

49

JULIAN

*W*onder's impassioned speech made Julian feel like an ogre who couldn't see further than the end of his nose. He had a feeling that if Ella didn't need him to show her how to fill out the applications, she would have gone home in a huff.

They walked in silence, with him brooding and feeling chastised, and her deep in thought about Fates knew what. Julian's sense of smell didn't detect anything overly troubling, but he'd learned that with Ella he could never be sure. The scents she emitted were so subtle that he often wondered whether she was a little like Turner, who didn't emit any at all.

The other option was that she wasn't letting herself feel, and since he knew she was adept at keeping up mental barriers, he speculated that it shouldn't be too difficult for her to block her emotions even from herself.

Surprising him, Ella threaded her arm through his and leaned her head on his bicep. "Don't mind what Wonder said. She got carried away. It's perfectly natural for you to want to keep me safe. I get it, because I feel the same about you.

Remember our fight from yesterday? I didn't want you to accompany me to Georgetown because I was afraid for you."

He arched a brow. "That was a fight? I wasn't aware of it."

"You were angry at me, and I didn't like it. I call it a fight."

He patted her hand. "I'm sorry."

"We also promised each other not to apologize so much."

Damn, she was confusing him. "What should I say then?"

"We need to find code words to replace sorry. I wouldn't mind you admitting to behaving like an ass."

He chuckled. "So instead of saying I'm sorry, I should say I'm an ass?"

"Or I was an ass. That works too."

He leaned and kissed the top of her head. "I was an ass. Happy?"

"Yes, thank you. And I was an ass too. Now we are even, and we can erase that silly spat from our memories."

As they neared his house, they were greeted by the sounds of piano playing. "Ray is up."

"He plays so beautifully." Ella sighed. "But he's such a different person than what he lets out through his music. Hearing those sounds, I would have expected a shy, gentle, artist type. Instead, he acts like a juvenile delinquent. He reminds me of that guy I dated in high school who offered to buy my panties from me."

Julian growled. "What sort of perverted game was he playing?"

She laughed. "Despite his panty fetish, he was actually not a bad guy. Jim was harmless, so you can stop making that weird sound in your throat."

"What sound?"

"You were growling, Julian."

"Oh, that sound." He winked and opened the door.

Acknowledging them with a nod, Ray kept on playing.

Ella waved. "Hi, Ray. Don't mind us. We will be in Julian's room."

That hadn't been Julian's plan. If he wanted to keep his hands off her, the living room was a better choice.

"That's where your computer is, right?" She headed down the corridor.

"It's a laptop. I could've brought it out to the living room. The place doesn't belong to Ray."

She pushed the door open and got inside. "I don't want to interrupt his practice." She sat on his bed and grabbed one of the decorative pillows. "And your room is always so neat. I wanted to see if it was messy at least on the weekends."

Julian went over to his desk. "My mother programmed me to never leave my room without making the bed first. She says it helps start the day right."

"There is something to that. Your mom is a smart lady. Bossy as hell, but I like her. She has a spot on my badass girl team."

He took the laptop and brought it over to the bed. "So now it's a whole team? Who are the members?"

"Eva, Carol, Tessa, Amanda, Wonder, your mother. I'm sure that when I get to know more people, I will find others to add to my list."

"What about your mother?"

Ella waved a dismissive hand. "Vivian is a scaredy cat. I love her, but she is not a badass. She is too nice and sweet for that."

"You are nice too."

Ella made a face. "I'm working on it."

"On not being nice?"

Kicking off her boots, she pulled her legs up on top of the bed and lay on her side. "It's a real handicap. Like when someone is rude to me, and I can't force myself to say something nasty back. I keep thinking about it later and getting angry at myself for not being assertive enough."

Trying to ignore the way her sweater was stretched tight over her breasts, Julian opened his laptop and searched for a mock application they could fill in. "Next time someone is rude to you, tell me, and I'll beat him up."

She chuckled. "I believe you. After what happened in the halfway house, I know you would. But what if the offender is a girl?"

"Then you're on your own. I'm not going to beat up a woman."

"That's chauvinistic."

Was she teasing him? It was hard to tell. The imp kept her expression neutral.

He arched a brow. "So, let me get it straight. To prove that I am a feminist I have to beat up a girl? That's absurd."

Ella plopped to her back. "If you haven't noticed, we live in an absurd world."

He lifted his eyes from the laptop. "What do you mean? Not that I disagree, but I'm curious to hear your observations."

She waved a hand and closed her eyes. "I'm too tired to think of all the examples. There are just too many, and then people get their panties in a twist if you don't agree with their opinions even when they don't make any sense. Democracy and free speech are dying." She yawned. "Someone needs to tell Brandon to start pushing dystopian movies and stories about the end of democracy as we know it before it's too late and we turn into Soviet Russia."

A moment later she was snoring lightly.

Sliding off the bed, Julian pulled out a blanket from the closet and covered Ella's small sleeping form.

Her hands tucked under her cheek and her pink hair sticking out in all directions, she looked so tiny and so sweet. But Wonder was right. Inside that fragile, small body lived a tremendous spirit.

50

ELLA

"*H*ello, gorgeous." Blocking the sun, Logan leaned over Ella and planted a soft kiss on her lips.

The dream was so realistic that she could feel the heat coming off his bare chest and smell his enticing male musk. Both were intensely alluring. The guy was made for seduction, with everything about him a feast for the female senses.

Or was he making her think that? Compelling her?

Crap. Dreaming about Logan while sleeping in Julian's arms was so bad. She needed to make herself wake up pronto.

Except, what if he had new information for her?

Besides, she needed to make her exit elegant so he wouldn't suspect her reason for escaping the dream. After all, she was supposed to like him.

Ella shielded her eyes with her hand. "I must've fallen asleep while filling out applications. I didn't expect you."

"I was surprised too." He sat next to her on her lounger and put his hand on her thigh.

Ella didn't react, pretending she hadn't noticed. "Are you sleeping now? Or are you napping too?"

"It's night time where I am. But before I went to sleep, I called my friend at Georgetown. I have an instruction for you."

She smiled. "I like a man who takes immediate action. What are the instructions?"

Her answer must have confused him because he just stared at her for a moment. "You are a confusing young lady, Ella. Or is it Kelly?"

She put her hand on his back. "To you, it's Ella." Hopefully, she wasn't laying it on too thick.

He smiled. "I like Ella better. But back to my friend. He said you should go through the motions like every other candidate. Which means filling out the application, sending out all the transcripts, etc. You need to schedule an interview too, but don't feel discouraged if it's for months from now. He is going to try and push it through sooner. He also said that your GPA and SAT should be very high for him to be able to do anything at all."

"Don't worry. They are."

He arched a brow. "Ella's or Kelly's?"

"Mine. But I can get them under Kelly's name."

"How?"

"I can't tell you, mainly because I don't know. But it's going to be done." She leaned up and kissed his cheek. "Thank you for helping me. I need to go now, though. The applications aren't going to fill out themselves."

He frowned, his body temperature suddenly dropping. "Are you applying anywhere else?"

"Of course. I heard Columbia has an excellent nursing program, and I'm also checking several other places. But Georgetown is my first choice. I just hope it pans out."

His smile returned. "It will."

"Anyway, I have to go. I hear my mom calling me." She waved at him. "Until the next time."

Forcing herself to wake up always resulted in a headache,

and this time was no different. It would've been nice to keep on sleeping a little longer, but Ella didn't want to spend time with Logan while snoozing on Julian's bed.

It was just wrong.

Where was he anyway?

"Julian? Are you in the bathroom?"

A moment later, he walked in with a mug of steaming coffee in each hand. "Hello, sleepyhead. Did you have a nice nap?"

Ella pushed up on the pillows and took the mug from him. "Yes and no. Thanks for the coffee."

Sitting on the bed next to her, he crossed his legs and propped his elbow on his knee. "You're welcome."

She took a sip, and then one more. "As soon as I slipped into dreamland, Mr. D was there. He informed me that he'd already spoken to his friend and that even with the inside help, I need an amazing grade point average. I also need to schedule an interview, which the friend is going to try expediting."

"The Doomer is tightening the noose. He is arranging it so you'll arrive at Georgetown on his schedule, not yours."

"Makes sense. He said that it was night time where he was, so I assumed he was on the island. It's supposed to be somewhere in the Indian Ocean, right?"

Julian nodded.

Ella took another sip of coffee. "He needs time to travel back to the States and organize the trap, so we probably have some time. And if not, I can stall by saying that my transcripts are not ready."

"Since he's not aware that you are onto him and that you have help, he doesn't need to do much preparation. I wouldn't be surprised if he doesn't know anyone at Georgetown and just arranges for you to get a fake invitation to an interview. Then all he has to do is show up and compel you and your mother to come with him."

Ella finished the rest of her coffee and put the mug on the nightstand. "That's true, but as I said, I can stall if needed. But we really need to take care of my nonexistent transcripts."

Julian reached for his phone. "Let me check if Roni is available to see us. This should be child's play for him."

"Wait, what time is it? How long was I asleep?"

By the empty feeling in her tummy, it should be dinner time. And just to prove it, her stomach made a gurgling sound.

"It's four-thirty. Why?"

"I don't want to intrude on Roni's dinner. It's Saturday, and he is probably having it with his fiancée, or girlfriend, or mate. I never know what to call the significant others."

Julian waved the hand with the phone. "You've just said it. Significant other covers all of the options."

"Nah, it sounds too formal. But anyway, how about we get something to eat before we invite ourselves to Roni's house?"

"You are too polite for your own good. What would you rather eat, another sandwich from the vending machine, or something fabulous that Ruth made?"

Ella scrunched her nose. "Isn't Roni's girlfriend's name Sylvia?"

Julian put his empty coffee mug next to hers on the nightstand. "Yeah, but Sylvia doesn't cook. Her mom does, and her name is Ruth."

"They live with her mom?"

"No, but they are very close, and Roni adores Ruth. Well, he probably adores her culinary skills, but in any case, she and her boyfriend, Nick, are always welcome at Roni and Sylvia's house."

"That's awesome." Ella put her hand over her chest. "It warms my heart to hear about a family that's so close. I hope we will be the same with my mom and Magnus, and Parker as well when he gets older and finds his love. I can imagine us all hanging out together, having Friday dinners and weekend barbecues at each other's houses."

Julian smirked. "That sounded like a proposal."

Embarrassed, she grabbed a pillow and tossed it at him. "I don't need to propose anything. It's you who keeps talking about us being fated for each other."

Naturally, Julian dodged the pillow.

"Do you object?" He lunged forward, trapping Ella under his big body.

She laughed and was about to tell him that his caveman antics were not going to wrestle an admission from her when he cupped the back of her head and smashed his lips over hers.

Holy Thor and all of Asgard, that was hot.

51

JULIAN

*J*ulian hadn't meant to attack Ella and do precisely what he'd promised her never to do. It seemed as if a combination of several small triggers had snuck up on him and awakened the beast in him.

When she'd talked about them being a family, his heart soared on the wings of hope, and then when she'd teased him by making their relationship sound one-sided and tossing a pillow at him, his aggression got triggered. He'd felt an overwhelming need to prove to her that they were indeed fated for each other, and that she believed it too despite her protests.

His kiss wasn't the polite and tentative affair that he usually forced it to be, he was devouring her, and Ella was responding to it very differently than what he'd come to expect from her. Her arms wrapped around his neck and her legs parted to accommodate him between them, and she was holding him to her and moaning into his mouth.

Ella was aroused, and it wasn't the anemic, barely-there scent Julian had gotten from her up until now.

For the first time, her aroma held the richness of a woman's passion, and not that of a young girl who was still fearful and not ready for sex.

Emboldened by her response, he pushed a hand under her sweater and rested it on her soft belly, just below the swell of her breast.

Ella arched up, which he took to mean that she wanted him to touch her, but since it was the first time, he needed more explicit permission. Letting go of her mouth, he lifted his head and looked into her eyes as he inched his hand up in slow motion.

If she wanted to stop him, all she needed to do was to say it, or just put her hand over his to stop its ascent. But Ella did none of those things.

Gazing up at his face with hooded eyes and parted lips, she panted in anticipation.

He held her gaze as his hand cupped her breast gently over her bra, and when she closed her eyes and bit on her lower lip, he thumbed her stiff nipple and retook her mouth.

Her scent was doing all kinds of things to him, none of which encouraged the slow and patient. He wanted to tear her clothes off and sink his shaft into what he knew was wet and welcoming.

If it were up to him, Julian wouldn't let her out of this bed for days. He'd feed her and wash her and then make love to her over and over again, biting her so many times that her scent would change and every immortal male would know who she belonged to.

Somewhere in the back of his mind, he knew those thoughts were crazy, and that he couldn't take Ella from five to one hundred in a single swoop. But right now the part of him that thought logically wasn't working that well, and the primitive part that had overtaken most of his synapses was roaring for him to ignore everything and make her his.

Letting go of Ella's mouth, he leaned back and pushed her sweater up, exposing her bra-covered breasts.

It was a lacy thing that didn't leave much to the imagination, but it was in the way nonetheless, and he had no patience to fumble with a clasp.

Instead, he pushed the cups up, freeing her breasts.

Sweet merciful Fates, what a sight. His mouth salivated as he swooped down and took one between his lips while lightly pinching the other.

Delicious. He sucked on the ripe berry, pulling as much of her breast into his mouth as he could, then letting go and flicking it with his tongue. Then he switched, feasting on the other one.

Careful not to scrape her with his fangs, he licked and sucked like a man possessed, the growls coming out of his throat a sound he'd only made once before, and it was when those humans had threatened his mate.

Something wasn't right, though, and it took him a couple of seconds to realize what it was.

Ella wasn't moving, and she wasn't making any sounds either. The scent of her desire still permeated the air, but that could've been from before.

Letting go of her nipple, he looked up at her face.

Her eyes were closed tight, and given her expression, he was willing to bet that her hands were balled into fists at her sides.

Ella was enduring, not enjoying.

The realization cooled Julian down faster than if he'd dipped his dick in a bucket of ice.

Moving up, he cupped her cheeks. "What happened?"

"Why did you stop?" she whispered.

"Because you froze up on me."

"I'm sorry." A tear slid down her cheek.

"No apologies, remember? I just want to understand."

She shook her head. "It's like you said. I froze up. Maybe I'm not ready yet."

As another tear slid down her cheek, he dipped his head and kissed it away.

"There is no reason to be upset. It's my fault. I got carried away and broke my promise to you by pushing you into doing more than you were ready for."

The haunted expression on her face was killing him, and he didn't know what else to do to make it better.

The soft growl Ella's belly made, gave him the out he needed. "You're hungry. Let me text Roni and see if I can get us invited to dinner at his house."

As he moved over to the side, Ella pulled down her bra and sweater. Wiping her tears away with the sleeve, she chuckled. "I'm glad I didn't put any eye makeup on."

His text got an immediate response, just not the one he'd been hoping for.

"We are out of luck. Roni and Sylvia went out to a restaurant."

Ella let out a relieved breath. "I'm glad. I didn't feel like socializing. Do you have anything we can make dinner from?"

"I have frozen pizzas."

"That would do. Are there any veggies to make a salad from?"

"There might be some lettuce and tomatoes."

"And an onion too?"

"I think so."

"I can make a garden salad from that."

He pushed to his feet and offered her a hand up. "Come on. Let me feed you."

52

ELLA

rap, crappity crap, and double crap.

Julian wouldn't be as understanding and sweet if he knew the real reason for her freeze-down.

Washing the lettuce leaf by leaf and then spending an inordinate amount of time chopping vegetables for the salad, Ella was buying herself a little time to sort out her thoughts and hide the maelstrom of confusing feelings away from Julian's attention.

One thing this episode had made abundantly clear was that Logan hadn't compelled her desire, and even if he had, he hadn't compelled the lack of it toward others.

As soon as Julian allowed his natural dominance to emerge, she'd responded.

Oh, boy, how she'd responded.

Ella had never been so aroused in her life. Up until now, the most intense cravings she'd experienced had been while reading some of the naughty romance novels she'd pilfered from her mother.

And that had been before her ordeal.

Since then, all she'd experienced were short-lived, anemic

flares that had fizzled out almost as soon as they'd started, and she hadn't touched a romance novel since her rescue.

Fictional alpha males excited her. Real-life alphas, less so.

Not Logan, not Romeo, and certainly not the Russian. Only Julian had ever gotten her so hot and bothered.

So why had she freaked out?

Some of it had been her bad memories of lying under the Russian and trying to dissociate her mind from what was happening to her. Her eyes shut tightly, she'd pretended that she was one of the heroines in her mother's novels, and that the man with her was one of those sexy billionaires.

Sometimes it had worked, making things a bit easier, but not always. Some of it had been about enduring and counting the seconds until it was over.

So yeah, that would have been the most likely explanation for her freak-out, and what Julian believed had caused it.

Ella wished it was.

The truth, however, was that her freeze-up had been mostly the result of shame and guilt.

If Logan wasn't compelling her attraction, then it was coming from her, and that was troubling on so many levels. If she could feel that way toward a monster clad in a pretty skin, then she really didn't deserve Julian.

She'd felt so much better about herself when compulsion had been the most likely culprit.

Now, it was back to the darkness theory.

She was attracted to Logan because something inside her resonated with him. Carol thought that it was his dominance, but that wasn't likely. Forcing a kiss on her hadn't aroused her, it had repulsed her.

Still, she couldn't deny that his uber-alpha quality played a big part in it.

And what was the deal with not responding to Julian until he'd turned caveman on her?

She was damaged goods, that was the deal.

Leaning over her shoulder, Julian glanced at the cutting board. "Are you making salad or confetti?"

"Oh, I wasn't paying attention." She looked at the tiny pieces. "It looks like salsa."

He chuckled. "Don't worry about it. I like salsa. I wonder how it will taste on top of a pizza."

"Ugh, gross. What kind of pizza are we having?"

"Mushrooms and sausage."

She made a face. "Sounds yummy."

"Do you want something else? I can heat up a marinara pizza."

"No, that's fine. Where do you keep your oil and vinegar?"

He opened one of the top cabinets. "Everything is here. Do you want salt and pepper?"

"Sure."

When the oven beeped, Julian pulled the pizza out and put it on a cutting board. "Do you want a movie with your pizza?"

"I would love to."

That way she wouldn't have to talk to Julian and answer his probing questions.

Perfect.

It would take some intensive and creative thinking to come up with plausible answers that weren't lies, but at the same time didn't reveal the embarrassing truth.

Creativity was not restricted to artsy pursuits.

Pulling out two large plates, Julian loaded each with three slices of pizza and brought them over for Ella to add the salad. "Only a little for me. I'm not that fond of salads."

She cast him a sidelong glance. "Perhaps I'll change your mind about that."

"I doubt it." He lifted the two plates and carried them to the living room coffee table. "My mother is a vegetarian, and she tried her best to convert me."

Ella followed him with the cutlery. "Yeah, I can see that. You even like meat on your pizza."

Which Ella thought was gross, but she was in the minority. Judging by the supermarket frozen pizza aisle, pepperoni was the most popular.

"Don't most people?" Julian went back to the kitchen. "Can I get you a drink?"

"Do you have Diet Coke or Sprite?"

"I have the non-diet variety."

"That's fine."

She eyed the Snake Venom beer he'd brought for himself. "Magnus likes that one too. I don't know how you guys can drink it."

"Immortal metabolism. Regular beer is like piss water for us."

Popping the lid of a coke can, Ella wondered whether she would develop a taste for that super-potent beer after her transition.

She certainly had a taste for the super-potent immortals, except she was too much of a chicken to do anything about it.

"Okay." Julian reached for his tablet. "Let's see what's playing on Netflix."

Too hungry to care about what they were going to watch, Ella picked up a pizza slice, flicked off the pieces of sausage, and took a big bite. It was very good, although in her state of hunger anything even remotely edible would taste gourmet.

Julian turned to her. "Did you see that Fifty Shades movie everyone was talking about?"

Mouth full of pizza, she shook her head.

"Do you want to watch it?"

Why was he suggesting such an awful movie? For sure he didn't want to watch it. Did he think she would get aroused by it?

Finishing chewing, she shook her head again. "I read the book, and I didn't like it."

He arched a brow. "It was all the rage."

"I know. That was why I picked it up. I'm not some literary snob. I liked the love story and the way it was told, but I didn't like the premise."

"The rich guy, poor girl thing? Or was it the dominant-submissive interplay?"

Julian seemed surprised, which was understandable after her intense reaction to his mild show of aggression from before. Apparently, though, he had only a vague idea about what went on in that book.

"The Cinderella trope is very common in romance, and it's an overused one, but I have no problem with that if the story is good. And I also have no problem with the kind of games the guy in Fifty Shades liked to play. What bothered me about it, though, was that the girl wasn't into pain, and she didn't enjoy it. What's sexy about that? To me, it seemed abusive."

Shaking his head, he raked his fingers through his hair. "I didn't know that. The movie trailers were misleading."

Ella picked up another slice. "Maybe they changed it in the movie and had her getting off on the abuse. But even if they did, I still wouldn't want to watch that. Just not my cup of tea."

There was a big difference between dominance and sadism, even a mild one like in that book. The first one aroused her. The second one repulsed her.

JULIAN

*I*f Julian was confused before, he was more so now. He needed time to piece together the crumbs of information Ella had revealed here and there, and from that to forge a key to unlock her secrets.

That she was keeping them, he was sure of. It was in her eyes when she averted them while answering his questions with half-truths, and it was in the sad expression that usually followed.

Whatever she wasn't telling him was eating her from the inside, and yet she was guarding it with fierce determination.

Scrolling through the selection, he chose a romantic comedy, something about a Valentine's Day mishap.

"Is that good?"

Ella nodded with a mouth full of pizza.

Feeding her made him feel as if he'd done at least one thing right by her, and wasn't that pathetic.

He was a twenty-six-year-old, well-educated guy who thought of himself as fairly intelligent and open-minded, and yet figuring out what made Ella tick was eluding him. Part of it was her great acting skill, and the other part was that he was predisposed to buying her badass, confident act because it was so much easier than digging deeper and discovering that she was suffering on the inside.

With a sigh, Julian clicked play and lifted his first slice, deciding to eat it slowly in case Ella was still hungry after finishing all three of hers. She hadn't been kidding about being hungry and was already on her second one.

Or maybe he should just put another one in the oven. Yeah, that was a better plan.

"I'll be right back. I want to heat up another pizza."

She smiled up at him. "Good idea. Ray will have some when he comes back."

A wave of jealousy washed over him. Why the hell was she concerned about fucking Ray?

Forcing a smile just until he turned around, Julian walked into the kitchen and pulled out a plain cheese pizza from the freezer.

Note to self. Stock up on meatless pizzas. And vegetables.

Back in the living room, he sat on the couch and lifted another slice. Pretending to watch the movie, he went over what he knew.

Up until today, Ella had responded to him with minimal excitement. The one time he'd momentarily lost control and had shown a little aggression, she'd lit up like a flare. But it hadn't lasted long, and she'd frozen up on him.

If her problem had been a troubling flashback, then how come she'd gotten into it in the first place?

Shouldn't any show of male aggression trigger her flight or fight response?

That had been the assumption he'd based his entire approach with her on, but apparently, he'd been completely off the mark.

Except, a girl who'd been forced into unwanted sex, who had her choices taken away from her, shouldn't respond to dominance, not unless it was something she'd enjoyed or rather craved before her abduction. Ella hadn't had any sexual experience prior to that, good or bad.

But evidently Ella had never been interested in those kinds of sex games. While every girl and her mother and grandmother had read the Fifty Shades book and enjoyed it, Ella hadn't.

It wasn't her thing.

Damn, he was so tired of guessing, tired of walking on eggshells, and tired of feeling like a martyr.

They had to have a frank talk, with Ella opening up and telling him what was going on with her. If she said she needed more time, he would wait patiently until she was ready. But he had to know where he stood.

Ella nudged his elbow. "Your pizza is ready."

The beeping hadn't registered because his mind had been somewhere else. "I'll get it." Julian rose to his feet.

Ella lifted her eyes to him. "Do you want me to pause the movie?"

"No. It's fine. I wasn't watching anyway."

In the kitchen, he pulled out the pizza, put it on the cutting board and sliced the hell out of it, dividing it into twelve tiny triangles just because he needed to keep his hands busy.

When he brought it to the living room, Ella clicked the television off. "Do you want to watch a different movie? I admit that this one is quite silly even for a chick flick."

"It's okay. You can keep on watching. I'm just not in the mood."

Ella put down the slice of pizza. "Is it because of me?"

His first instinct was to protect her fragile feelings and lie. But he was so done with that.

"You are confusing me, Ella."

She nodded. "I'm confusing myself."

As her despondent expression twisted his gut, he took her

hand and entwined their fingers. "What's holding you back? Are you still fearful? Does intimacy with me scare you?"

Looking at their conjoined hands, she lifted them both to her lips and kissed his knuckles. "I'm not afraid of you, Julian. I never was."

The sweet gesture melted his heart, but he was adamant about getting to the bottom of this and going soft would be counterproductive. "So, what's the problem? Are you still getting flashbacks?"

"I do, but that's not the problem. At least not all of it. I'm stuck."

"What do you mean?"

She pulled her hand out of his and raked her fingers through her messy hair. "I'm stuck with the dream-walker. I need to pretend to like him, and I can't be intimate with you while I'm doing it. I just can't."

Why the hell not? He didn't like the idea of her playing nice with the Doomer, but it was unavoidable. And besides, it was only pretend.

Or maybe it wasn't?

What kind of liking was she talking about? Was she having dream sex with that son of a bitch?

Even though it was going to kill him if she was, Julian had to know. At least the guesswork would be over. Unless he got a straight answer, he was going to torment himself by imagining what went on in those dreams, and that was much worse.

Except, he wanted Ella to fess up without having to force the admission out of her. Instead, he cast a bait. "Why not? Being with me doesn't mean that you can't smile at other guys. I wouldn't like it, but that's my problem."

ELLA

"What if I have to do more than smile?" As soon as the words left her mouth, Ella's heart had plummeted to somewhere deep in her gut.

Why the hell had she let it out, committing herself to reveal what should've remained hidden?

And if her guilt and fear weren't enough, Julian's expression added another ton of bricks to the heavy load in her gut. He looked as if she'd plunged a dagger in his heart and then twisted it.

If only she could go back in time and stop herself from opening her big mouth.

"I'm sorry," she whispered.

"Define more."

Cringing, she averted her eyes so she wouldn't have to watch his anger flare up. "I had to kiss him."

Surprising her, he let out a breath. "That's all?"

Okay, maybe she was making a big deal out of nothing, torturing herself over something Julian considered insignificant. Perhaps his age and experience made him more tolerant. If Julian had told her that he kissed a girl in a dream, she would have been majorly pissed. Especially a dream that was not a fantasy but a real mind connection between two people.

"Isn't it enough? You have no idea how guilty it made me feel."

"Because of me?"

She nodded.

He clasped her hand. "I won't lie to you. I'm jealous. But knowing that you have no choice and that you're not enjoying it helps."

God, this was hard.

Should she tell him the truth?

To what end? She would be just hurting his feelings and souring their relationship.

Except, lying added another thick layer of sludge to her guilt, making her feel dirty and not worthy of someone as good and as pure as Julian.

He was so understanding, so mature about this, maybe he would be able to accept her misguided attraction to Logan too?

"The thing is…" She grimaced. "I would be lying if I said that he had to force me, or that I suffered terribly while doing it."

As Julian's face started turning red, she quickly added, "I was convinced that he was using compulsion on me, artificially making me feel attraction toward him and preventing me from feeling it toward anyone else."

Julian's eyes softened. "It might be true."

Crap, she was doing it again. Hiding behind an excuse she now knew wasn't true. "I wish it were," she murmured under her breath. "That would have explained so much." And transferred responsibility for her actions from her shoulders to Logan's, effectively eradicating most of the guilt.

Unfortunately, she could no longer use that to ease her conscience.

"How do you know he is not compelling you to feel things

for him?" Hope shining in his soft, blue eyes, Julian scooted closer to her. "If he could so easily compel your silence, I don't see why he wouldn't do this. Doomers are not known for their high moral standards."

She should just let him believe that and shut up. It would save them both unnecessary heartache.

Except, Julian was a smart guy, and eventually he was going to realize the same thing she had less than an hour ago. If Logan's compulsion had been blocking her from feeling attraction toward other men, then she wouldn't have gotten so aroused by Julian's show of assertiveness, or anything else for that matter.

And once Julian figured that out, he would think that she was a liar in addition to being damaged goods who lusted after the worst possible guy.

With a sigh, she pulled her hand away and slumped against the sofa's plush pillows. "As I said, I wish it were true, but after reacting to you the way I did, I can no longer use this as an excuse. That's what really freaked me out, not some disturbing flashback. Not this time, anyway. I realized that the only reason I haven't been responding to you as strongly before was that apparently I've been craving intensity, while you've been walking on eggshells around me."

For some reason, Ella had trouble using the term dominance. Maybe because it suggested things that were further up the spectrum from what she craved. All she wanted was an alpha type male who was sexually assertive but not a caveman, and she was definitely not interested in the sort of games she'd read about in the Fifty Shades book.

It was so damn confusing. Was it like this for everyone?

She doubted it. Otherwise most would have not found compatible partners. In her case, it was like only one very particular shade could unlock her desires, and all the rest were ineffective.

In short, it was a recipe for disappointment.

He chuckled sadly. "The road to hell is paved with good intentions. I've been suppressing my caveman urges because I believed they would scare you. But now that we've figured it out, it should no longer be a problem."

If only the solution could be so simple. But nothing in Ella's life was.

"The thing is, you weren't wrong. Not entirely."

Shaking his head, Julian let go of her hand. "Now you've got me completely confused. One moment you say that you crave my inner caveman, and then you admit that he scares you. What am I supposed to do?"

Did he think that he was the only one who was frustrated by this?

"I can't help it, Julian. I crave something that scares the hell out of me, and I'm in a Catch 22 situation. For reasons I can't understand, I need to yield control to get aroused, but I'm terrified of letting anyone have that much power over me. It's not that I don't trust you, or that I'm afraid of you, but I just can't let go. I have to stay in control."

Hooking a finger under her chin, he lifted her head so she would look into his eyes. "Why do you need to stay in control? You are safe with me, and you are safe here in the village. I'm sure you realize it."

"I do. That's not the problem."

"Then what is?"

God, he was killing her. Forcing her to dig deep into what made her tick and look at what she didn't want to see.

"If I let go, I'll fall apart. The only thing holding me together is my control over what I allow myself to feel and what I don't. Numbness is my friend. Can you understand that?"

She was being unfair to him. Julian couldn't possibly know how it felt to be her. He'd never been humiliated, sold like a piece of property, and used. He hadn't felt helpless and hopeless, and he hadn't been touched by evil.

"I think I do." He scratched his short beard. "You keep everything bottled up inside and plow through by the sheer force of your will. That's your survival mechanism. But you are tired of pretending and of carrying this burden alone. It's like holding up a ton of bricks. They are too heavy for your arms, and you wish there was a way for you to put them down, but you can't stoop without breaking your back, and you are forced to keep trudging onward."

That was such an insightful analogy that she could actually visualize herself walking with a huge pile of bricks, not in her arms but tied to her back. If she crouched, her knees were going to buckle, and if she bent forward, the bricks were going to crash into her head and smash it.

There was no way out from under them.

Not now, and not ever. She was stuck with that impossibly heavy cargo weighing her down.

Unbidden, tears started pooling in the corners of her eyes, and a moment later they were streaming down her cheeks in twin salty rivulets.

"I can't see a way out, Julian. I'm stuck."

"Blast them, one at a time." He made a finger gun and aimed it at her invisible cargo.

Julian was trying to cheer her up, but once the dam had burst, there was no stopping the flood. The tears just kept coming.

Besides, she couldn't visualize his suggestion.

"How can I blast them when they are on my back? I can't aim." The words came out in a sob.

"What I mean by blasting is talking to me about them. As long as you keep them inside, they feed on you and gain substance. But putting them out there, not all at once, but one at a time, will suck that substance out of them and they will dissipate into thin air. Eventually, as the load gets lighter, you'll be able to stand up tall and shake the rest off."

Again, she could visualize that happening, but instead of the bricks falling off, they would just transfer onto Julian's back. His empathetic nature made working in a human hospital impossible because he couldn't take the suffering of strangers. Her suffering would be so much worse for him to carry.

"I wish I could. But I can't."

"Why not?"

"Because those bricks are not going to dissipate. They are going to land on your back. I don't want to do it to you."

Leaning, he kissed her tear-stained cheek. "My back is pretty sturdy, and my thigh muscles are strong. Once you transfer your bricks to me, I'll just crouch down and put them on the ground. Then we will take a big sledge-hammer and blast them all the way to hell where they belong."

JULIAN

*E*lla had reached a breaking point. Or perhaps it was a breakthrough?

Trying to comfort her and stop the crying, Julian had been pulling nonsense out of his ass.

He'd never had to deal with an emotional meltdown before. His mother was a pillar of strength who he hadn't seen shed a single tear, and in the hospital, it hadn't been his job to provide comfort or counsel.

It was his fault.

If he hadn't pushed and probed, she wouldn't be sobbing right now like her world was ending.

Except, maybe it was good for her to let it all out, cathartic?

He just wished Ella would talk to him instead of sobbing. She'd been suppressing her feelings so well, probably from herself as well, because he hadn't sensed the turmoil in her.

Tears alone weren't going to purge the load she was carrying, and once the crying stopped, she would go back to showing strength she apparently didn't possess.

"I lost my virginity to a guy old enough to be my grandfather, and he wasn't an immortal with a perfect body. But that wasn't the worst of it." As another sob rocked her, Ella waved a hand and then bolted up.

Thinking she was running away from him, he reached for her hand.

"I need a tissue." She yanked her hand away and dashed to the powder room.

He was such an idiot. The girl was crying her eyes out, and it hadn't crossed his mind that she needed something to blow her nose into?

Idiot, he murmured under his breath.

The thing was, all he could offer her was a roll of toilet paper because he didn't have a box of tissues. But he could at least offer her water, or wine, or both.

In the kitchen, he suddenly remembered the stash of Godiva chocolates Ella had given him for safekeeping. If anything could lift her spirits, it was that.

Armed with his secret weapon, a bottle of wine, two bottles of water, and two glasses, Julian returned to the couch and organized everything on the coffee table.

As he waited for the nose blowing and sniffles to stop, he fought the urge to barge into the bathroom and take Ella into his arms.

Obviously, she was trying to get over her crying alone in there, and once she succeeded, she would come out and pretend like everything was alright.

It would be the end of their talk, and the weight of nasty she was carrying around would keep festering inside her.

Perhaps he should knock on the door and ask if she was okay?

Right. Talk about stupid.

She obviously was not.

When Ella finally opened the door, she was much more composed. Her eyes and nose were red, but she wasn't crying anymore.

"Sorry about that." She sat next to him on the couch. "I didn't mean to have a meltdown like that."

Wrapping his arm around her shoulders, Julian pulled Ella closer. "No apologies, remember? And besides, I want you to let it all out. No more keeping things from me and feeling guilty about it."

He leaned, opened the box of chocolates, and brought one to her mouth. "I can promise you this. No matter what you tell me, or how bad you think it is, nothing will make me walk away from you."

Chewing on the chocolate, she arched a brow. "What if I told you I had dream sex with Mr. D?"

His gut clenched with fury, but it wasn't directed at Ella. He was just going to kill Lokan. "Dream sex doesn't count. But I will have to kill him."

She chuckled. "Please don't. At least not until Turner and Kian finish interrogating him. And no, I didn't have dream sex with him. I would never go that far."

"How far did you go? I'm just asking, so this issue no longer creates a divide between us. I don't want you to carry guilt on top of that ton of bricks."

Reaching for another chocolate, she motioned at the wine. "Can you pour me a glass?"

"With pleasure."

Taking the wineglass, she sniffed it. "The Russian got me into wine drinking. I thought I wouldn't want to touch it because of the memories it brought, but I still like it." She chuckled. "I'm just glad he didn't feed me Godiva chocolates. If that put me off them, it would've been a disaster of epic proportions."

Ella was reverting to her old self, joking and making sarcastic comments, and Julian wondered whether she was doing it to change the subject and end confession time.

But she continued, "I let him kiss me, that was all. But it wasn't like with the Russian. With him, I was just enduring it."

She took another sip. "I feel so shallow and dirty, but I can't stay indifferent to the Doomer. Maybe it's because he's so handsome, and it's only physical. And maybe it's because he is intelligent in a cunning and evil way, and that makes him intriguing."

Looking into his wine glass, Julian's entire focus was on keeping his fangs from elongating, his eyes from glowing, and his throat from growling. He'd promised Ella he would keep his cool, and it was crucial that he didn't break that promise even in the slightest.

She was opening up to him, telling him things she'd feared were going to upset him, and he wanted her to keep talking.

Ella took another sip of wine, reached for another chocolate, but didn't pop it into her mouth. "I could've lived with that. None of it was too horrible for a human girl who didn't buy into the whole true-love mates thing immortals believe in." She took a little bite off the chocolate and chewed, probably buying herself some time to think.

Emptying the wine down his throat, Julian poured himself another glass.

This talk was illuminating on more than one level.

Apparently, the guilt she was feeling was his fault. After all, he'd been the one who'd pressed the issue of her being his true-love mate. No wonder she'd resisted accepting it.

When she finished chewing, Ella took another sip of wine and then continued in a near whisper. "What bothers me is that I might be attracted to his darkness because there is so much of it in me. I'm tainted, and so is he. Even when I was still terrified of him, I felt the pull. It felt to me as though like was recognizing like."

She chuckled without mirth. "I even called him Darth Sidious, and joked about him tempting me over to the dark side."

Julian's initial response was an intense need to get his hands on Lokan and tear his throat out. Luckily, not all of his brain had been taken over by the caveman, and some of the logic synapses were still operational.

"The pull you initially felt toward him had to be affinity. Amanda speculates that Dormants and immortals feel a special connection, and that is another indicator for identifying Dormants. That feeling of like recognizing like is exactly how she describes it. But because you didn't know what it was, you interpreted it as sexual attraction. And since the Doomer is, unfortunately, very good-looking, you had no reason to question that interpretation."

ELLA

*H*mm, could he be right?

It would be so nice if it were true.

Perhaps it was?

Amanda was a scientist, a neuroscience professor who was researching Dormants and ways to identify them. She must know what she was talking about.

Except, affinity had several meanings, and Amanda might have been referring to the sexual one.

"Affinity, eh? If I remember the definition correctly, it can also mean attraction."

"That's true, but what Amanda is referring to is the feeling of belonging to a group—the mutual origins that Dormants and immortals share. Most Dormants report a lifetime of feeling different than other humans, like they don't belong. But with immortals they experience that sensation you get when meeting someone for the first time and hitting it off right away. It's the like recognizing like you've talked about. That's what got me thinking about Amanda's affinity theory."

Feeling as if the boulder sitting inside her stomach had

shrunk a little, Ella took in her first deep breath since this conversation had started.

"So, I'm off the hook? You're no longer jealous?"

"I didn't say that. Of course, I'm jealous. But I can live with that." He winked.

The boulder shrank by several more inches.

"You have no idea what a relief this is. You've just blasted half of those damn bricks, and I feel so much lighter. I was so sure something was really wrong with me. How could I feel a pull toward a despicable guy?"

She threw her hands in the air. "Even before I knew he was a Doomer, I knew that he was a warlord and that he was buying weapons from the Russian. He didn't even try to make himself look nice, admitting to being as bad as they come. Good looks shouldn't have been enough to blindside me, and neither should his smarts or his dubious charm. I saw through all of that down to the rotten core of him and still couldn't stop the bloody attraction."

"You know what your biggest problem is?" Julian refilled her empty wine glass.

The boulder started expanding again.

She should've known that Julian couldn't be as accepting as he'd seemed. After hearing her confession, any normal guy would've been foaming at the mouth or walking away, and as understanding and compassionate as Julian was, he wasn't a saint. Now he was going to tell her what he really thought.

Pretending nonchalance, she shrugged and lifted her feet onto the couch, tucking them under her long skirt. "There are so many of them that I wouldn't know which one you're referring to."

"You are stubborn."

That wasn't what she'd expected.

Ella lifted a brow. "How so?"

"If you'd talked to Vanessa when you'd just gotten here and

told her what you've told me, she would have figured out immediately that what you felt for Lokan was affinity and would have explained it to you. You could've saved yourself weeks of needless fear and self-doubt."

That was a relief. She could live with Julian thinking that she was stubborn. It was much better than the other personality flaws he could have accused her of.

Grimacing, Ella took a long sip of wine. "I hate shrinks."

The box of chocolates was still mostly full, and she was tempted to reach for another. It had such a calming effect on her, but her stomach wouldn't appreciate it.

"You didn't give her a chance."

Ella waved a dismissive hand. "I knew she was going to suck the moment she tried to convince me that I was raped."

He arched a brow. "You weren't?"

"No. I was coerced. There is a big difference. I wasn't attacked, and I wasn't beaten up. I cooperated. I had no choice, but it was my decision to agree."

Julian shook his head. "I don't see the difference. What if you were at a club and someone slipped you a roofie or a similar date-rape drug? You wouldn't have resisted then either, but I'm sure that as soon as the drugging effect was over, you would've marched into the nearest police station to report it as rape."

"That's different.'"

"How so?"

"Because if I were drugged, I wouldn't have been able to make a conscious decision to cooperate."

"So, what you are saying is that your decision-making ability would have been taken away from you?"

In a shrink-like manner, he'd restated what she'd said in the form of a question, and that was no doubt leading somewhere.

Ella put her wine glass down and crossed her arms over her chest. "It would have been impaired by the drug."

"An impaired ability to make a choice."

He was starting to annoy her. "Where are you going with this, Julian? I hate the shrink-ish roundabout talk. Just say what you mean."

Raking his fingers through his hair, he sighed. "I was trying to lead you to the conclusion without having to say it myself, but you are more stubborn than a clan of badgers. So here it goes." He took a deep breath and pinned her with a hard look. "When your only choice is to cooperate, then it is like not having a choice at all. It is rape."

"I could have said no. I could've fought."

"Could you have really?"

Crap.

He was right.

She couldn't.

Not without risking her family, and not without sustaining significant injuries. And since it would have been utterly stupid to resist, the choice hadn't been really a choice.

It had been an illusion.

She'd been raped.

As the tears started falling anew, Julian wrapped his arms around her and lifted her onto his lap.

"I'm so sorry, love. I know it hurts, but I believe that the only way to put it behind you is to let it out."

She slapped his chest. "What would you know about it? Have you ever been humiliated? Violated? Treated like an object for sale? You know nothing, Julian."

It wasn't his fault, she knew that, but she hated that he was right, and she hated feeling like a victim, and he was the only one she could take out her frustration on.

"Shh, it's okay. You can hit me as many times as you want. Use me as your punching bag. I'll take anything if it helps you even a little bit."

Crap, why did he have to be so nice?

Now she couldn't hit him, and she needed to hit something.

"Stop it! I don't want you to be nice to me!"

"Why not?"

"Because I can't punch you when you're being so sweet."

"I can make you mad in a heartbeat."

"Oh, yeah? How?"

"I want you to promise me that you'll talk to Vanessa."

"She can't help me."

"I want you to give it a try. For me. Payment for turning me into your punching bag."

"The price is too high." She grabbed a throw pillow. "I'd rather punch this inanimate object and not talk to a freaking shrink."

He shook his head. "Then do it for love, for us."

Talk about playing dirty. "What do you mean?"

"It means that I love you, and that I want you, and that I want us to be a couple in all ways, and that I want you to transition so we can spend the rest of our immortal lives together. But first, you have to heal, and it would take much less time with Vanessa's help."

Ella felt a lump form in her throat.

Without saying the actual words, Julian had told her countless times and in so many ways that he loved her, but until now he had never said it explicitly, and hearing those three little words coming out of his mouth had made a world of difference.

There was no more guessing, or doubting, or disbelieving.

This was it, the real deal, and what she'd been waiting for without realizing that she had.

Suddenly, the boulder inside her gut felt as if it had shrunk to a size no larger than an apple, and after hauling such a huge weight around for so long, Ella felt buoyant.

"I love you too."

Crushing her to him, Julian kissed her as if he was trying to pour all of his love into that kiss. It wasn't gentle, and it wasn't elegant, and she was pretty sure her lips would be bruised from it, but it was so worth it.

When Julian finally let go of her mouth, she sucked in a long breath, filling her lungs with much-needed oxygen.

"If you keep kissing me like that, I'll heal in no time."

He nipped her lower lip. "Nice try. Are you going to see her?"

Ella still didn't believe in shrinks, and talking to Vanessa was as appealing as having a bikini wax one hair at a time. But it was important to Julian. And if there was even the slightest chance that the shrink could help her get her shit together faster, so she could be with Julian without dragging excess baggage into their nascent relationship, it was worth a try.

Any sacrifice was worth a clean start.

"I'm going to give her a chance. That's all I can promise."

"That's all I'm asking for."

The end...for now...

COMING UP NEXT
THE CHILDREN OF THE GODS BOOK 28
DARK DREAM'S TRAP

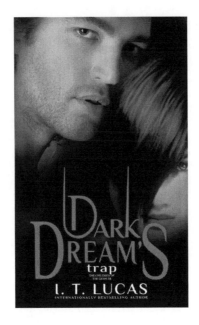

FOR EXCLUSIVE PEEKS AT UPCOMING RELEASES
JOIN MY *VIP CLUB* AND GAIN ACCESS TO THE VIP PORTAL AT
ITLUCAS.COM
CLICK HERE TO JOIN
(OR GO TO: http://eepurl.com/blMTpD)

(If you're already a subscriber and forgot the password to the VIP portal, you can find it at the bottom of each of my emails. Or click **HERE** to retrieve it. You can also email me at isabell@itlucas.com)

Dear reader,

Thank you for joining me on the continuing adventures of the *Children of the Gods*.

As an independent author, I rely on your support to spread the word. So if you enjoyed the story, please share your experience, and if it isn't too much trouble, I would greatly appreciate a brief review on Amazon.

Click here to leave a review

Love & happy reading,

Isabell

THE CHILDREN OF THE GODS ORIGINS

1: Goddess's Choice

When gods and immortals still ruled the ancient world, one young goddess risked everything for love.

2: Goddess's Hope

Hungry for power and infatuated with the beautiful Areana, Navuh plots his father's demise. After all, by getting rid of the insane god he would be doing the world a favor. Except, when gods and immortals conspire against each other, humanity pays the price.

But things are not what they seem, and prophecies should not to be trusted...

THE CHILDREN OF THE GODS

1: Dark Stranger The Dream

Syssi's paranormal foresight lands her a job at Dr. Amanda Dokani's neuroscience lab, but it fails to predict the thrilling yet terrifying turn her life will take. Syssi has no clue that her boss is an immortal who'll drag her into a secret, millennia-old battle over humanity's future. Nor does she realize that the professor's imposing brother is the mysterious stranger who's been starring in her dreams.

Since the dawn of human civilization, two warring factions of immortals—the descendants of the gods of old—have been secretly shaping its destiny. Leading the clandestine battle from his luxurious Los Angeles high-rise, Kian is surrounded by his clan, yet alone. Descending from a single goddess, clan members are forbidden to each other. And as the only other immortals are their hated enemies, Kian and his kin have been long resigned to a lonely existence of fleeting trysts with human partners. That is, until his sister makes a game-changing discovery—a mortal seeress who she believes is a dormant carrier of their genes. Ever the realist, Kian is skeptical and refuses Amanda's plea to attempt Syssi's activation. But when his enemies learn of the Dormant's existence, he's forced to rush her to the safety of his keep. Inexorably drawn to Syssi, Kian wrestles with his conscience as he is tempted to explore her budding interest in the darker shades of sensuality.

2: Dark Stranger Revealed

While sheltered in the clan's stronghold, Syssi is unaware that Kian and Amanda are not human, and neither are the supposedly religious fanatics that are after her. She feels a powerful connection to Kian, and as he introduces her to a world of pleasure she never dared imagine, his dominant sexuality is a revelation. Considering that she's completely out of her element, Syssi feels comfortable and safe letting go with him. That is, until she begins to suspect that all is not as it seems. Piecing the puzzle together, she draws a scary, yet wrong conclusion...

3: Dark Stranger Immortal

When Kian confesses his true nature, Syssi is not as much shocked by the revelation as she is wounded by what she perceives as his callous plans for her.

If she doesn't turn, he'll be forced to erase her memories and let her go. His family's safety demands secrecy – no one in the mortal world is allowed to know that immortals exist.

Resigned to the cruel reality that even if she stays on to never again leave the keep, she'll get old while Kian won't, Syssi is determined to enjoy what little time she has with him, one day at a time.

Can Kian let go of the mortal woman he loves? Will Syssi turn? And if she does, will she survive the dangerous transition?

4: Dark Enemy Taken

Dalhu can't believe his luck when he stumbles upon the beautiful immortal professor. Presented with a once in a lifetime opportunity to grab an immortal female for himself, he kidnaps her and runs. If he ever gets caught, either by her people or his, his life is forfeit. But for a chance of a loving mate and a family of his own, Dalhu is prepared to do everything in his power to win Amanda's heart, and that includes leaving the Doom brotherhood and his old life behind.

Amanda soon discovers that there is more to the handsome Doomer than his dark past and a hulking, sexy body. But succumbing to her enemy's seduction, or worse, developing feelings for a ruthless killer is out of the question. No man is worth life on the run, not even the one and only immortal male she could claim as her own...

Her clan and her research must come first...

5: Dark Enemy Captive

When the rescue team returns with Amanda and the chained Dalhu to the keep, Amanda is not as thrilled to be back as she thought she'd be. Between Kian's contempt for her and Dalhu's imprisonment, Amanda's budding relationship with Dalhu seems doomed. Things start to look up when Annani offers her help, and together with Syssi they resolve to find a way for Amanda to be with Dalhu. But will she still want him when she realizes that he is responsible for her nephew's murder? Could she? Will she take the easy way out and choose Andrew instead?

6: Dark Enemy Redeemed

Amanda suspects that something fishy is going on onboard the Anna. But when her investigation of the peculiar all-female Russian crew fails to uncover anything other than more speculation, she decides it's time to stop playing detective and face her real problem—a man she shouldn't want but can't live without.

6.5: My Dark Amazon

When Michael and Kri fight off a gang of humans, Michael gets stabbed. The injury to his immortal body recovers fast, but the one to his ego takes longer, putting a strain on his relationship with Kri.

7: Dark Warrior Mine

When Andrew is forced to retire from active duty, he believes that all he has to look forward to is a boring desk job. His glory days in special ops are over. But as it turns out, his thrill ride has just begun. Andrew discovers not only that immortals exist and have been manipulating global affairs since antiquity, but that he and his sister are rare possessors of the immortal genes.

Problem is, Andrew might be too old to attempt the activation process. His sister, who is fourteen years his junior, barely made it through the transition, so the odds of him coming out of it alive, let alone immortal, are slim.

But fate may force his hand.

Helping a friend find his long-lost daughter, Andrew finds a woman who's worth taking the risk for. Nathalie might be a Dormant, but the only way to find out for sure requires fangs and venom.

8: DARK WARRIOR'S PROMISE

Andrew and Nathalie's love flourishes, but the secrets they keep from each other taint their relationship with doubts and suspicions. In the meantime, Sebastian and his men are getting bolder, and the storm that's brewing will shift the balance of power in the millennia-old conflict between Annani's clan and its enemies.

9: DARK WARRIOR'S DESTINY

The new ghost in Nathalie's head remembers who he was in life, providing Andrew and her with indisputable proof that he is real and not a figment of her imagination.

Convinced that she is a Dormant, Andrew decides to go forward with his transition immediately after the rescue mission at the Doomers' HQ.

Fearing for his life, Nathalie pleads with him to reconsider. She'd rather spend the rest of her mortal days with Andrew than risk what they have for the fickle promise of immortality.

While the clan gets ready for battle, Carol gets help from an unlikely ally. Sebastian's second-in-command can no longer ignore the torment she suffers at the hands of his commander and offers to help her, but only if she agrees to his terms.

10: DARK WARRIOR'S LEGACY

Andrew's acclimation to his post-transition body isn't easy. His senses are sharper, he's bigger, stronger, and hungrier. Nathalie fears that the changes in the man she loves are more than physical. Measuring up to this new version of him is going to be a challenge.

Carol and Robert are disillusioned with each other. They are not destined mates, and love is not on the horizon. When Robert's three months are up, he might be left with nothing to show for his sacrifice.

Lana contacts Anandur with disturbing news; the yacht and its human cargo are in Mexico. Kian must find a way to apprehend Alex and rescue the women on board without causing an international incident.

11: Dark Guardian Found

What would you do if you stopped aging?

Eva runs. The ex-DEA agent doesn't know what caused her strange mutation, only that if discovered, she'll be dissected like a lab rat. What Eva doesn't know, though, is that she's a descendant of the gods, and that she is not alone. The man who rocked her world in one life-changing encounter over thirty years ago is an immortal as well.

To keep his people's existence secret, Bhathian was forced to turn his back on the only woman who ever captured his heart, but he's never forgotten and never stopped looking for her.

12: Dark Guardian Craved

Cautious after a lifetime of disappointments, Eva is mistrustful of Bhathian's professed feelings of love. She accepts him as a lover and a confidant but not as a life partner.

Jackson suspects that Tessa is his true love mate, but unless she overcomes her fears, he might never find out.

Carol gets an offer she can't refuse—a chance to prove that there is more to her than meets the eye. Robert believes she's about to commit a deadly mistake, but when he tries to dissuade her, she tells him to leave.

13: Dark Guardian's Mate

Prepare for the heart-warming culmination of Eva and Bhathian's story!

14: Dark Angel's Obsession

The cold and stoic warrior is an enigma even to those closest to him. His secrets are about to unravel...

15: Dark Angel's Seduction

Brundar is fighting a losing battle. Calypso is slowly chipping away his icy armor from the outside, while his need for her is melting it from the inside.

He can't allow it to happen. Calypso is a human with none of the Dormant indicators. There is no way he can keep her for more than a few weeks.

16: Dark Angel's Surrender

Get ready for the heart pounding conclusion to Brundar and Calypso's story.

Callie still couldn't wrap her head around it, nor could she summon even a smidgen of sorrow or regret. After all, she had some memories with him that weren't horrible. She should've felt something. But there was nothing, not even shock. Not even horror at what had transpired over the last couple of hours.

Maybe it was a typical response for survivors--feeling euphoric for the simple reason that they were alive. Especially when that survival was nothing short of miraculous.

Brundar's cold hand closed around hers, reminding her that they weren't out of the woods yet. Her injuries were superficial, and the most she had to worry about was some scarring. But, despite his and Anandur's reassurances, Brundar might never walk again.

If he ended up crippled because of her, she would never forgive herself for getting him involved in her crap.

"Are you okay, sweetling? Are you in pain?" Brundar asked.

Her injuries were nothing compared to his, and yet he was concerned about her. God, she loved this man. The thing was, if she told him that, he would run off, or crawl away as was the case.

Hey, maybe this was the perfect opportunity to spring it on him.

17: Dark Operative: A Shadow of Death

As a brilliant strategist and the only human entrusted with the secret of immortals' existence, Turner is both an asset and a liability to the clan. His request to attempt transition into immortality as an alternative to cancer treatments cannot be denied without risking the clan's exposure. On the other hand, approving it means risking his premature death. In both scenarios, the clan will lose a valuable ally.

When the decision is left to the clan's physician, Turner makes plans to manipulate her by taking advantage of her interest in him.

Will Bridget fall for the cold, calculated operative? Or will Turner fall into his own trap?

18: DARK OPERATIVE: A GLIMMER OF HOPE

As Turner and Bridget's relationship deepens, living together seems like the right move, but to make it work both need to make concessions.

Bridget is realistic and keeps her expectations low. Turner could never be the truelove mate she yearns for, but he is as good as she's going to get. Other than his emotional limitations, he's perfect in every way.

Turner's hard shell is starting to show cracks. He wants immortality, he wants to be part of the clan, and he wants Bridget, but he doesn't want to cause her pain.

His options are either abandon his quest for immortality and give Bridget his few remaining decades, or abandon Bridget by going for the transition and most likely dying. His rational mind dictates that he chooses the former, but his gut pulls him toward the latter. Which one is he going to trust?

19: DARK OPERATIVE: THE DAWN OF LOVE

Get ready for the exciting finale of Bridget and Turner's story!

20: DARK SURVIVOR AWAKENED

This was a strange new world she had awakened to.

Her memory loss must have been catastrophic because almost nothing was familiar. The language was foreign to her, with only a few words bearing some similarity to the language she thought in. Still, a full moon cycle had passed since her awakening, and little by little she was gaining basic understanding of it--only a few words and phrases, but she was learning more each day.

A week or so ago, a little girl on the street had tugged on her mother's sleeve and pointed at her. "Look, Mama, Wonder Woman!"

The mother smiled apologetically, saying something in the language these people spoke, then scurried away with the child looking behind her shoulder and grinning.

When it happened again with another child on the same day, it was settled.

Wonder Woman must have been the name of someone important in this strange world she had awoken to, and since both times it had been said with a smile it must have been a good one.

Wonder had a nice ring to it.

She just wished she knew what it meant.

21: DARK SURVIVOR ECHOES OF LOVE

Wonder's journey continues in *Dark Survivor Echoes of Love*.

22: DARK SURVIVOR REUNITED

The exciting finale of Wonder and Anandur's story.

23: DARK WIDOW'S SECRET

Vivian and her daughter share a powerful telepathic connection, so when Ella can't be reached by conventional or psychic means, her mother fears the worst.

Help arrives from an unexpected source when Vivian gets a call from the young doctor she met at a psychic convention. Turns out Julian belongs to a private organization specializing in retrieving missing girls.

As Julian's clan mobilizes its considerable resources to rescue the daughter, Magnus is charged with keeping the gorgeous young mother safe.

Worry for Ella and the secrets Vivian and Magnus keep from each other should be enough to prevent the sparks of attraction from kindling a blaze of desire. Except, these pesky sparks have a mind of their own.

24: DARK WIDOW'S CURSE

A simple rescue operation turns into mission impossible when the Russian mafia gets involved. Bad things are supposed to come in threes, but in Vivian's case, it seems like there is no limit to bad luck. Her family and everyone who gets close to her is affected by her curse.

Will Magnus and his people prove her wrong?

25: DARK WIDOW'S BLESSING

The thrilling finale of the Dark Widow trilogy!

26: Dark Dream's Temptation

Julian has known Ella is the one for him from the moment he saw her picture, but when he finally frees her from captivity, she seems indifferent to him. Could he have been mistaken?

Ella's rescue should've ended that chapter in her life, but it seems like the road back to normalcy has just begun and it's full of obstacles. Between the pitying looks she gets and her mother's attempts to get her into therapy, Ella feels like she's typecast as a victim, when nothing could be further from the truth. She's a tough survivor, and she's going to prove it.

Strangely, the only one who seems to understand is Logan, who keeps popping up in her dreams. But then, he's a figment of her imagination —or is he?

27: Dark Dream's Unraveling

While trying to figure out a way around Logan's silencing compulsion, Ella concocts an ambitious plan. What if instead of trying to keep him out of her dreams, she could pretend to like him and lure him into a trap?

Catching Navuh's son would be a major boon for the clan, as well as for Ella. She will have her revenge, turning the tables on another scumbag out to get her.

28: Dark Dream's Trap

The trap is set, but who is the hunter and who is the prey? Find out in this heart-pounding conclusion to the *Dark Dream* trilogy.

29: Dark Prince's Enigma

As the son of the most dangerous male on the planet, Lokan lives by three rules:

Don't trust a soul.

Don't show emotions.

And don't get attached.

Will one extraordinary woman make him break all three?

30: Dark Prince's Dilemma

Will Kian decide that the benefits of trusting Lokan outweigh the risks?

Will Lokan betray his father and brothers for the greater good of his people?

Are Carol and Lokan true-love mates, or is one of them playing the other?

So many questions, the path ahead is anything but clear.

31: Dark Prince's Agenda

While Turner and Kian work out the details of Areana's rescue plan, Carol and Lokan's tumultuous relationship hits another snag. Is it a sign of things to come?

32 : Dark Queen's Quest

A former beauty queen, a retired undercover agent, and a successful model, Mey is not the typical damsel in distress. But when her sister drops off the radar and then someone starts following her around, she panics.

Following a vague clue that Kalugal might be in New York, Kian sends a team headed by Yamanu to search for him.

As Mey and Yamanu's paths cross, he offers her his help and protection, but will that be all?

33: Dark Queen's Knight

As the only member of his clan with a godlike power over human minds, Yamanu has been shielding his people for centuries, but that power comes at a steep price. When Mey enters his life, he's faced with the most difficult choice.

The safety of his clan or a future with his fated mate.

34: Dark Queen's Army

As Mey anxiously waits for her transition to begin and for Yamanu to test whether his godlike powers are gone, the clan sets out to solve two mysteries:

Where is Jin, and is she there voluntarily?

Where is Kalugal, and what is he up to?

35: Dark Spy Conscripted

Jin possesses a unique paranormal ability. Just by touching someone, she can insert a mental hook into their psyche and tie a string of her consciousness to it, creating a tether. That doesn't make her a spy, though, not unless her talent is discovered by those seeking to exploit it.

36: Dark Spy's Mission

Jin's first spying mission is supposed to be easy. Walk into the club, touch Kalugal to tether her consciousness to him, and walk out.

Except, they should have known better.

37: Dark Spy's Resolution

The best-laid plans often go awry...

38: Dark Overlord New Horizon

Jacki has two talents that set her apart from the rest of the human race.

She has unpredictable glimpses of other people's futures, and she is immune to mind manipulation.

Unfortunately, both talents are pretty useless for finding a job other than the one she had in the government's paranormal division.

It seemed like a sweet deal, until she found out that the director planned on producing super babies by compelling the recruits into pairing up. When an opportunity to escape the program presented itself, she took it, only to find out that humans are not at the top of the food chain.

Immortals are real, and at the very top of the hierarchy is Kalugal, the most powerful, arrogant, and sexiest male she has ever met.

With one look, he sets her blood on fire, but Jacki is not a fool. A man like him will never think of her as anything more than a tasty snack, while she will never settle for anything less than his heart.

39: Dark Overlord's Wife

Jacki is still clinging to her all-or-nothing policy, but Kalugal is chipping away at her resistance. Perhaps it's time to ease up on her convictions. A little less than all is still much better than nothing, and a couple of decades with a demigod is probably worth more than a lifetime with a mere mortal.

40: Dark Overlord's Clan

As Jacki and Kalugal prepare to celebrate their union, Kian takes every precaution to safeguard his people. Except, Kalugal and his men are not his only potential adversaries, and compulsion is not the only power he should fear.

41: Dark Choices The Quandary

When Rufsur and Edna meet, the attraction is as unexpected as it is undeniable. Except, she's the clan's judge and councilwoman, and he's Kalugal's second-in-command. Will loyalty and duty to their people keep them apart?

42: Dark Choices Paradigm Shift

Edna and Rufsur are miserable without each other, and their two-week separation seems like an eternity. Long-distance relationships are difficult, but for immortal couples they are impossible. Unless one of them is willing to leave everything behind for the other, things are just going to get worse. Except, the cost of compromise is far greater than giving up their comfortable lives and hard-earned positions. The future of their people is on the line.

43: Dark Choices The Accord

The winds of change blowing over the village demand hard choices. For better or worse, Kian's decisions will alter the trajectory of the clan's future, and he is not ready to take the plunge. But as Edna and Rufsur's plight gains widespread support, his resistance slowly begins to erode.

44: Dark Secrets Resurgence

On a sabbatical from his Stanford teaching position, Professor David Levinson finally has time to write the sci-fi novel he's been thinking about for years.

The phenomena of past life memories and near-death experiences are too controversial to include in his formal psychiatric research, while fiction is the perfect outlet for his esoteric ideas.

Hoping that a change of pace will provide the inspiration he needs, David accepts a friend's invitation to an old Scottish castle.

45: Dark Secrets Unveiled

When Professor David Levinson accepts a friend's invitation to an old Scottish castle, what he finds there is more fantastical than his most outlandish theories. The castle is home to a clan of immortals, their leader is a stunning demigoddess, and even more shockingly, it might be precisely where he belongs.

Except, the clan founder is hiding a secret that might cast a dark shadow on David's relationship with her daughter.

Nevertheless, when offered a chance at immortality, he agrees to undergo the dangerous induction process.

Will David survive his transition into immortality? And if he does, will his relationship with Sari survive the unveiling of her mother's secret?

46: Dark Secrets Absolved

Absolution.

David had given and received it.

The few short hours since he'd emerged from the coma had felt incredible. He'd finally been free of the guilt and pain, and for the first time since Jonah's death, he had felt truly happy and optimistic about the future.

He'd survived the transition into immortality, had been accepted into the clan, and was about to marry the best woman on the face of the planet, his true love mate, his salvation, his everything.

What could have possibly gone wrong?

Just about everything.

47: Dark Haven Illusion

Welcome to Safe Haven, where not everything is what it seems.

On a quest to process personal pain, Anastasia joins the Safe Haven Spiritual Retreat.

Through meditation, self-reflection, and hard work, she hopes to make peace with the voices in her head.

This is where she belongs.

Except, membership comes with a hefty price, doubts are sacrilege, and leaving is not as easy as walking out the front gate.

Is living in utopia worth the sacrifice?

Anastasia believes so until the arrival of a new acolyte changes everything.

Apparently, the gods of old were not a myth, their immortal descendants share the planet with humans, and she might be a carrier of their genes.

48: Dark Haven Unmasked

As Anastasia leaves Safe Haven for a week-long romantic vacation with Leon, she hopes to explore her newly discovered passionate side, their budding relationship, and perhaps also solve the mystery of the voices in her head. What she discovers exceeds her wildest expectations.

In the meantime, Eleanor and Peter hope to solve another mystery. Who is Emmett Haderech, and what is he up to?

———

THE PERFECT MATCH SERIES

PERFECT MATCH 1: VAMPIRE'S CONSORT

When Gabriel's company is ready to start beta testing, he invites his old crush to inspect its medical safety protocol.

Curious about the revolutionary technology of the *Perfect Match Virtual Fantasy-Fulfillment studios*, Brenna agrees.

Neither expects to end up partnering for its first fully immersive test run.

PERFECT MATCH 2: KING'S CHOSEN

When Lisa's nutty friends get her a gift certificate to *Perfect Match Virtual Fantasy Studios*, she has no intentions of using it. But since the only way to get a refund is if no partner can be found for her, she makes sure to request a fantasy so girly and over the top that no sane guy will pick it up.

Except, someone does.

Warning: This fantasy contains a hot, domineering crown prince, sweet insta-love, steamy love scenes painted with light shades of gray, a wedding, and a HEA in both the virtual and real worlds.

Intended for mature audience.

Perfect Match 3: Captain's Conquest

Working as a Starbucks barista, Alicia fends off flirting all day long, but none of the guys are as charming and sexy as Gregg. His frequent visits are the highlight of her day, but since he's never asked her out, she assumes he's taken. Besides, between a day job and a budding music career, she has no time to start a new relationship.

That is until Gregg makes her an offer she can't refuse—a gift certificate to the virtual fantasy fulfillment service everyone is talking about. As a huge Star Trek fan, Alicia has a perfect match in mind—the captain of the Starship Enterprise.

PERFECT MATCH 1: VAMPIRE'S CONSORT

Perfect Match is a series of quick, stand-alone reads with a touch of sci-fi and a lot of sizzle.

When Gabriel's company is ready to start beta testing, he invites his old crush to inspect its medical safety protocol.

Curious about the revolutionary technology of the *Perfect Match Virtual Fantasy-Fulfillment studios*, Brenna agrees.

Neither expects to end up partnering for its first fully immersive test run.

Perfect Match 1: Vampire's Consort is a short two-hour read.

(20400 words)

EXCERPT

Gabriel

Gabriel turned his swivel chair around and gazed out of his office windows at the darkening sky. In less than an hour, he would know whether his and Hunter's insane dream was all over.

The future of the revolutionary technology they'd been developing for past six years depended on the decision of one man.

Their enigmatic investor was either going to pour more money into the startup or cut his losses short and pull out.

William, the programmer the guy had sent to help them out, had been working on the software for the entire week. Hopefully, his recommendation wasn't going to be the death sentence Gabriel feared.

When William had scheduled the first-ever meeting between them and his boss, he hadn't provided any hints, and his expression had been impossible to read.

Hunter was sure that it was a negotiating tactic, and that the guy had managed to solve their problem but wasn't going to share unless they capitulated to his boss's demands.

The investor wanted a controlling share in their company, and if his programmer held the key to its survival, they would have no choice but to sell their brain-child in order to keep it alive.

Gabriel hoped that Hunter was right, and that the big man himself was coming to meet them to close the deal and not as a courtesy to a dying enterprise.

In addition to the millions of personal funds that he and Hunter had sunk into the startup, which had been everything they'd gotten from selling their successful virtual gaming software, they had used up all the additional millions the mystery investor had put into the development.

And yet, they were a year behind schedule.

The beta testing should've been done by now, and the company should've been up and running.

Turning the swivel chair around, Gabriel glanced at the

bottom drawer of his desk. The bottle of scotch he kept there was calling to him.

Except, drinking before an important meeting was a bad idea. He needed to be sharp.

Fortunately, scotch wasn't his only stress management strategy. There was another way he could relax.

Pulling out his phone, Gabriel found the right channel on YouTube, pressed play, and got comfortable in his chair. When nothing else worked, listening to his favorite doctor explain anatomy and physiology to young children did. Brenna's soothing, melodic voice always managed to calm his nerves.

"Stalking the pretty doctor again?"

Immersed in the Brenna experience, Gabriel hadn't heard the door open, or Hunter come in.

"It's not stalking when I watch videos that she puts out for the general viewing public."

Plopping on one of the visitors' chairs, Hunter put his Frappuccino cup on Gabriel's desk. "You've been obsessing about this woman since high school. I don't understand why you haven't called her up already. Since when are you afraid of making a move?"

When he and Hunter had met senior year in Caltech, Gabriel was no longer the awkward, gangly and pimply kid he'd been in high school. Not that he'd been a great looker at twenty-one, but at least the damn pimples were gone.

"She didn't know I was alive back then, and she doesn't now. What am I going to tell her? That I'm a fan of her YouTube videos?"

Hunter shook his head. "That's why you should've gone to your high school reunions. There is no better place to meet an old crush, and you know that she's not married because you stalk her Facebook page as well."

That was true. But there had been plenty of reasons not to attend. At first, it had been about his uninspiring looks. So yeah, he'd lost the pimples, but not much else had improved until he'd started a rigorous Krav Maga training regimen.

The thirty-pound muscle gain had turned him from a six feet three inches hunched-over scarecrow into someone women desired, even without knowing that he was a successful entrepreneur and loaded.

Not that he was. Not anymore. That money was long gone, all spent on his and Hunter's crazy idea to provide a different kind of fully-immersive virtual experience. A fantasy fulfillment for adults.

They had dove into it head first, not surfacing until six years later when they'd gotten stuck and couldn't find a way over the hurdle they'd encountered. The code they needed just didn't exist.

Until William showed up.

Hunter rubbed his chin. "You can hire her as a medical advisor. We need someone to test the monitoring equipment."

It had been done already, but only during the limited alpha stage. They needed to run more tests during the full-immersion beta testing. It could be a good excuse when they were actually ready for beta, which they were nowhere near.

"There is nothing for her to check until we can hook up volunteers to the machines. And since the machines are not working, I have nothing to show her."

But Hunter's suggestions to attend a reunion wasn't a bad idea, and his timing was perfect. There had been an email about it a week or so ago. Gabriel's next high school reunion was coming up in less than two months.

His fascination with Brenna Hutchison had started in their junior year, and fourteen years later Gabriel was still just as obsessed with her as ever, if not more.

It was time he did something about it.

Hunter smirked. "At some point, they will work, and then

there will be plenty for you to show her." He waggled his brows.

Gabriel ignored the insinuating remark. Even if the virtual machines were up and running, he wasn't going to hook Brenna up to one and chance her finding her perfect match from the pool of volunteers.

"You're an optimist, Hunter. You should brace for the possibility that this is never going to work. Our investor might pull the plug."

"No, I'm a realist. I've peeked over William's shoulder while he was working on fixing the code. I've never seen anything like it. The guy must be an alien with coding skills lightyears more advanced than ours."

"Right." Hunter and his alien theories. "I hope your alien is not going to sell our proprietary technologies to our competitors."

To guard against piracy, the *Dream Encounters* team had been working offline for the entire six years of its existence. There were too many stories in the startup universe about people investing endless time and resources into a new product, and then someone stealing the work from them and going to market with it before them.

Still, word of what they were working on had gotten out, and four burglary attempts had been made in the last year alone. Evidently, when hacking didn't work, the crooks resorted to old fashioned thievery.

Hunter snorted. "As far as William is concerned, we have nothing worth stealing. As I said, he rewrote in one week what several of our teams have been working on for six years."

"If that was true, he and his boss wouldn't be interested in our company. They'd be doing it themselves. William might be a genius coder, but it doesn't make him an inventor." Gabriel tapped his temple. "That requires vision, imagination, and a hefty dose of crazy."

That got Hunter thinking. "Yeah, you're probably right. We came up with the revolutionary idea for virtual experiences and almost figured out a way to make it happen. William just fixed what we did wrong." He smiled. "Don't worry, though. I had him sign the same confidentiality agreement that we have all of our team members signed on. It's ironclad."

Nothing was ironclad. And if information found its way to their competitors, it would be difficult to prove who'd leaked it.

When the intercom buzzed, Gabriel's gut clenched.

"Showtime," Hunter said.

Their receptionist came on line. "William and his boss are here."

Was it his imagination, or did his sixty-five-year-old aunt Barbara sound a little flustered?

"We will be right out."

"Okay."

Gabriel got up, put his suit jacket on, and smoothed a hand over his hair. "Ready?"

Hunter nodded.

Plastering twin friendly expressions on their faces, Gabriel and Hunter walked out of his office and then stopped dead in their tracks.

Damn.

No wonder Barbara was blushing like a schoolgirl.

While his aunt gazed dreamily at William's boss and the two guys who were probably his bodyguards, the object of her fascination looked like he was about to kill something. Or someone.

Gabriel felt as if he was facing off with a tiger and wondering whether he was hungry. In comparison, the body-guards seemed tame. Well, maybe not the blond. That guy looked lethal. The huge redhead, on the other hand, smiled and winked at Barbara, causing her to giggle like a young girl.

Who were these people?

Maybe they were actors? Or rather movie stars with millions to invest in promising startups?

One could never tell in Los Angeles. And that would also explain why no names had been provided. Up until now, they'd been dealing with an investment company and the executives representing William's boss.

Regrettably, though, Gabriel hadn't been watching much of anything for the past six years, and he was unfamiliar with Hollywood's latest stars. Given the way Hunter was staring at their guests, neither had he.

"Hello, I'm Gabriel Barnes." He offered the boss his hand.

The guy was taller than him by an inch or so, and his blue eyes were so intense that Gabriel was sure he was wearing contacts. That, and what must have been many hundreds of thousands in plastic surgery done by the best surgeons in the world, made him look otherworldly.

Hunter was probably mumbling "alien" under his breath.

"Kian." The god-like man shook what he'd been offered.

Weird name that was probably fake. "It's a pleasure to finally meet you in person, Mr. Kian."

"Just Kian." The guy didn't smile.

"As you wish." Gabriel turned to Hunter. "And this is my partner, Hunter Anderson."

Brenna

"Brenna! Oh my gosh!" Sally barreled toward her. "You haven't changed a bit!" Pulling her into a crushing hug, she kissed her on both cheeks.

"You too. I mean, you haven't changed at all." Except for the fifty pounds or so weight gain. "It's so wonderful to see you after all these years."

Poor Sally.

She'd always been on one diet or another, but nothing had ever worked. She'd lose a bit and then gain double as much back.

"You have to meet my husband, Drew." Sally waved a chubby guy over. "Drew, come say hi to my friend Brenna."

"Nice to meet you." He offered her his hand.

Shaking it, Brenna smiled. "Same here." She pretended to look for someone. "I'll have to catch you later. I think I see Jana." She scurried away before Sally had a chance to stop her.

They hadn't seen each other in twelve years, and even before that, they hadn't been great friends. But Sally had always been like that. Sweet and well-meaning, but overbearing in her exuberance.

In contrast, Brenna was quiet and bookish, and excitable people like Sally overwhelmed her.

After several more encounters like this, Brenna was itching to put on her big sunglasses and gather her long curly hair in a bun so no one would recognize her. She hated having to pretend that she'd missed people she barely recognized and with whom she'd exchanged no more than a few words throughout high school.

Attending a high school reunion without a date had been a stupid idea, which was why she'd skipped all the previous ones. Well, that and not having time to take a break from the rat race.

For the past twelve years, her life had been all about her goal of becoming a doctor, and while she'd been chasing that dream, it seemed like life had passed her by.

Almost everyone was married or already on their second round after a divorce. She was probably the only idiot who'd come alone. In lieu of a husband, she should've glued her diploma to her forehead. At least it would have saved her from having to explain why she was still single at thirty.

She should have known it would suck.

The truth was that Brenna had come for only one reason.

For years she'd wondered what had become of Gabriel, the boy whose gaze had followed her around throughout junior and senior years, but who'd never gathered up the nerve to approach her.

Not that she would've dated him if he had.

Her life had been all about getting the best grades and participating in as many extracurricular activities as possible. The acceptance rate to top-notch colleges had been and still was ridiculously low, and Brenna's singular focus in high school had been a college application that would stand out from the crowd.

Still, she'd never stopped thinking about Gabriel and imagining what he was doing with himself.

Such an interesting guy.

Confident academically and competitive as heck, but so shy with girls. Other than his intense, intelligent eyes, he hadn't been much to look at, but she'd seen potential others hadn't. As a teenager, he'd been much too thin for his tall body, spindly and a little hunched over. But she'd noticed that his shoulders were broad and that the face under all the pimples was handsome.

While the guys who'd been popular in high school were now padded around the middle and balding, Gabriel's looks had probably improved with age.

Mostly, though, Brenna was curious about what he had done with himself. Such a smart and driven guy must have achieved a lot over the last twelve years. She had even googled his name, but had found nothing.

Maybe he'd changed it?

With a sigh, Brenna snatched a cup of punch off a tray and found a vacant chair to sit on. Her feet were killing her. She couldn't wait to kick off the torturous shoes she'd bought for this occasion.

She was a sneakers and clogs kind of girl. Not stilettos.

Regrettably, her efforts to look good had been wasted because Gabriel hadn't shown up. In fact, the entire trip was senseless. The guy was probably married with two kids and a dog.

Blessing the long table cloth, she slid her aching feet out of the high-heeled shoes and stretched her toes. Barely able to stifle the moan of pure bliss, Brenna closed her eyes and took in a deep breath. She'd give her feet a few moments of rest and then head back to her hotel room.

"Hello, gorgeous," a familiar voice said, one she'd hoped not to hear tonight. "Looking even better than I remembered. How have you been?" Corey reached for her hand and lifted it. "I don't see a wedding ring." He sing-songed.

She plastered a sweet smile on her face and glanced at his hand. "But I see one on yours. Where is your wife, Corey?"

He waved a dismissive hand. "Running to pee for the twentieth time tonight. Didn't you see a hippo lumbering around?"

"I see that you're as charming as ever, Corey. But calling your pregnant wife a hippo is a new low even for you."

Apparently, people didn't change much over the years, and Corey was still the same asshole he'd been in high school, just minus the good looks.

"And you're still a stuck-up bitch. Nothing new there. But I'll do you anyway." He lifted her hand to his lips and licked the back of it.

She yanked it away. "Ugh, gross."

Laughing like a hyena, he rose to his feet. "See ya, Brenna."

It was time to go even though it meant pushing her poor feet back into the torturous shoes. She needed to find a bathroom, wash her hand, and call an Uber.

The line to the bathroom was more than twenty ladies long, and even though she only needed to get to the sink, Brenna waited her turn while shifting her weight from foot to foot to try and ease the discomfort.

"Heels are a pain in the butt, but they make it look good." The woman behind her chuckled. "I'm Cheryl, Matt Grager's wife."

"Brenna." She lifted her hand but then remembered why she was standing in line. "I would offer you my hand, but I spilled punch all over it."

"Bummer. At least it didn't get on your dress."

Brenna forced a smile. "Lucky me."

Finally, when her turn arrived, she rushed to the sink and scrubbed her hands and forearms all the way to the elbows as if she was prepping for surgery.

What a complete and utter failure this night had been. She was never attending another reunion.

Heading out, Brenna pulled out her phone and scrolled until she found the Uber application. As it opened, though, something, or rather someone, caught her eye.

A tall guy in a suit exited a taxi, and when he leaned inside the cab to pay, she took a moment to admire his well-defined backside. She was still standing and gawking when he straightened up and turned around.

No way.

Brenna would recognize those dark eyes and that intense gaze no matter how much everything else had changed.

"Gabriel?"

PERFECT MATCH 1: VAMPIRE'S CONSORT
IS AVAILABLE ON AMAZON

Also by I. T. Lucas

THE CHILDREN OF THE GODS ORIGINS

THE CHILDREN OF THE GODS

DARK STRANGER

DARK ENEMY

KRI & MICHAEL'S STORY

DARK WARRIOR

DARK GUARDIAN

DARK ANGEL

DARK OPERATIVE

45: Dark Secrets Unveiled
46: Dark Secrets Absolved
Dark Haven
47: Dark haven Illusion
48: Dark Haven Unmasked

PERFECT MATCH

Perfect Match 1: Vampire's Consort
Perfect Match 2: King's Chosen
Perfect Match 3: Captain's Conquest

The Children of the Gods Series Sets

Books 1-3: Dark Stranger trilogy—Includes a bonus short story: **The Fates take a Vacation**

Books 4-6: Dark Enemy Trilogy —Includes a bonus short story—**The Fates' Post-Wedding Celebration**

Books 7-10: Dark Warrior Tetralogy
Books 11-13: Dark Guardian Trilogy
Books 14-16: Dark Angel Trilogy
Books 17-19: Dark Operative Trilogy
Books 20-22: Dark Survivor Trilogy
Books 23-25: Dark Widow Trilogy
Books 26-28: Dark Dream Trilogy
Books 29-31: Dark Prince Trilogy
Books 32-34: Dark Queen Trilogy
Books 35-37: Dark Spy Trilogy
Books 38-40: Dark Overlord Trilogy
Books 41-43: Dark Choices Trilogy

BOOKS 44-46: DARK SECRETS TRILOGY

MEGA SETS

THE CHILDREN OF THE GODS: BOOKS 1-6—INCLUDES CHARACTER LISTS

THE CHILDREN OF THE GODS: BOOKS 6.5-10—INCLUDES CHARACTER LISTS

TRY THE CHILDREN OF THE GODS SERIES ON AUDIBLE

2 FREE audiobooks with your new Audible subscription!

FOR EXCLUSIVE PEEKS AT UPCOMING RELEASES & A FREE COMPANION BOOK

Join my *VIP Club* and gain access to the VIP portal at
ITLUCAS.COM
CLICK HERE TO JOIN
(or go to: http://eepurl.com/blMTpD)

Included in your free membership:

- **FREE** Children of the Gods companion book **1**
- **FREE** narration of Goddess's Choice—Book **1** in The Children of the Gods Origins series.
- Preview chapters of upcoming releases.
- And other exclusive content offered only to my **VIPs.**